BOOKS BY JOHN O'HARA

THE INSTRUMENT

THE
INSTRUMENT

A NOVEL BY

JOHN O'HARA

RANDOM HOUSE

NEW YORK

First Printing
© Copyright, 1967, by John O'Hara
All rights reserved under International
and Pan-American Copyright Conventions.
Published in New York by Random House, Inc.,
and simultaneously in Toronto, Canada,
by Random House of Canada Limited.
Library of Congress Catalog Card Number: 67–12717
Manufactured in the United States of America
by The Book Press Incorporated, Brattleboro, Vermont

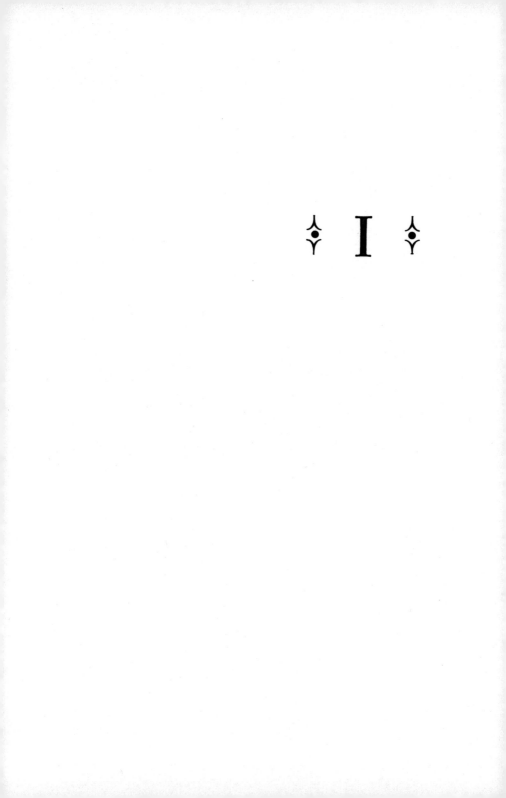

I

Yank Lucas fell asleep late one night and left the gas burning on the kitchen range. He was heating some water for coffee, and when the water boiled over it extinguished the flame and allowed the gas to escape. In a short while the odor of the gas passed under the door of Yank's flat and out into the hallway. Jiggs Muldowney, on his way upstairs, got a whiff of the gas and decided it must be coming from Yank's flat. He did not know Yank Lucas, did not even know his name, was not sure who occupied the flat, did not want to get mixed up in anything. The tenants of the building preferred to mind their own business. But after hesitating a moment or two, Jiggs knocked on the door, got no answer, tried the door and found it was unlocked. He went in and saw Yank Lucas sprawled on the kitchen floor.

Jiggs opened a couple of windows and dragged and lifted Yank to one of the windowsills and propped him up against it. Then he turned off the gas. The thing to do was to call the police. That was the proper thing to do. But Jiggs had no love for the police. Even in a situation like this he wanted to think twice before having anything to do with them. He put his own head out the window to get some fresh air. A pretty strong draft had been created by his opening the windows; it was a cold, windy night. It did not take long for the kitchen to get cold, but the flat needed a thorough airing, and Jiggs needed time to think. Putting the facts together, Jiggs observed that a half-empty can of coffee was on the kitchen table and that the coffee percolator was stained. A man who was going to commit suicide would probably not want to have a cup of coffee if he was going to take gas. People who committed suicide that way usually opened the oven door and simply turned the valve. Therefore the facts indicated that this man was not trying to kill himself, and Jiggs placed him face down on the floor and knelt over him and began giving him artificial respiration. He put his hands under the man's chest and lifted him and lowered him, up and down, up and down. That was all that Jiggs remembered about artificial respiration, but it was enough. The man muttered, "Cut it out, will you?" The words were not distinct, but the meaning was plain.

"All right, I'll cut it out," said Jiggs, and got to his feet. The man lay there, but he was at least half awake, coming back to consciousness. Jiggs took out a cigarette and was about to light it when he remembered not to. The man rolled over on the floor and looked up at Jiggs. He wanted to say something, but he could not. He dozed off for about a minute, then reopened his eyes. "Cold," he said.

"Yeah, but you need the air," said Jiggs. "I said you need the fresh air."

"God damn cold," said Yank Lucas. "I'm sick."

"You're alive, quit squawking," said Jiggs. He sat on the single kitchen chair and twirled his unlit cigarette with his thumb and fingers. He got up and soaked a tea towel with cold water and put it on the man's face. The man brushed it off, but it had had a reviving effect.

"Who are *you?*" said Yank Lucas.

"Muldowney, from the flat above," said Jiggs.

"Well, fuck you," said Yank Lucas.

"Sure, you ungrateful bastard," said Jiggs. "By rights I oughta left you there."

"Who *are* you?"

"I'm the guy that saved your miserable God damn life," said Jiggs.

"You save' my life," said Yank Lucas. He raised himself to a sitting position, supporting himself with one hand. Slowly he looked about the kitchen, and gave an involuntary shudder. "God damn cold," he said.

"You'd a been a lot colder if I didn't come along," said Jiggs.

The change in position made Yank Lucas cough. "So fuckin' weak," he said. "I smell gas."

"Boy, you're quick," said Jiggs.

"Who *are* you, anyway?"

"I'm John J. Muldowney, Esquire," said Jiggs. "You want my serial number? You wanta see my union card? Get some air in your lungs and stop wasting your breath. I wanta go to bed."

"Are you a fag?"

"I oughta give you a good kick in the teeth," said Jiggs. "I never saw such a miserable, ungrateful bastard in my whole life. I saw some pips, but you top them all."

"What the hell are you doing here?"

"Yeah, what am I? That's a good question," said Jiggs. "Don't worry, as soon as you can stand up, I'll blow."

Yank Lucas looked at the can of coffee, then at the gas range. He was beginning to put his own facts together.

"Figuring it out, hey?" said Jiggs.

Yank Lucas nodded. "Uh-huh."

"Little by little," said Jiggs.

"You smelled the gas, huh?"

"Little by little, he's figuring it. Yeah, I smelt the gas."

"I put the coffee on. I sat down there for a minute. I must have fallen asleep." Yank Lucas was talking to himself. He looked at his wristwatch. "Twenty-five after four, or twenty after five. I can't focus."

"Well, it's twenty-five after four," said Jiggs.

"How long have you been here?"

"Oh, I guess a little over a half an hour," said Jiggs.

"Would you care for a drink?"

"Sure," said Jiggs. "Where is it?"

"In the other room," said Yank Lucas.

"I'll get it," said Jiggs. The other room was the only room, aside from the kitchen and bath. It contained a studio couch, opened for the night, some imitation Danish chairs and a desk, a portable typewriter, numerous books in piles on the floor, and a bottle of gin, a bottle of cheap rye, and a bottle of domestic vodka. Jiggs chose the rye.

"I don't know if you ought to have any," said Jiggs. "I ain't sure it's good for you."

"I don't want any. I couldn't keep it down," said Yank Lucas. "I think I'll try a glass of milk."

"I bet you don't hold that down," said Jiggs.

"Maybe not," said Yank Lucas.

"On the other hand, maybe if you put some rye in with the milk, maybe that'll do you some good. You want to try it?"

"I'll try anything to get rid of this gas taste," said Yank Lucas.

Jiggs poured some rye into half a glass of milk and handed it to Yank Lucas. It stayed down, but not for long. While Jiggs was drinking his rye and water Yank went to the bathroom and vomited.

"Well, anyway, you're moving around," said Jiggs.

Yank Lucas came out of the bathroom, shaking his head and wiping his face with a washcloth. "Not so good," he said.

"You know any doctor in the neighborhood?" said Jiggs.

"No," said Yank Lucas. "I don't know any doctor in New York."

"Well, if they're not a friend of yours they're sure as hell not coming here this hour of the night."

"I'll be all right," said Yank Lucas. "I owe you an apology."

"Well, I owe you a punch in the nose, so we'll call it even. Boy, this is raw whiskey. If you can take this, a little gas ain't gonna hurt you."

"I don't drink it. I stick to vodka," said Yank Lucas. "Have a drink of vodka. I only have the whiskey for a friend of mine. She likes it."

"Some broads will drink anything. Yeah, I'll try the other. Are you a writer?"

"Supposed to be," said Yank Lucas.

"What, books?"

"No, plays," said Yank Lucas.

"There's a broad up over me, she's a writer. I hear that fuckin' typewriter of hers."

"No, she's not a writer. She's a professional typist. She types manuscripts, so much a page."

"Oh, that's it? I was wondering to myself, Jesus, nine o'clock in the morning or earlier. All day long. Anybody that wrote that much ought to be a millionaire by this time. Never stops."

"She stops, when she doesn't get scripts to type," said Yank Lucas.

"Yeah, and she has to hump that jig she got living with

her," said Jiggs. "That's my nickname. Jiggs. But I wouldn't give her a hump, I'll tell you. Did you ever take a look at her?"

"I've seen her," said Yank Lucas.

"You'd have to be awful hard up to stick it in her," said Jiggs. "Oh, maybe I would of welcomed her at certain times. Yeah, I guess at certain times."

"Like when you were in the service," said Yank Lucas.

"Well, yes. I wasn't thinking of the service, exactly."

"Prison?"

"Where else? When I was in the service I never went except basic when I couldn't get a piece of tail. Woman tail. The most I ever went was maybe a month. Not that that ain't long enough, mind you. What a terrible thing to get so hard up and you have to take what you can get. Just as long as it has a snatch. How you feeling?"

"Better," said Yank Lucas.

"If I's you I'd go see a doctor in the morning. I administered the artificial respiration, but I don't know if I did it right. Maybe'd be a good idea if you got your broad to come over and stay here the rest of the night."

"Not her," said Yank Lucas.

"I got my wife upstairs'll be yelling her silly head off because I'm this late."

"You have your wife upstairs? I never heard her yell," said Yank Lucas.

"Well, you're lucky. In more ways than one, you're lucky."

"I guessed that there was a woman in the flat above. The footsteps are different. But she never yelled."

"Well, it isn't so much she yells so loud. But she starts out calling me a mother-fucker and that's for openers. She likes to see how far she can go before I take a poke at her."

"Uh-huh."

"A stoolie or a fag," said Jiggs. "Either one of them she calls me and she gets it, right in the kisser."

"And still I never heard her yell," said Yank Lucas.

"You know why? Because there's some women built that way, and she's one of them."

"Oh, yes," said Yank Lucas. "Aren't you cold? I think we can close the windows now."

"You want to make sure all the gas is out of here," said Jiggs. "And there's one other thing. The super. You don't want the super finding out you went to sleep with the gas on. He'll tell the landlord, and they'll get rid of you. Nobody lives here if they don't have to, and I guess you're no different than the rest of the tenants. So if you want to keep living in this dump, don't mention to the super how you left the gas on."

"Don't worry, I won't," said Yank Lucas.

"This is a real dump. And it ain't even cheap. What do you pay, if you don't mind me asking?"

"A hundred a month."

"I pay the same. I got another room, but I'm another flight up and we don't have the open fireplace. Forty a month used to be high for a flat like this. I could tell you rents all over this part of the city. I ought to. I skipped enough of them." He took out a single cigarette from the pack in his pocket and lit it. "Jesus, you notice that, what I just done?"

"You lit a cigarette," said Yank Lucas.

"Nothin' happened. A little while ago if I lit a cigarette in here you know wudda happened. So I guess we're safe to close the windows."

"Yes, I don't want to be saved from asphyxiation and then freeze to death."

"That's the word I was trying to think of. Asphyxiation. I knew it began with an *a* and had an *x* in it."

"Axiomatic," said Yank Lucas.

"What's that?"

"Oh, just a word," said Yank Lucas. He closed one of the windows.

"Here, I'll help you with the other one," said Jiggs. "You look peak-ed. You don't want that coffee now, do you?"

"No, I wanted to stay awake, but now I'd rather sleep."

"You hit the sack and I'll leave the windows open enough to give you a little fresh air."

"All right," said Yank Lucas. He took off his shirt and slacks and shoes, and got into bed in his socks and underwear. Jiggs watched him. "I'm gonna leave the light on in the kitchen, in case you have a nightmare. I get the fuckin' things and I don't know where I am. You'll be having them. Maybe not tonight, but you'll be having them."

"Uh-huh," murmured Yank Lucas. His eyes fell shut and he slept.

He was accustomed to sleeping through the morning noises of the neighborhood: the bouncing trucks on Ninth Avenue; the children arriving at the parochial school across the street; the whistles of the ferryboats and tugs; the bells and sirens and Mack Bulldog engines of the fire apparatus; the more immediate sounds of the typist upstairs and the heavy unidentifiable footsteps in the hall. They were morning sounds, but most of them went on all through the day. Yank Lucas awoke and first blamed the noises, but a moment later he knew that the noise was inside his aching head and was not coming through his ears. He was having a little trouble breathing. His chest was sore. His lungs were sore. Then his slowed-down brain recalled the events of a few hours earlier. It was twenty of nine or a quarter of eight by his wristwatch. One of his first thoughts was of something he had heard or read somewhere about brain damage to people who had been deprived of oxygen, and the thought was terrifying. His terror compelled him to action, and he got out of bed. He went to the refrigerator and looked for something to take the gas taste out of his mouth and nose. A can of pears. A jar of tomato juice. Some milk in a quart bottle. A half-pint container of light cream. The milk seemed safest but did not have a strong taste. He mixed some milk and tomato juice in a tumbler, and it was strong enough, but it made him sick, and the strain of vomiting it brought back the pains in his chest. But strangely enough the regurgitation produced one desirable effect: the taste of gas, the lingering smell of it, was gone.

He closed the windows and sat at the kitchen table. His head ached and he was weak, but he knew he would live. Quite seriously he knew he would live, as quite seriously he had been wondering if he would die. He felt no gratitude to the oaf who had saved his life, and he never wanted to see him again to thank him. He knew that later on he would see him and thank him properly. He hoped that he would be able to thank him in a tangible way that would dismiss the man. He disliked the man and everything about him. He was a cheaply evil man. A small-time criminal and a brute. In all likelihood a pederast. Quite possibly, from the way he had spoken of his wife, a pimp, married to a whore. He had thick black hair with some grey in it, bushy black eyebrows, hair in abundance growing out of his ears, mats of hair on the back of his hands and stubby fingers. He had worn a topcoat with buttonholes that were too wide for the buttons, and like most of the Irishmen in the neighborhood, he wore a cloth cap. To this man Yank Lucas owed his life, and he suspected that the man was not going to let him forget it. He was afraid of the man, his brutishness, his low-grade guile.

Yank Lucas went to the bathroom and brushed his teeth. He ran the tap water over the toothbrush and squeezed a fresh ribbon of the toothpaste on it and brushed his teeth again. It made his mouth feel clean and cool, and helped further to dispel the smell and taste of gas and tomato juice and vomit. After staring at the percolator and hesitating, he rinsed out the aluminum pot and put in some coffee and water and placed it on the stove. He remembered to relight the pilot. "This time I'll stay awake," he said aloud. While the coffee was cooking he shaved, and when he had shaved and drunk his first cup of coffee he felt better. His head still ached, his chest was still sore, but he was coming around.

It was a quarter after nine. Ellis Walton always got to his office at eleven o'clock, or so he said. Today he would be there at eleven o'clock and expecting Yank Lucas to be there. "For my part I'm not hurr'ing you, Yank," Ellis Walton had said. "I just as soon from my own personal point of view, if you took a couple weeks. But you want Zena as much as I want Zena, and Friday's the longest she'll wait. You bring in the new third act Friday, she takes it away and reads it over the weekend, and then it's in the lap of the gods. She reads it Saturday, that muzzler of a husband reads it and sticks in his two cents' worth, and Sunday we know if we got her or David Salmon. Monday she signs the contract with us or with Salmon. She told me herself she'd rather come with me, but Salmon has the inside of the track with her husband. Somehow or other Barry Payne got her mesmerized, and just now she'll do anything he says. Next year maybe it'll be different, but just now it's Barry Payne. So maybe I'm asking the impossible, Yank. You gotta pressurize yourself to finish by Friday, and even then I can't promise you Zena. But I'm a son of a bitch if it isn't worth the try."

"I'll make the try," said Yank Lucas. "I know what she can mean to this play."

"If I can come out in next Tuesday's *Times* and announce that I signed Zena, this office'll be pandemonium I guarantee you. The theater parties. Picture companies. And you'll be able to write your own ticket financially. When a performer is hot the way she is, it takes a real dog to denigrate her, and your play isn't a dog. I got every confidence in your play, Yank. Every. But where another woman has to be twice as good in the part, Zena Gollum right now can do no wrong. Personally, I don't say she's that good. I can pick numerous flaws in Zena. I had her sitting in this office, right where you're sitting now, four years ago, and I gave her a small part more because I took pity on her. I got her for a hundred and seventy-five dollars a week, and I could of got her for less, but I took pity on her. We opened and closed in Boston, through no fault of hers. No fault of hers, I'll give her that. Once the curtain rises this woman is transformed from a common, ordinary little dame with a nice little ass, and she turns into a real artist. She'd fuck a donkey, too, you know, back there three or four years ago. More guys can lay claim to scoring there and I don't happen to be one of them merely because I just plain didn't want it. It was there if I wanted it, but I didn't want it. Maybe that's why she's willing to work for me now, and maybe that's the only chance we have with Barry Payne. He don't like going into Sardi's and half the guys there give her that I-was-there

[15]

look. Not that he's in love with her, God knows, but she's an important property now and he don't want anybody lousing up his program, whether it be some new guy or whether it be some guy back for a retake. Watch him the way he won't let any other guy get near her. Always got the arm around her. One of these days she'll get wise to him, but in the meanwhile he holds the whip handle."

"I haven't got anything, but if I had anything I'd give it to have her in my play," said Yank Lucas.

"Well, then give everything between now and Friday, Yank, and remember this, my friend. Barry Payne is a no-goodnik, a louse from way back. But if he thinks your play is better for his property than David Salmon's, he'll ditch Salmon."

"Does he know anything, this Barry Payne?" said Yank Lucas.

"I gotta give the son of a bitch that much. Yes. He knows what's right for her. Two plays, two blockbusters. And he picked both of them."

That was Tuesday; this was Friday. Tuesday, Wednesday, Thursday had been work and coffee, a little sleep, more coffee and more work and finally a degree of exhaustion that nearly had cost him his life. The worst of the work lay on the bedroom floor in squeezed-up balls of paper, and Yank Lucas had known that the best of it was not going to be good enough for Barry Payne because it was not good enough for him; he was forcing it to please a man for whom he had nothing but contempt. Now, with a couple of hours remaining before the deadline, he gave up. At eleven o'clock he would telephone Ellis Walton that he could not work that way; he could not write to order. Whatever had been good in the play had been his. The third act had been wrong, and he had known it before anyone else saw it, but now a Broadway sharpie was bullying him from a distance.

Yank Lucas, upon his decision to give up, enjoyed a sense of relief, of a vague triumph over the bully, and of renewed fondness for the play that since Tuesday he had been hating. At eleven o'clock he would have his conversation with Ellis Walton. He owed Ellis Walton an expression of regret; Walton had treated him decently. He did not know, or much care, whether Walton would understand how the pressure had made him hate a play that he had lived with and loved for two years. If Walton behaved well, he would go back to work on it, improve the third act, and no matter how long it took, Walton would get the play when it was right. They had lost Zena Gollum, but that loss meant as much to him as to Ellis Walton. More. Ellis Walton had other plays by other authors lined up; Yank Lucas had one play, no job, and less than two hundred dollars in the world.

But he had something else. He had his life, the spark of it that had been extinguished by a boiling-over coffee pot. There was a nice irony in the scoundrelly character of the man who had revived the spark. It was irony of the kind that was already in his play. He was amused by that. He thought about it, he breathed over it, and then he knew what he must do with his play.

"You must have worked your ass off," said Barry Payne. "When did you get this idea for the gas stove? It's a gimmick, but it's a good gimmick."

"Barry, I told you this man had a genuine sense of the theater," said Ellis Walton.

"If it's all the same to you, Ellis, let me hear it from him," said Barry Payne. "I'm curious, Lucas. Did you have this gas stove bit in an earlier version and discarded it?"

"No," said Yank Lucas.

"I can guarantee you it wasn't," said Ellis Walton. "I been with this play since Peggy McInerney brought me the first draft last April. There was never the slightest hint of the gas stove bit. I was as much surprised as you were. Not surprised by Yank being able to come up with it, but I was just as taken with it."

It was Saturday afternoon, and they were sitting in the living-room of the Barry Payne–Zena Gollum apartment on Central Park West. "Well, Lucas, you're not going to tell me, or Ellis isn't going to let you tell me. But it sure makes all the difference. What I like about it, I turned down two plays that had Zena committing suicide. This woman don't commit suicide. I don't mean the girl in your play, I mean the actress by the name of Zena Gollum. You hear these silly bastards say Zena Gollum can play anything. The phonebook bit, you know. Zena Gollum would be enchanting reading the phonebook. Balls to that! She might want to do this or do that, but I won't let her. I got nothing against suicide in a play, but suicide for Zena Gollum is out. Out. You know why? Because it won't ring true. This isn't just an actress. Actresses I can get, Ellis can get, anybody can get. But this is a real stage personality. And what kind of a stage personality? Better I should tell you what kind of a stage personality she isn't. A lady she isn't. Ethel Barrymore. Tallulah Bankhead, she isn't. Maybe you never saw Sylvia Sidney in her younger days, but I did, and some of the same quality Zena has inherent in her. Every slob woman in the audience can identify with Zena. They can identify with her for three acts, and suffer with her. But they don't identify with her if she commits suicide. If I put her in a play where she knocks herself off, we lose them. We absolutely lose them. Why? I tell you why. Because the slob women don't commit suicide, that's why. Maybe you say, so what? There's only two matinees a week. Your evening audience is part men. Yeah? Well, men go to musicals. Women are the ones that buy the tickets for plays. Your men in the audience can watch her tokus. Explain to him a tokus, Ellis."

"He can guess," said Ellis Walton.

"I happen to know what it is," said Yank Lucas.

"So all right. So I just want to tell you, Lucas, if you ever want to write another play for Zena Gollum, leave out the suicides."

"I think I ought to tell you, Mr. Payne, I didn't write this play for Miss Gollum."

"He means—" said Ellis Walton.

"I know what he means. Give me credit for that much, Ellis. No author wants to admit he writes a play for a star. All right, so maybe he didn't. But he *re*wrote it for her, didn't he? And he did a great job. Four days. If you can come up with a whole new third act in that amount of time, I gotta go along with Ellis. You have a real, genuine theater sense. We'll open in Boston and stay there two weeks. Maybe they'll make us cut out some of the dirty stuff, but we can put it back in for New York. Where the Negro comes in and finds her passed out on the kitchen floor, we gotta watch the direction there. We don't want the slightest hint that the Negro sneaks a feel or makes any kind of a pass at her."

"There's no such hint in my script."

"I know there isn't, but you don't know some of these directors," said Barry Payne. "The girl is gonna be bothered the rest of her life by her feeling for the Negro. Gratitude and all that. The only decent thing ever happened to her, and so on. Therefore we don't want to spoil that scene with the Negro getting hot nuts for her. You see what I mean?"

"I see what *you* mean? I wrote the play," said Yank Lucas. "*You* see what *I* mean."

"Right," said Barry Payne. "Well, Ellis, give the man some money and let him go out and celebrate."

"I think he was hoping to meet Zena. Weren't you, Yank?"

"Yes," said Yank Lucas.

"I didn't want her here. I sent her out to get rid of her

so we could talk. But don't worry, Lucas. You got her for your play. What'll it be, Ellis? In Monday's paper?"

"Oh, sure. Why?"

"In case I run into David Salmon, I want to know what to say."

"You wouldn't want to tell him the truth?" said Ellis Walton.

"Let him find out about it when he reads the paper. The son of a bitch thinks he owns me and it'll do him good to slap him down. You heard about me, Lucas? I'm supposed to be the Number One Shitheel on Broadway."

"I heard you were a candidate," said Yank Lucas.

"Yeah, well I glory in it. I'm with Durocher. Nice guys don't win, and I knew that before I ever heard of Durocher. But me you know about. Wait till you have some kind of a falling-out with Ellis, here. Then you'll find out about *him*."

"He's been all right so far," said Yank Lucas.

"All right, don't say I didn't warn you," said Barry Payne. "Speaking of warning, I don't know how much Ellis told you, but I don't like anybody getting ideas where Zena is concerned. That goes for all departments, not only the hay department."

"Such as what other departments?" said Yank Lucas.

"Such as like telling her she ought to be more independent. Such as like telling her she ought to pick her own scripts. You could ruin three years' work I put in on her and her career. Somebody will, eventually, but I need two more years and from then on it's a breeze. After that, I don't have to worry."

"Nobody's got any such designs on your wife, Mr. Payne, or at least I haven't and Ellis hasn't," said Yank Lucas.

"Right, Yank, right," said Ellis Walton.

"Listen here, Lucas. I been studying you, and I know what goes on in your mind. Ever since you came in this apartment you've been looking at me and thinking, 'I'd like to put this snotty little Jew-boy in his place,' that's what you were thinking."

"Fellows, fellows," said Ellis Walton.

"And what was the snotty little Jew-boy thinking?" said Yank Lucas.

"Fellows, please. *Good taste*," said Ellis Walton.

"I'll tell you what I was thinking, if that's what you want to know. If you really want to know, I was thinking if I didn't want this play for Zena I wouldn't waste five minutes of my time talking to you. I was also thinking, he needs Zena. So we arrive at a stalemate. Temporar'ly a stalemate. But I want to be the first to tell you, Lucas, as soon as I see you proselytizing Zena in any manner, shape, or form whatsoever, and regardless of whether we're sold out ten weeks ahead, I take her out of the play."

"Regardless of contract," said Yank Lucas.

"Contract? Don't be naïve, Lucas. Don't be naïve. If I want to take her out of the play, she comes out. I'll have her operated on if necessary."

"You say all that in front of Ellis and me?"

"I'll say anything in front of Ellis and you. Two against one. But two happening to be the producer of the play and the author, whereas I'm the husband of the star. So maybe a jury would think you two were ganging up on me. Regardless, you'd have to close the play, and by the time you ever got us into court the court calendars are so crowded these days it'd be two or maybe three years from now."

"Who's talking lawsuits, Barry? You're the only one is talking lawsuits. You always have to make things unpleasant, even such a happy occasion."

"What's with this happy occasion, Ellis? We're three cutthroats talking business. Four cutthroats, only Zena don't happen to be present. So now I hope we all understand one another."

"Perfectly," said Yank Lucas.

"Ellis, I'll be in your office eleven o'clock Monday morning and you'll have a cheque ready for the sum we agreed upon, made out payable to me for personal services."

"Will Zena be there? It'd be nice if my p. a. could get a photographer in to take some pictures."

"The contract won't be all ironed out for another couple weeks. We can take the pictures then," said Barry Payne.

"But we could fake them on Monday. The sooner we start getting publicity."

"The pictures have to come later. I'm getting new caps put on her teeth, for TV. I had to turn down over a hundred thousand dollars for TV appearances. Those cameras are ten times more relentless than the movie cameras. She looks like she had more gums than teeth. Her complexion isn't all that good, either, right now. Plenty of people were willing to teach her how to act, but nobody ever told her how to take off her makeup. I should have got hold of her about six or seven years ago."

"Well, you could have," said Ellis Walton. "She was around."

"Yeah, she was around, all right," said Barry Payne. "But I didn't know it. I was too busy with a certain other party to be bothered about an unknown named Zena Gollum. And Zena Gollum was pretty busy herself. Unprofitably. Getting a hundred and a half from big men like Ellis Walton."

"A hundred and seventy-five, and could have got her for less," said Ellis Walton. "Everybody gives you credit, Barry. She was getting nowhere fast till you entered the picture."

"You'll have me crying in a minute," said Barry. "All the credit *I* want—"

"Take the cash and let the credit go, eh Barry?" said Ellis Walton. "Well, Yank?"

"I'm ready when you are," said Yank Lucas.

On the way down in the elevator Yank Lucas said, "I've heard about people like him. I even heard about *him.* But he's something. He really is something. He's probably on the phone to David Salmon this very minute."

"No," said Ellis Walton. "He'll knife you and everything else. He'll try to put things over on you. But once he says yes to a deal, you can rely on it. That's the only reason why people put up with him. A very complicated man, full of contradictions, but we're in business, Yank. How are you for money?"

"Low," said Yank Lucas.

"If you'll excuse me saying so, you look like something the cat dragged in. Take a few hundred dollars and go away for a rest somewhere. I'll advance you the money, up to a couple thousand. I don't want to have a sick author on my hands."

"I wouldn't know where to go," said Yank Lucas.

"When the paper comes out Tuesday, Peggy McInerney won't have any trouble getting you a job in Hollywood."

"I don't want to go to Hollywood," said Yank Lucas.

"Where is your home town?"

"Oh, Christ I don't want to go there. I come from a town called Spring Valley, out in western Pennsylvania. But I have no desire to go back there."

"What do your people do?"

"My father teaches History of Art in the college there. Spring Valley College."

"Oh, I heard of it. They have teams play in the basketball tournaments at Madison Square Garden."

"Why do you say Madison *Square* Garden? Is there a Madison *Round* Garden?"

"Do I say Madison *Square* Garden? I never took notice. I don't have much of an ear for dialog. I know it's good when I read it, but I don't hear it. That's why I produce plays instead of write them. Anyway, Yank, you ought to go hole up in some hotel and get a good rest. Eat good food, like steaks. Drink a lot of milk. Take a girl with you. Relax and rest. As far as that goes, if you only wanted a girl for like one night, if you wanted to leave that up to me I'll be glad to take care of it for you. What do you like? Blondes? Brunettes? Redheads?"

"I have no special preference," said Yank Lucas.

They got in a taxi. "Can I take you somewhere? Let's go back to my office and I'll get some cash out of the safe."

"All right," said Yank Lucas.

Ellis Walton gave the driver the address on Sixth Avenue, and explicit directions on how to get there.

"Are you trying to tell me Sixth Avenue is a one-way street? Because I know that, mister," said the driver.

"Yeah, well some don't," said Ellis Walton.

"Then they oughtn'ta be driving a hack," said the driver.

"I quite agree with you," said Ellis Walton. "Yank, I sincerely trust this'll be the real beginning of a real mutual association. Don't go taking any stock in Barry Payne putting the blast on me back there."

"I didn't," said Yank Lucas.

"I appreciate you coming to my defense. He's a great divide-and-conqueror. That's why he said what he said about me. He'll have you fighting with the director, and me fighting with the set designer, and the set designer fighting with the costume people. And Zena fighting with everybody. She doesn't want to make the trouble, but he makes it for her so she has to depend on him. Halfway through the rehearsals you're gonna ask yourself is it worth it. Well, it is, if we have a hit. And it is anyway. For you this will be your baptism by fire. What the hell is a baptism by fire? Is there some Gentile religion that actually does that?"

"Baptism *of* fire. In World War One I think they used the expression the first time a man went into action, under fire."

"Yeah, it had to be something like that. I always meant to inquire. I couldn't see them burning a little infant unless they wanted to get rid of him."

"No, it isn't like cutting off the foreskin," said Yank Lucas.

"You have a very interesting mind, Yank. It interests me. You ever been married?"

"Yep."

"Is that why you don't want to go back to Spring Valley?"

"Partly."

"She's still living there, huh?"

"Still living there, married again. Two children."

"It's gonna all come out when your play's a hit," said Ellis Walton.

"All right, if you want to hear about it. I married a girl in my class, in sophomore year."

"You mean your college class or your class socially?"

"My college class. Socially—that's a laugh. Socially, I never belonged to any class, rich or poor. To the rich I was poor, and to the poor I was poor pretending to be like the rich. My father was a college professor. History of Art. If he ever got a couple of hundred dollars ahead, he'd buy a painting with it."

"Some of them pay off."

"Not the ones he bought. He did it to encourage unknown artists, and they stayed unknown. He was full of
shit. A poseur. But he knew all the dates and the periods,
the influence of one school on another, and there was nobody on the faculty that could argue with him, because if
he said a painter was born in 1812 and died in 1865, it
checked out every time. So there he stayed, partly because
he didn't cost much. And he had a beard. It isn't easy to fire
a professor that has a beard. They had another old prof with
a beard, that should have been castrated or locked up, but
they kept him on forever too. My father didn't have that
kind of trouble, but I don't know where he could have got
another job if they'd fired him. My sister and I would have
had to go without a college education. As it was, I quit when
I got married, in the middle of sophomore year, and went to
work on my father-in-law's paper. It came out once a week.
I was 4-F because I had a history of polio when I was ten
years old, and my wife's father was delighted that I could
come and work for him. We had to move in with them, no
place else to live. We'd have been better off living in a tent,
or I would. I had to be with my father-in-law twenty-four
hours a day, which was about twenty-three and a half hours
too much for both of us."

"What was your wife like?"

"She was still going to college, for Christ's sake. She was
pretty, not too bright, but they insisted on her staying in
college so she'd get a degree. So part of the day she was a

pretty co-ed, and then came home late in the afternoon and was supposed to be a young married woman. No go."

"Why did you happen to marry her, if you don't mind me asking."

"Because she miscounted. She was late, and thought she was pregnant. She wasn't."

"And what finally broke it up?"

"Another guy. And a combination of things. Living with her people, and spending all that time with her father at work and in the evenings. The other guy was an army officer, assigned to the college, and he had a car and plenty of gas. I only had the use of a car that belonged to the paper, and I wasn't supposed to use it for my own pleasure. The army guy was a major, in command of the whole set-up, and perfectly understandably he was screwing everything he could get his hands on. Which included my wife. So I quit the paper and she got a divorce, stayed in college, and I moved to New York."

"Did she marry the major?"

"Hell, no. He had a wife and children in—I don't know —out West somewhere. No, she married a town boy."

"Why are you so dead set against going back?"

"Because I lived there for twenty-one years, winter and summer, and in all that time I realized that there wasn't one person, man or woman, that I cared enough about to worry whether they lived or died. Alice, my wife, named after Theodore Roosevelt's daughter, provided me with the only real excitement I ever had there. The first time I ever got in bed with her without any clothes on, I thought this was a joy that would last forever. Inexhaustible. But when she told me that she was going down on the major two or three times a week, and would have continued to if I hadn't got suspicious, I had to get away from her and the town and the first twenty-one years of my life. The story back home is that I'm impotent. She begged me not to tell her parents why we were separating, and I didn't. I suppose she and her parents cooked up the impotence story."

"It didn't jibe with the reason why you married her," said Ellis Walton.

"Oh, we never told them that, either," said Yank Lucas. "I'm not sore at her. When she told me about the major, she said if I wanted to play around it was all right with her. Just as long as her family didn't find out. There she drew the line. If they found out, she was going to have to divorce me. And as far as I know, she's settled down to married life with her husband and kids, and I wouldn't be at all surprised if she's convinced herself that I was impotent and that the major and God knows who else were part of growing up. And if she thinks that—they were. I wrote a bum cheque to get the money to leave town, but that never became a public scandal. I left a note for my father, telling him I was doing it, and promised him I'd never ask him for another cent. Three hundred dollars. He made good on it, and my conscience has never bothered me, considering the fact that he'd spent a lot more than that on lousy pictures by total strangers. I don't say I'm proud of screwing him out of three hundred bucks, but it also served the very useful purpose of giving me a cloud to leave home under. He doesn't have to like me any more, and I don't have to go back. And there you are."

"How did you keep alive while you were writing those other plays?"

"Bus boy and dishwasher. Good enough pay, and all you want to eat."

"Oh, yeah? I would have thought a newspaper job," said Ellis Walton.

"The guys were beginning to come back from the war, and anyway I didn't want a job that involved writing. I wanted to do my writing at night, at home. I've never had to starve. I could go to any of a half a dozen agencies and get a dishwasher or bus boy job the same day I showed up. You save money on clothes and food, so all you really need is carfare and your rent. Another thing, they treat you well. If a bus boy quits his job during the rush hour, the manager or the owner has to do the dirty work. We know that, and they know we know it. I took a job parking cars but I quit after one day. Too strenuous. My neck muscles were so sore I couldn't turn my head the next day. My bus boy experience has improved my Spanish enormously. I spent two Christmases in East Harlem since I've been in New York."

"You'll never have to do that again," said Ellis Walton. They were in his office, and he took some money out of the safe. "Five hundred dollars. More if you want it."

"This is the most money in cash I've ever had in my life," said Yank Lucas.

"Six months from now I'll remind you of that," said Ellis Walton.

"No, I'll never feel richer than I do at this moment. Six fifty-dollar bills and two hundreds," said Yank Lucas. "I hope I don't get rolled on the way home."

"You better give me your IOU for this," said Ellis Walton.

"Why?"

"Because otherwise you'll owe Peggy McInerney fifty bucks' commission. You're going to have to start thinking about those things, Yank."

"I'll try to get used to it," said Yank Lucas.

"The hard part won't be having the money to spend," said Ellis Walton.

"No?" said Yank Lucas, laughing.

"No. That's what money is for, to spend and enjoy life. It's the *idea* of money, getting rid of the *idea* of money that'll be tough. I'm speaking of talented men like yourself, Yank. If you can spend the money and forget about it, you're safe. Your talent is safe. But that remains to be seen."

"I may have only this one good play in me," said Yank Lucas.

"You don't believe that, not for a minute you don't. Neither do I. I wished I didn't have to pay you money. I wish there was some system whereby you never touched money. But we don't live under any such system, so take the money and get a rest, have a good time, and let's hope for the best."

"Ellis, it's nice of you, but you don't have to worry about me and money. Money and I have been strangers all my life. I really don't think it's going to make that much difference to me now."

"I'm glad to hear you say that," said Ellis Walton.

"You're dubious."

"No, I'm Doctor Cronkhite," said Ellis Walton.

"What?"

"You never saw Smith and Dale. A vaudeville act. The one says to the other, 'You're dubious,' and the other one says, 'No, I'm Doctor Cronkhite.' I saw that act a hundred times."

"I never saw much vaudeville. Twice in Altoona and twice in Pittsburgh. I've never been anywhere but Spring Valley, P A, and New York, N Y."

"You never had to go anywhere. Your play proves it. But from now on you can just about go where you please. And you won't have to wash any more dishes."

"The confidence you have in the success of this play," said Yank Lucas.

"You know where I get this confidence from? From that shitheel Barry Payne. My own personal judgment I got plenty of confidence in. But already Barry is kind of afraid of you, and he never was of me. He walks all over people he isn't afraid of, but for you he has a begrudging respect, meaning he's afraid of you."

"Well, as you say, we'll see," said Yank Lucas. "I have another favor to ask you."

"Name it."

"Could you break one of these bills? I want to go home in a taxi, and I only have a dollar and twenty-one cents in my pocket. I don't know how much a taxi costs, but if I gave the man a dollar I'd still have to break a fifty-dollar bill. And in my neighborhood that's asking for it."

Ellis Walton reached in his pocket. "Here's three ones, a five, and a ten-spot."

"Now I owe you five hundred and eighteen dollars. Let's change the IOU."

"No, I'll let you take me to lunch someday. Your eighteen bucks won't go very far then," said Ellis Walton.

Yank Lucas took a taxi, but on an impulse of caution he paid the driver and got out at the Ninth Avenue corner and walked to his building. It was just as well. Coming out as he went in was Jiggs Muldowney.

"Wuddia say, boy? How do you feel?" said Jiggs.

"Pretty good, thanks."

"You don't feel good enough to come down the corner and have a snort?"

"No, I don't feel that good," said Yank Lucas.

"You don't happen to have a couple bucks on you."

"Yes," said Yank Lucas.

"Or a five'd be even better."

"All right," said Yank Lucas. Jiggs Muldowney, with his mouth hanging open, looked down at the ten, the five, and the two singles that Yank Lucas took out of his pocket.

"That ten-spot looks pretty nice," said Muldowney.

"It looks pretty nice to me, too," said Yank Lucas. "The five'll have to do."

"Okay, I'll take the five," said Muldowney. He closed his fist over the bill. "See you."

To himself Yank Lucas said, "Not if I can help it." And now, with $512.21 on his person, he *could* help it. He went upstairs and packed his suitcase and within the hour he was on a train bound for Boston. Although he had never been to Boston, and knew no one there, he had heard a lot about it at home, and his play was going to open there, and it was the destination of the next train.

His total ignorance of Boston revealed itself in his first conversation with the Pullman porter, who asked him if he was getting off at Back Bay. He had heard of Back Bay, but what he had heard had led him to believe that Back Bay was a fashionable suburb, related to Boston as Sewickley was to Pittsburgh. The porter set him straight and did so with patience. Later, as the train was pulling out of Providence, Yank Lucas said to the porter, "What's a good hotel in Boston?"

The porter sized him up for the second time; his tweed jacket and flannel slacks, his unpolished loafers and knitted black tie, his untrimmed hair. Yank Lucas could almost read the porter's opinion of his scratched and banged-up suitcase that lay at the bottom of the pile in the Pullman vestibule. "What's a good hotel in Boston?" said the porter. "Well, we got several first-class. People speak very well of the Ritz Hotel, and then there's the Copley-Plaza, the Statler, the old Parker House hotel. Require reservations, most of them, but being a Saturday you may not have any trouble. Largely depends on how much you care to spend. And the location. Was you thinking you might wish to be closer to Harvard?"

"Harvard, why?"

The porter smiled. "I had it in my mind you might be transacting your business there or the M. I. T. Just a guess on my part."

"No, I have nothing to do with education. And education had very little to do with me."

"In that case, you probably be better off in a central location, like the Statler. I'll let you off at Back Bay and a taxi will take you there. Anything else, sir?"

"No, you've been very helpful, thank you," said Yank Lucas. And he had been; by mistaking his shabby-collegiate clothes for those of a man who might be transacting his business at Harvard, the porter had provided him with a false identity that was more desirable than that of retired dishwasher. It gave him some confidence when he asked for, and got, a room at the Statler. "There was to be a reservation for me," he told the plastic individual behind the desk.

"We have no record of it. What was the firm name?"

"Harvard University," said Yank Lucas.

"They might have made the reservation someplace else."

"Oh, well. If you have a room, I'll stay here and straighten it out Monday."

"Very well. That's Mr. R. Y. Lucas, Spring Valley College, Spring Valley, P A."

"Dr. Lucas."

"I beg your pardon. Doctor. Doctor R. Y. Lucas? I seem to recognize the name."

"Well, it's been in the papers. I'm not a medical doctor, if that'll give you a hint."

"I know! Atomic physics," said the plastic individual.

Yank Lucas nodded wearily. The plastic individual looked at him as though he were capable of disappearing in a mushroom cloud. It was a small enough triumph over a small bully, but it was gratifying nonetheless. "I may want to have a private phone put in my room later on," said Yank Lucas.

"I'm sure that can be arranged, Dr. Lucas," said the plastic man, now a fellow conspirator.

"Oh, it can be arranged, all right," said Yank Lucas.

He had a sumptuous dinner in his room, ordered newspapers and magazines and a box of bonbons, and for two days and nights tried to make an effortless change from the old life to the one that had already begun. He ate and slept and took taxi rides to the blank buildings of Harvard and went for a walk in the Public Garden. He put in the time and postponed thought, especially thought that was related to the pull toward New York that began after the first good night's sleep. On Monday the people of Boston went back to work and their industriousness told him to go away, and he did. But he had had a good time in Boston, away from everybody and everything he had ever known before. He had never had a box of candy all to himself, and he had never known how a room-service waiter treated an atomic scientist. Back to reality.

The moment he opened the door of his flat he smelled gas. He closed the door behind him and knew that the smell of gas was all in his imagination. He went about sniffing the air and there was no true trace of gas. But he also knew that for as long as he lived in the flat the association would be there, and he did not unpack his suitcase. He telephoned Ellis Walton. "I want to move to a hotel. Can I afford to?"

"As long as you weren't thinking of the Waldorf-Astoria," said Ellis Walton. "You mean someplace like the Algonquin?"

"That's where Peggy McInerney took me to lunch. I liked it."

"They know how to charge you there, too, but you can swing it. You want me to handle it for you?"

"Will you? They don't know me."

"Not yet they don't, but they will," said Ellis Walton.

"Can I move in tonight?"

"Tonight already?" said Ellis Walton. "Gee, Yank, I don't promise you but let me see what I can do."

Ellis Walton called back with a favorable report; he could move to the Algonquin that night. He unpacked his suitcase and tossed his old bathrobe and shirts in the wastebasket, and used the space for the manuscripts of finished and unfinished plays. He had one final look about the flat and found nothing else he wanted to keep. He went downstairs and flagged a taxi at the corner, and he tried not to be overdramatic as he told himself that he had seen the flat for the last time.

Somewhat like Byron, he awoke the next morning and found himself famous. That is, he opened his paper and read the announcement that Zena Gollum had agreed to appear in a new play by a hitherto unknown author named Yank Lucas, under the aegis of Ellis Walton. The article went on to say that Miss Gollum had a penchant for choosing vehicles by new playwrights, and that her husband, Barry Payne, had brought the manuscript to her attention after a chance meeting with Lucas in the Automat, where Lucas was working as a bus boy. Mr. Payne had subsidized Lucas during the revisions of the play and would be associated with Mr. Walton in the production.

"You see the New York *Times?*" said Ellis Walton on the telephone.

"I just finished it," said Yank Lucas. "I liked the part about Barry Payne subsidizing me. That must have pleased you, too. I was wondering if I ought to call them and straighten them out."

"It wouldn't do any good. Getting a correction out of the *Times* is next to impossible."

"All the news they see fit to print," said Yank Lucas. "Well, if you're not annoyed and I don't suppose I should be."

"Oh, you get used to those things. And already I got a half a dozen calls from people wanted to put money in the play."

"The magic name of Yank Lucas, retired bus boy. That must have done it."

"By the way, my press agent, Sid Margoll, wants to see you as soon as he can. He says he needs a bio of you."

"I gave you my life story the other day."

"I know, but we might have trouble getting it in the papers."

"And plenty of trouble if you did," said Yank Lucas. "All right, send him over."

"Are you free for lunch?" said Ellis Walton.

"Say that again, please?"

"Are you free for lunch?"

Yank Lucas laughed. "I had to hear it twice. You have the distinction of being the first man that ever said that to me, Ellis. How quickly things change. Even you wouldn't have asked me that yesterday."

"No, but are you? If you are, I could bring Sid and then leave you two together. He wants to get started lining up interviews and all that. You'll like Sid. He knows his way around, widely acquainted. Underneath it all, a great little guy."

"Underneath it all?"

"The con. The bullshit," said Ellis Walton. "Shall we say downstairs at one o'clock. Downstairs there, I mean."

"Not Sardi's?"

"If you'd rather, but you'll be seeing plenty of Sardi's and 21 and I want to show my appreciation. They did me a favor giving you that room last night, and one hand washes the other, so they say."

"I don't have a clean shirt," said Yank Lucas.

"As long as you wear a tie nobody's stopping you," said Ellis Walton.

"Wait'll you see my tie," said Yank Lucas.

At ten minutes of one he went downstairs to the lobby and

could not find a place to sit. He recognized and half-recognized some of the men and women: two movie stars, four or five leading women of the theater, a girl who picked up strangers in Village joints, a famous novelist, a man with a monocle who was either an actor or a writer, a little man who wrote a chatter column.

"There we are. Yank, I want you to meet Sid Margoll."

"I'd of found you myself," said Sid Margoll. "I hear we got a really great script, Yank. Really great. By the way, I want to get where the name Yank originated from."

"Let's grab our table first and have a little libation," said Ellis Walton.

Sid Margoll stopped and spoke to six people on the way to the table. "Broad says she knows you," he said.

"She does," said Yank Lucas.

"She said maybe you wouldn't remember her, but she knows you from the Village."

"That's right."

"She's in here every day, but you don't often see her stay for lunch. She's trying to promote the English guy, but I got news for her. He's a salesman at Mark Cross, the leather goods store. You don't often see him here. He's a piss customer at the 21. I seen him there a thousand times, standing at the bar, nursing one drink. He don't bother anybody, but he takes up space. Well, Yank, bon voyage. You're off on the big journey. Going up, take Broadway. Going down, take Sixth."

"The hell kind of a remark is that?" said Ellis Walton.

"You want to fire me? Yank don't mind. It's actors that

mind. Not actresses. Actors. I could name you on two fingers all the actors I got any use for. One finger is Walter, and the other finger is Huston. Walter Huston. And who knows? Maybe if I knew him better I wouldn't need any fingers. Where'd you get the name Yank from?"

"My middle name. My full name is Robert Yancey Lucas. My mother's people came from the South, and that's how I happened to be named Yancey. When I was little some kids thought Yancey was Yankee, and I grew up with that nickname. Yankee, and then Yank."

"Oh, we gotta do better than that," said Sid Margoll. "Why did you keep calling yourself Yank?"

"There was another Robert Lucas in town, no relation, but around the same age. I was never known as anything but Yank Lucas."

"It doesn't fit you," said Sid Margoll. "You ought to be playing trombone with a name like that."

"Maybe so, but I'm used to it, and I have reasons for wanting to keep it."

"I don't mind the name, but we have to cook up a better excuse for it. You're from Pennsylvania. Anywhere near Shamokin? I got two uncles there in the haberdashery business. I could fix you up with a half a dozen shirts, wholesale. The one you got on has seen its better days."

"Lay off the personal remarks," said Ellis Walton.

"I'm testing him out and you keep interrupting while I'm studying his reactions. I think Yank happens to be a fellow with a sense of humor, but I can't tell some reporter he has a sense of humor and they start asking personal questions and Yank blows his top. You worked on a paper, Yank. You know how they tell you beforehand about such-and-such."

"I usually interviewed undertakers and people like that. I was on a weekly, and all we cared about was names. Lists of pallbearers. People who attended church suppers. Once in a while we had a fire, an automobile accident. The visiting celebrities the editor kept for himself."

"Now you go back there and *he'll* interview *you*," said Sid Margoll.

"That's extremely doubtful," said Yank Lucas.

"Oh? Anything there? A story?"

"He was my father-in-law," said Yank Lucas.

"*Was*. You got a wife now, Yank?"

"No."

"What's this about you being a bus boy? A dishwasher? Is that for real?"

"Very much so."

"Give me the names of some of the hashhouses. Not now. Later. Where did you live?"

"In the Chelsea district."

"We'll make that the Village," said Sid Margoll. "Your average reader doesn't think Chelsea is colorful."

"It was where *I* lived."

"Oh, I know some mobbies came from that district. Some of the toughest. But who knows that in Shamokin, P A? They never even heard of Chelsea, but they sure as hell heard of Greenwich Village. You were 4-F because you had polio. How about if I say you were in the Merchant Marine? You weren't, were you?"

"I've never even been to Staten Island."

"I'd like to send out a bio that feature editors will *go* for. They'll go for the dishwasher-bus boy bit, but I need more than that."

"I'm not a very good subject for feature stories."

"You're telling me. You don't even look very unusual. A typical Nordic Anglo-Saxon. You could be an English teacher in a high school. If you were a conscientious objector, or a fag with a beard. You make it tough, Yank. Got any hobbies?"

"No."

"That broad that said she knew you. She inferred that you gave her a jump. Are you a tail man?"

"I guess I get my share."

"If it was anybody but Zena Gollum I could have you romancing her, but Svengali Payne would never hold still for that. Ellis, what a great break for everybody if Yank actually did romance—"

"No! You cut that out! You want to blow the whole bit before we even signed a contract?" said Ellis Walton. "You must be off your rocker."

"Only trying to get you your money's worth, Ellis," said Sid Margoll. But he looked lengthily at Yank Lucas with the thought of Zena Gollum still in mind. "What if I was to plant a blind item, like Kilgallen, she runs a lot of blind items. Now wait a minute, Ellis. I go to Kilgallen and I say to her, 'Listen, Dorothy May, I got something for you. Exclusive. Way ahead of time. You run it blind now, and later on I'll give it to you complete before anybody else has the straight facts.' She might go for it. First she'll try to figure out who it concerns, from the people I represent. She'll want to know, and I'll tell her she just has to play it my way for the time being. She may go for it, she may not. If she don't, I wasted five minutes. But she may go for it, because she figures if *she* don't go for it, I'm gonna go right away and give it to somebody else. So let's say she goes for it. She runs a blind item, so blind that it could be any number of people in show business. Then I feed her a little more, that the newly discovered playwright genius Yank Lucas has a major heart interest."

"Listen to him. Such crap," said Ellis Walton.

"No clue as to who the heart interest is. Not the slightest. But supposing Yank and Zena do get together? Which I don't say is impossible. By that time, say a couple or three months from now, I don't rule out the possibility. I don't rule it out one bit. Yank is a kind of a clean-cut type, and that's something new for Zena. Especially a clean-cut type that has talent. Most of your clean-cut types don't have any talent. When they get done washing their face in the morning that's about the end of their contribution. But Yank is a clean-cut type that it just so happens he gave her the words to say in her new play. As for you, Yank, I understand you never met Zena. You only seen her work. But I want to tell you something. In spite of what you may hear to the contrary, Yank, Zena Gollum has something offstage. A dumb broad she may be, and I don't see you wanting to marry her. But I bet you a good dinner at the Colony restaurant that sooner or later you get in the kip with her. And that's the time for me to go to Kilgallen and break the whole story."

"The whole thing leaves me cold," said Ellis Walton.

"I'm ignoring your remarks," said Sid Margoll. "Kilgallen breaks the story. Like, 'The whole town will soon be talking about Yank Lucas and his heart interest. The Sardi Set knows the lady's name.' Et cetera. And Mr. Barry Payne is out on his ass. Because once Zena Gollum finds out what it is to be independent again, once she breaks the magic spell, and furthermore we got Kilgallen on our side."

"You jump around from one idea to another," said Ellis Walton. "That's one of the troubles with your schemes, and I don't buy any part of this one. Except the part where Barry Payne is out on his ass. That I like. What's your reaction, Yank?"

"I'm fascinated," said Yank Lucas.

"You want to take me up on that bet, a good dinner at the Colony restaurant?" said Sid Margoll.

"Sure. If I don't get laid, I get fed. I don't see how I can lose there," said Yank Lucas.

Sid Margoll laughed. "This guy I like. I told you he had a sense of humor. If I don't get laid I get fed."

"What do you get out of it, Sid?" said Yank Lucas.

"Me, I get the satisfaction. Don't you worry about me. It wouldn't be the first time I masterminded something sensational. I don't always get the credit, when the thing happens, but even your Ellis Waltons find out about me sooner or later.

I got a young fellow working for me, I pay him a yard and a half a week. Write? He can write as good as Ernest Hemingway right this minute."

"Oh, come on," said Yank Lucas.

"Well, he don't have Hemingway's reputation but if he keeps at it. Anyway, I got him working for me for a hundred and fifty dollars, turning out my press releases. Great. But a hundred and a half is as high as he'll ever get. He's not a press agent. He's a writer. I can't write worth a shit, but I'm a press agent. Tell him what chutzpa is, Ellis."

"What you got plenty of," said Ellis Walton.

"What you got none of, Yank. Coupled with imagination, a different imagination than the one you got, Yank."

"How do you spell that word?" said Yank Lucas.

"Chutzpa? How would you spell chutzpa, Ellis? I wouldn't know how to go about spelling it. It isn't a word you write, it's a word you say, like in conversation. Why do you want to know how you spell it?"

"I like to know how to spell things," said Yank Lucas.

"No, you don't want to infringe on Clifford Odets. That's his territory," said Sid Margoll. "Well, there we are."

"Where is that?" said Ellis Walton.

"I mean we still got Barry Payne to contend with. I wanda dispose of him. Maybe if we kept you under wraps awhile. What would you think of that, Ellis? If we kept him under wraps? I could line up a very few interviews for when we open in New York. A very few. You ever talked on the radio, Yank?"

"Yes."

"You did? That surprised me," said Sid Margoll. "What kind of a program?"

"WSVC, Spring Valley, P A. The news and the weather. Five minutes of the latest news and the weather for our listening area. Your breakfast program brought to you for your listening pleasure through the courtesy of Schumacher-Chevrolet, who also bring you play-by-play descriptions of all home games."

"A fifty-watter," said Sid Margoll.

"I never counted the watts," said Yank Lucas. "I wouldn't know how. I got there at twenty minutes of seven every morning and a man handed me three or four sheets of paper and I read it into the microphone, with interruptions for the commercials. I was paid thirty dollars a week, and was all set to buy a car when my career ended. Three glorious weeks and then the manager of the station gave the job to a veteran. Who happened to be his wife's brother. But a veteran. Yes, I've been on the radio. If you figure it out, it comes to six fives are thirty, times three is ninety. An hour and a half, with time out for the commercials."

"Not exactly Gabriel Heatter," said Sid Margoll. "But you don't get mike-fright or any of that."

"What is there to be afraid of? Except veterans who take your job away, just when you have a car all picked out."

"Would you like to go on with Zena?" said Sid Margoll.

"You can't make any arrangements for Zena, Sid. You know damn well Barry controls all that," said Ellis Walton.

"I'm supposing maybe Barry is out of the picture," said Sid Margoll.

"Oh, for Christ's sake," said Ellis Walton. "Stop it already."

"Well, without Zena," said Sid Margoll. "Maybe we do a Garbo. No interviews. No pictures. You refuse to be photographed, Yank. You don't speak to the press. It'll only work if you cooperate, mind you. If you say no to one, you say no to them all. They try to take your picture, you duck. You wear dark glasses in public. They come to me and they say, 'What's with this jerk?' And I tell them I got strict orders, no personal publicity. Allergic to publicity."

"Already I can visualize you hinting at some sinister reason," said Ellis Walton.

"So I hint? Who knows him? Peg McInerney. You. Barry Payne. Me. The broad out in the lobby promoting the salesman from Mark Cross's. We'll do it that way."

"It shouldn't be very hard," said Yank Lucas.

"We don't want to overdo it," said Sid Margoll. "You don't go into hiding or like that. Far from it. You go to Sardi's and the 21 and all like that. But none of your press conferences, none of your interviews, no talks on the radio. How much does McInerney know about you?"

"Not much."

"You never gave *her* a little jump, did you?"

"*Peggy?*"

"Oh, back there fifteen-twenty years ago you'd be surprised some of the well-known literary lights. She used to come in here for lunch every day, dressed like a dike. Brown suit with a scarf around her neck. But she didn't have that big fat belly then. You didn't have to have a thing ten inches long to get the red part in. I gave her a bang one day, we got talking dirty in her office and the first thing you knew she had it out and I had it in. Only that once. But I remember it even if she doesn't. Does she still have all those writers' pictures in her office?"

"Yes."

"She don't have my picture in her office. But maybe she only counts writers. And publishers. And critics. Good old Peggy. She had a mother she took care of, and then by the time the old lady cooled, Peggy had a shape like Alexander Woollcott. Now she got a belly that sits on her lap. A shame. It is, you know. A woman likes her hump as much as she did, she's only in her late fifties and plenty of dough, but who could get that near her? A wall of fat between you and home plate, and I didn't get any thinner either, or I would of gone back for more. Mention my name to her sometime and see what she says, just out of curiosity."

"I'll do that," said Yank Lucas.

"I'll give you a little tip. When I first knew Peggy, she was put together better than Zena Gollum is now. So don't lose any time. Fifteen-twenty years from now there's no telling what Zena will look like. The two of them are very much alike when I think of it."

"In build," said Ellis Walton.

"Not only in built. Plenty other ways."

The publicity strategy on Yank Lucas was summarized in

a vague agreement between Ellis Walton and Sid Margoll, concurred in by Yank Lucas, that they were to do nothing for the time being. It was a useful and instructive experience in the custom of the business luncheon, the first of its kind for Yank Lucas, and one of the last. The three men had met for a specific purpose, in this case the preparation of a biographical sketch of Yank Lucas. At the conclusion of the luncheon the sketch had been forgotten, nothing was said of it, but meanwhile the three men had eaten some food and had some conversation.

"Where are you going from here, Yank? Can I take you somewhere?" said Ellis Walton.

"As a matter of fact, I'm on my way to Peg McInerney's office. Three o'clock," said Yank Lucas.

Sid Margoll nodded slowly, with a deadpan expression that was supposed to have various meanings but in truth had none, and therefore could have had whatever meaning Yank Lucas and Ellis Walton wished to read into it.

"I'll be in my office, in case you and Peg have anything you want to contact me," said Ellis Walton.

The men shook hands and separated, and Yank Lucas arrived at Peg McInerney's office five minutes ahead of time. She called to him from her revolving chair. "Come on in."

It was now possible to scrape away the fat, to resculpture her on the basis of his recently acquired information. Yes, behind the lard, beneath it, might have been a woman who once had been at least attractive enough to have joined in sex with all those authors and editors and critics whose photographs lined her office wall.

"I've been on the phone all day about you," she said. She put on her black-rimmed glasses and looked down at a piece of paper on her blotter. "I turned down four offers for your personal services. Studios wanting to sign you up at five hundred a week. Would you care to hear the names and so on?"

"I don't think so," he said.

She slapped the piece of paper contemptuously. "One of them was Charley Van Allen. I reminded him that he could have had you for two hundred a year ago, when you needed the money. The old story. A few lines in the papers and you're a desirable property, although he still has never seen a line you've written. The hell with them. But I did turn down one offer that interested me. A pre-production deal. Not enough money now, but I left it open. I could get you twenty-five thousand dollars tomorrow, but you're in a very fortunate position. You've been poor so long that you don't need twenty-five thousand. A name writer who'd had a couple of flops might be tempted, because of their scale of living. This business is full of contradictions. They buy that house in Bucks County and start spending money, and you'd be surprised what some of them will work for to meet their commitments. One of my best authors is taking seven-fifty where only two years ago he was getting twenty-five hundred on the Coast. Too many commitments he has to meet. I hope it doesn't happen to you, but it probably will. You had lunch with Ellis Walton."

"Ellis Walton and Sid Margoll."

"Sid Margoll. The press agent. That's a name I haven't thought of in years."

"He said he knew you."

"I don't suppose he told you I had to throw him out bodily one day."

"No, he didn't mention that."

"Bodily. Chorus girls probably had to put up with his exhibitionism, but I was never a chorus girl. So I had to tell him to put that little thing back where it belonged or I'd throw him out. And I had to throw him out. So he's working for Ellis. Well, never tell him anything you don't want to appear in Kilgallen's column. All these press agents make trades with the gossip columnists. It's their bread and butter, they'll tell you. He'll take money from Ellis, but you see, Ellis isn't a big enough operation to hire Margoll on a yearly basis, so Sid has to have other clients. Not one of them he wouldn't knife in the back to stay in the good graces of the gossip columnists."

"What's the point of telling me all this?"

"Because I expect to make a lot of money with you, and I don't want you to make any foolish mistakes. Such as telling Sid Margoll in confidence that you've turned down twenty-five thousand dollars." She leaned forward in her chair and waved a finger at him like a politician waving a cigar in an off-the-record interview. "You'll hear the same kind of thing about us, agents, if you haven't already." She leaned back again, touching her fingertips to each other. "The story on us is that we'll give a client a screwing to keep in with the picture companies. You'll hear stories about our giving kickbacks to movie executives. A story editor buys a novel or a play, say for fifty thousand dollars, but the author only sees a fraction of that. Part of it finds its way back to the story editor."

"What's the point of telling me that?"

"So that you don't waste any time being suspicious of me. There *was* a time when I made under-the-table deals, but I don't have to any more. I can afford to have ethics. I can even afford to help young writers if I think they have something, and you have." She stopped speaking, as though waiting for him to speak.

"I think I ought to tell you—I think I'd *better* tell you—I took five hundred dollars from Ellis. A personal loan."

"To avoid paying me a fifty-dollar commission. It's a good thing you told me, Yank. If I'd found it out later—and I would have—I could very easily forget my ethics and cost you a lot more than fifty bucks. I practically forced that confession out of you, but I had to give you a chance to tell me. That's the way Ellis works. He disapproves of Barry Payne when Barry does the same kind of thing, but when *he* does it it's an act of friendship. B, a, l, l, s. Balls. I know them all, every God damn one of them. Some of them I learned about the hard way, as they're only too ready to tell you. But if I'm a son of a bitch it's because I had to be, to survive."

"I don't think you're a son of a bitch," said Yank Lucas.

"You haven't seen me in action. I can be when I have to be, and it's all the fun I have left now that I'm an ugly fat slob. A bit of motherly advice. Always be on the level with me and I'll fight for you in ways that you don't know how to fight. Once in a great while I come across a talent I respect. You happen to be one of them. This isn't con. I don't have to con you. No-body has to, although they will. I can tell from your writing and what I know about you that you wouldn't fall for con, simply because you don't con yourself and therefore you don't go for it when you get it from someone else. That's a rare thing among writers, especially playwrights. There's so much ma-larkey connected with show business that even the writers get hammy. I don't know how you can avoid it or I'd tell you. But maybe I don't have to tell you. Stay as sweet as you are, Yank."

"Me, sweet?"

"Not icky sweet. God forbid. But do you know who the sweetest man I ever met in the theater was? Eugene O'Neill. It didn't show in his plays, either, but he was. Don't try to be another O'Neill—but you won't. I *know* that. You're one of the rare ones, and I'll slap down any son of a bitch that tries to change you. Male or female. If I were twenty years younger I'd ruin you, but I'm not twenty years younger. I take it you haven't met your leading lady yet."

"Still haven't met her," said Yank Lucas.

"That will be very interesting. I wonder how that little monkey is going to play it."

"Isn't that pretty much up to the director?"

"I wasn't thinking about your play. I was thinking about the play she's going to make for you."

"I thought she was bound and gagged by Mr. Payne."

"Everybody thinks so. Everybody but me. You know what the fags say—it takes one to tell one. That's why I'm probably the only man, woman, or child in show business that understands Zena Gollum. She's me twenty years ago. Jewish where I'm Irish, an actress where I wanted to be a writer. But she's me. I understand her. I even had a figure like hers when I was her age, and I had a guy that I allowed to run my life as she does with Barry Payne. In my case it was a writer, a poet no less. He didn't try to make money out of me or anything like that. But I had to be at his beck and call, any hour of the day or night. For sex, or not for sex. Sometimes for nothing but sex, and when that was over he'd beat me. Other times he just wanted to talk, and he was quite a talker. Then I wouldn't hear from him for a couple of weeks at a time and I'd worry about him."

"Did you ever figure out what the hold he had over you was?"

"Of course. I didn't know it, and he'd never admit it, but he needed me. That's all. For a woman, love is nothing compared to what being needed can do to you. Women had teats millions of years before anybody ever heard about love, and in spite of the sweater girls, the original purpose of the teat was to give milk. Not necessarily to your own child. You're a small-town boy. You know how a cow moans and groans when she needs to be milked. The son of a bitch needed me."

"Did he milk you, Peggy?"

"The same as, if there'd been any there. We'd better get off that subject or I'll lose my dignity. Oh, we had sex aplenty. But the only time love was ever mentioned was when he was reciting one of his poems. He dominated me by simply being the one person in the world, besides my mother, that I was indispensable to. Thereby, for over two bloody years *he* was indispensable to *me*. I had other men, but when he whistled I came a-running. Got him out of Bellevue, went his bail, changed his sheets, made him take a bath. And screwed him when he was up to it."

"And then came the day that what?"

"Then came the day that I hadn't heard from him for about two weeks and I began to get the worries. He never had a phone. The phone company had learned their bitter lesson. So I went down to his room on Avenue B, and there he sat, in his old Morris chair. Dead as a mackerel and smelling worse. In those days there was a thing called smoke. They drained the alcohol out of a can of Sterno and strained it through cheesecloth, and drank it."

"Oh, I've heard of smoke," said Yank Lucas.

"Well, he'd heard of it too, but he hadn't learned the technique. If he'd gone down to the Bowery he could have got them to show him how it was done, but he was such a wise guy he never asked anybody's advice on anything. That particular trait cost him his life, that and his great desire to be independent. He used to beat me to show me how much he didn't need me. But if he had sent for me, I'd have brought him a bottle of gin. I always did, automatically."

"There really isn't a hell of a lot of similarity between him and Barry Payne, is there?"

"No, but between me and Zena Gollum there is. I don't expect her to go home some day and find Barry Payne dead in a Morris chair. But Barry Payne will go home some day and he won't find Zena Gollum."

"Because somebody else needs her more?"

"Could be. More to the point, because he convinces her that he doesn't need her. How that will happen I have no idea, but remember, she's a big star. I only had my mother, but Gollum has her public. They need her, too. Barry Payne is overprotective of his property, Miss Gollum, and he has a way of coming between her and her public. Oh, hell, she's an ignorant little monkey, never finished high school, and Payne is depriving her of the fun she's entitled to. If she ever stops to think along these lines, she'll tell him to go screw. You can't keep someone like that locked up forever. She's entitled to a better time than he gives her. Everybody is. I don't like her. I couldn't care less what happens to her after your play's had a run. But I feel sorry for anybody that's not getting all they can out of life, especially when they're young. I look around this office. This is where I've spent most of the last fifteen years, right in this room. I have a beautiful apartment on

East Fifty-second, near the river. A cooperative. It's full of
lovely things, and I have a colored woman takes care of me.
Cleans and does the cooking when I want her to. Once a year
I give a party there, the top celebrities, and I blow myself to
a dress at Bergdorf's or Hattie's. Champagne. Caviar. Somebody once called it 'the secret life of Peg McInerney,' as if I
lived that way all the time. Well, I don't. I'm in here at half
past nine five mornings a week, and I'm often here till eight
o'clock at night, talking to people on the Coast. I could
phone them from my apartment, but if I have to look anything
up it's all here. My files. Contracts. Copyrights. I can't ask
my secretary to keep those kind of hours. So I finish up here
and go down and grab a cab and go home, have a couple of
blasts by myself and heat up what my maid left for me. I'm a
good agent because I'm a miserable woman. I could retire
now, but to what? What in Christ's name would I do all day?
I wouldn't have anybody to fight with except people like the
doorman at my apartment. And I wouldn't have anyone to
fight *for*. Watch me go into action on your next play. This one
I had to play it a little cool. Ellis Walton isn't the greatest
manager that ever lived, but you're not Tennessee Williams.
At least not yet. So I got you a deal that I'm not taking any
bows for. You're assured of a first-class production, with a hot
star, and you come in third in the money department. Ellis
Walton and Mr. and Mrs. Barry Payne will come in ahead of
you. But on your *next* play! The names I've been called before
will seem like valentines."

"All you people—if I were superstitious I'd be worrying my head off. The play isn't even in rehearsal."

"You put your finger right on it when you said, 'All you people.' Starting with me, the first one to read it, everybody had the same feeling about this play. Practically actor-proof and director-proof except for the third act. Then when you came up with the new third act, there were no more reservations."

"When did you read the new third act?"

"Last night. If you had been there I'd have eaten you," she said. "I'd have devoured you. I'll bet it had the same effect on Zena Gollum, and don't think she won't try. Well, if you ever want to use my apartment, Barry Payne doesn't know where it is."

"That's another thing you're all so sure of," said Yank Lucas.

"I'm more sure of it than the others. I told you, she's me twenty years ago. Just remember that I'm her twenty years from now."

"You have me married to her before I know her."

"Well, I may be wrong about that. And if you did marry her, I doubt if it would last twenty years. Or twenty months."

"It's not going to last, because it's not going to happen. As far as marriage is concerned, I've had it."

She squinted and gazed at him steadily. "Maybe you don't need anybody. I've never thought of that, but maybe you don't. That goes with genius sometimes, and maybe you're a genius. Are you?"

He waited a long while before answering. "Ask me ten plays from now."

"That's a good answer. I'll buy that."

He smiled. "I'm a genius now, but ten plays from now I may not even be good."

"Don't elaborate. I knew what you meant," she said. She half turned and looked over her shoulder at the photographs of the men of letters she had known.

"What?" said Yank Lucas.

"They weren't all lovers of mine but I loved them all, and I think you belong up there. You'd be the first new face in ten years. Look at those collars and ties. How did they ever breathe?"

"Heavily, some of them, I gather."

"You son of a bitch. You're so right," she said.

"Which one was the poet?"

She shook her head. "He's not there. I have him in my bedroom at home."

"Oh," said Yank Lucas.

"With his shirt open at the neck. I can't bear to remember him the way he was the last time I saw him."

"You don't have to explain. I knew when you were talking about him."

"I believe you did. I'd believe almost anything you told me, Yank. Let's keep it that way."

"All right," said Yank Lucas. It was time to go. He had nothing to do, but it was time to go.

He was to look back upon the next few months as a period of numbness. From the signing of the contract to the beginning of rehearsals he was comfortable, with nothing to do but wait, and nothing he could do to hasten things. They could not begin rehearsals until Zena's play closed, and the play would not close until the gross receipts fell below a figure that was known to Barry Payne but not to Yank Lucas or to Ellis Walton. The announcement that Zena was to be in a new play had the effect of stimulating interest in the current play, and business picked up for a while. Then one day Ellis Walton called Yank Lucas and told him that Zena would be ready to begin rehearsals in three weeks. The news did not altogether dissipate the numbness of comfortable waiting, but two days before the first reading his lethargy vanished. In two days he would be called upon to speak his piece to the world. The world, as it happened, was a tacky ballroom in a seedy old hotel, and the human race was represented by a few actors and the non-acting men and women whose presence was required at the rehearsal.

There was the star, Miss Gollum; the leading man was Scott Aubrey. Miss Gollum's father was to be played by Joseph W. Grossman. Her sister was Shirley Dick. Her brother was Rick Burtyne. Her mother was Ada-Anne Allen. The Negro in the third act was Jasper Hill. All but Miss Gollum had been cast in Ellis Walton's office, in the presence of

Walton, Yank Lucas, and Barry Payne. They were all solid, dependable Broadway actors. Even Rick Burtyne, the youngest in years, had a long list of successes and failures, some motion picture experience and, like the others, profitable appearances in radio soap opera. Yank Lucas had seen them all on stage and remembered them. Two or three of them had worked for Ellis Walton in other plays. Yank Lucas suspected that each name had been submitted to Barry Payne before the actor was asked to read for a part. It did not matter. It was better to let Barry Payne give his secret approval now than to find fault with the actors later. It was a case of happy casting all around. "When you send for an actor, the reading is just a formality," said Ellis Walton. "Not to them, though. They come here in a sweat, especially when they never met the author before. And of course you have the right to say no to any of them. But when they go out of here knowing they have a job lined up, without waiting too long, you have what I call happy casting. They go out of here feeling that they're members of the company, which they are. If you have to fire them later, that's something else again. Then you have to have what I call unhappy casting. You got to go looking for an actor to take their place, and the one you finally hire is sore at you because you didn't send for him in the first place. That's what I call unhappy casting. Here we got happy casting."

The director was Marc DuBois. "I shouldn't tell you this, but he wasn't even my second choice," said Ellis Walton. "He's nobody's first choice, not even very many's second choice. But he's the best we could get. The ones you want are all tied up five years ahead, and even if they weren't they're starting to shy away from Zena. Not on account of Zena, but because on account of Barry Payne. That left us with Marc and any number of dogs. He's dying to get his hands on Zena—not to screw her but to direct her. For him it's a very good opportunity. He's smart enough to know that if she's great, which she should be, he gets some of the credit for getting a good performance out of her. If she bombs, he has the greatest out in the world—interference by Barry Payne."

"Well, he's done some good things," said Yank Lucas.

"Exactly. And I honestly think everybody connected with this play is going to move a step forward career-wise. Including Zena."

"Whom I finally get to meet—"

"Monday morning, ten o'clock, the second floor of the Judson Arms."

"Is there anything I ought to do? Anything in particular?"

"You could make a little speech if you wanted to, but if I were you I'd just go and shake hands with the various actors and then sit down. Let Marc make the speeches."

The ballroom of the Judson Arms Hotel was half filled with the chairs and planks and horses of the previous night's banquet. For a stage the bandstand was an adequate substitute. Yank Lucas and Ellis Walton shook hands with each of the actors, who, with the exception of Zena Gollum, arrived before ten o'clock. Marc DuBois arrived at five minutes before the hour, shook hands with Yank Lucas and Ellis

Walton and the actors, and looked at his wristwatch. "In this rain it's tough getting a cab, so I won't say anything today. But I might as well tell you, Ellis, I don't want her to make a habit of being late," said DuBois.

"No, don't say anything today," said Ellis Walton.

"The star's prerogative—only I don't happen to go for that crap. The way I look at it, the star ought to be here first, to set a good example."

Awkwardly, with no lines to speak and nothing to do, the actors stood about and made small talk until nearly half past ten. DuBois looked at his watch. He and his male secretary were sitting apart from the others, with playscripts in their laps while DuBois muttered to the secretary. DuBois, having looked at his watch, slapped the playscript shut, put it on his chair and went to Ellis Walton. "I suggest we send downstairs for some coffee."

"She'll be here any minute," said Ellis Walton.

"Is it all right if *I* send down for coffee?" said DuBois. "Teddy's used to being my gofer."

"Your what?" said Ellis Walton.

"You never worked in radio. A gofer goes for coffee," said DuBois.

"A new expression to me," said Ellis Walton.

"Well, if we're going to have to wait for *her*, we might as well have a coffee klatsch. You're paying for the use of the hall."

Ellis Walton called to his secretary. "Coffee and Danish for how many there are. You can use that phone over there."

"Tell them don't forget napkins," said DuBois. "I don't want to get my script all stickied up."

"Napkins," said Ellis Walton to his secretary. "We should of heard by now. Maybe she went to the wrong hotel. But Barry wrote it down."

"Wrote it down? I wouldn't be surprised if he used to be a bellhop here," said DuBois.

"You know him better than that," said Ellis Walton.

"Some things I know better. Some things I don't," said DuBois. "Oh, look! We're here."

Barry Payne, with his hand under Zena Gollum's elbow, came toward the threesome of Ellis Walton, Yank Lucas, and Marc DuBois. "Now don't anybody start looking at their watches. It was all my fault. I had to go back for my reading glasses. Hello, Ellis. Lucas. Marc. You all know Zena."

"I don't," said Yank Lucas.

"You were introduced to her at the apartment," said Barry Payne. "No, that's right, you weren't. Well, may I present my wife, Miss Gollum, this is the author, Yank Lucas."

"My pleasure," said Zena.

"How do you do," said Yank.

"Go on over and say hello to the others," said Barry. "Tell them it was my fault we're late."

"I won't tell them anything," said Zena. She moved away.

"Got a fig up her ass," said Barry. "We were all the way down to Columbus Circle and I reached in my pocket for my glasses. You'd think she never forgot anything. Well, anyway she's a quick study. She doesn't forget lines. So we didn't lose very much time."

"She *is* a quick study? I didn't know that," said Marc.

"You never heard anything to the contrary," said Barry.

"No, but I didn't hear that she was, either. Fortunately the lines in this play evolve, one line from the preceding line. I'm not just saying that because the author's here. It's true. The dialog is very naturalistic. Maybe just a little too naturalistic, but we can work on that later."

"I don't think so," said Yank Lucas.

Oh? Aren't we going to have *any* changes, Mr. Lucas?"

"We're probably going to have a lot of changes. But not on the grounds that the dialog is too naturalistic," said Yank. "Specific changes, yes. When we want to speed up an exit, for instance. But the naturalistic dialog stays naturalistic."

"Are you slapping me down, Mr. Lucas?"

"I don't like statements like the dialog is too naturalistic."

"Even if you find out that it is, for dramatic purposes?" said Marc.

"I repeat, when changes are necessary, for dramatic purposes, I'll make them. Most likely. But only then. As far as slapping you down—I'll slap anybody down if they start monkeying around with my play."

"He's learned his rights awfully soon," said Marc.

"That's a good thing," said Yank. "That way we understand each other from the very beginning. You're here to direct the play, Mr. DuBois, not to rewrite it. The actors are here to act in it. This may be my first *and* last play on Broad-

way, but I know what actors try to do to plays, too. I can
walk out of here and take my play with me, and go back to
washing dishes. But everybody please understand that the
play you've all read is the play that goes on."

The first to break the silence was Barry Payne. "He's right.
I'm for no changes till we go before a live audience."

"I think I know Yank Lucas pretty well. He's a reasonable
man," said Ellis Walton.

"I don't think I'm very happy here, three against one,"
said Marc DuBois. "Four against one, if you count Zena, who
arrives for the first rehearsal thirty-five minutes late. I'm perfectly willing to bow out if that's the way it's going to be."

"Nobody wants you to bow out, Marc," said Ellis Walton.

"Zena's lateness was my fault," said Barry.

"Huh?"

They turned at the sound of Zena Gollum's voice.

"Did someone mention maybe Zena Gollum? Let's go to
work, people. This is a good bunch, Ellis. Come on, Marc, let's
quit farting around. You know, on the way downtown I kept
thinking, what do they mean *re*hearsing? We haven't even
hearsed yet. So how can we *re*hearse? That's a joke, son."

"She listens to Fred Allen," said Barry.

"Well, I don't forget my reading glasses," she said, and
took out a pair of heavy black-rimmed glasses and put them
on. "God damn it, I feel good. I want to get my new choppers
into Mr. Lucas's play."

"I think you saved the day, Miss Gollum," said Yank.

"How?" said Zena.

"Later," said Barry.

"All right, everybody," Marc called out. "Onstage, please. Everybody seated and we'll have a reading. A milk run. Never mind the pear-shaped. Just a reading so we'll all have some idea of what the play's all about."

"Coffee and Danish," said Walton's secretary, as a bellboy arrived.

"Forget the Danish. Serve them the coffee," said Ellis Walton.

Yank Lucas watched the actors mounting the bandstand, with chairs dangling from their arms, scripts and coffee containers in their hands, and reading glasses on the tops of their heads or clenched in their teeth. It was a very unlikely beginning.

"Remember this, Yank. Remember it all," said Ellis Walton. "It positively only happens to you once. Till the next time."

Yank Lucas nodded. He wanted to hear Marc DuBois. "Act One, Scene One. At Rise—" he read from the script.

"A real ham, you know," said Ellis Walton. "He gives out with the pear-shape even just reading the directions. And the swish comes out as soon as he opens his mouth. Listen to him."

"I am," said Yank Lucas.

"I never wanted to be an actor, but I love everything about—"

"Sh-sh."

Marc DuBois took off his glasses and stepped to the edge of the bandstand. "I'm sorry, but if we're going to have these distractions out front—I must have quiet . . . Let's begin again. Act One, Scene One."

They read the play straight through, without taking time out for the intermissions. When they finished the reading—superstitiously leaving out the last line—they sat quiet for a moment, then took deep breaths that were nearly sighs.

"I'd like to have everybody back at two o'clock, please," said Marc DuBois. "Can you all be here at two?"

They all said they could.

"This is a great, great play, and we're all going to have to work our little asses off," said Marc. "Thank you."

The actors came down off the bandstand and went their various ways. Zena Gollum's way was to seat herself in a chair next to Yank Lucas. She did not speak nor look at him, and in a few seconds—fewer than ten—she got up and went to her husband. "Let's eat here, they must have a restaurant downstairs," she said.

"They have. I noticed it coming in," he said.

"I'm not very hungry, but I guess I ought to eat *something*," she said. "Could you hear me all right?"

"Sure I could hear you," he said.

"How was I otherwise?"

"How were you otherwise?" he said. "This was just a reading. You didn't have to be anything otherwise."

"I was hoping he'd say something to me," she said.

"Who? Lucas?"

"I was hoping he would, but he didn't," she said.

"Oh, that's why you went and plunked yourself down next to him," he said.

"I *wanted* him to say something," she said.

"Come on, you're not that insecure," he said.

"Maybe he's afraid of you," she said.

"Him? Not that fellow. Do you want to go downstairs, or do you want something sent up here?"

"You decide," she said.

"Let's go downstairs," he said.

"I was as good today as I'll ever be. I was *in* it," she said.

"Crap. You were in it like reading a book, maybe, but I don't call that acting."

"It didn't get across to you, but I hoped it would to him. If it's gonna take this much out of me every time I'll be worn out soon."

"Let's go eat," he said.

"I don't like this play, especially in the third act. You didn't notice, but we were all—I don't know. We all got coughing, as if we could smell the gas."

They headed for the elevators. "What do you mean, you don't like this play?"

"Jasper doesn't like it either. I could tell," she said.

"You're psychic."

"Nobody was trying to act," she said. "Shirley Dick. But none of the others. Even Scott Aubrey, he was taken by it. We weren't just waiting for cues up there. Do you know what I think? I think we could all sit there, without any scenery, never move out of our chairs, and just read this play, and it'd get across. They're always talking about innovations. We could do that with this play. No acting at all."

"And I think you're off your rocker," he said. "I sat there for the better part of two hours, and it didn't have any effect on me. This play has to be acted and acted strong."

"In other words, I'm completely wrong, as usual," she said.

"In other words, you're afraid of this play and you'd like to get out of working in it. Why? Because compared to this one you've been walking through plays, but you can't do it with Lucas's. What *about* Lucas?"

"What about him?"

"Are you, uh, like getting a message from him?"

"Him? I wouldn't hardly know him if I saw him on the street," she said.

"That's for the birds," he said. "The minute the reading was over you made a beeline for him. Is he gonna be the one?"

"What one?" she said.

"The one I have to watch out for."

"Maybe he is," she said.

He slapped her. They were in the corridor, waiting for the elevator. She touched her chin where the slap had grazed her. "You should have saved that," she said. "Till you had something to go on."

"I have something to go on," he said. "I don't have to see you in bed with him. I know when it's starting to itch you."

"Do you? Then you know before I do," she said.

"You're exactly right. I know before you do. All I have to do is see you look at a guy. You look right at their fly."

"Well, that's the place to look," she said.

He would have slapped her again, but the elevator car, an old-fashioned grillwork type, halted for them. "Down," said the operator.

"Down is right," she said. "Any way you look at it." She smiled at her husband, and he could tell—because she was telling him—that he had lost her. By the time they reached the lobby she was radiant. "You go on uptown. I'll eat by myself," she said.

"You starting to give orders all of a sudden?" he said.

"If I's in your place I'd take the hint," she said.

"If you think it's gonna be that easy, Zena, are you ever wrong," he said.

"Ta ta, dear. I'll see you when I see you," she said.

The Judson Arms had a coffee shoppe, now crowded with men from the fur industry. Many of them recognized her, and she heard her name. The headwaiter, who did not recognize her but knew a sable coat when he saw one, said, "I don't have a table right now, if you want to wait in the lobby."

She scanned the room for a familiar face, and saw Ellis Walton with Marc DuBois. "I see who I'm looking for," she said, and went to them.

"Will you join us? Where's Barry?" said Ellis.

"He had to go uptown. Now that you're up, don't get up," she said. "What'd you order?"

"I'm having the double lamb chops and the mixed green salad," said Ellis. "Marc is having the yogurt."

"I'll have the chops," she said. "But no salad. Maybe some

stewed tomatoes, if they have them." The waitress wrote down the order and departed. "Well, so what's new?"

"I don't know. What's new with you?" said Ellis.

They laughed a little. "You know, I felt so God damn depressed, but it wasn't depressed I was feeling. Where is Lucas?"

"He went to get a haircut," said Ellis.

"Was I wrong, Marc? I had the feeling that we were getting into something, and I wasn't sure I wanted to be in it."

"Jesus, don't say that," said Ellis.

"She's right, though. It describes it. I never got that from a reading before, in my whole career. Let's hope it augurs well for the future, and I'm sure it does."

"I'll tell you what Scott Aubrey said to me," said Ellis. "He said he was absolutely terrified. He said if he did anything to harm this play, he was going to give up the theater."

"For once I believe him," said Marc. "We all got a truly wonderful feeling of esprit, didn't you think, Zena?"

"What do you mean by a spree? You mean like going on a spree? No, I didn't," she said.

"I meant esprit de corps. All working together for the common good, as it were."

"Oh, I sure did," she said. "Yes."

"I think Zena means a sense of foreboding," said Marc.

"Be interesting to see how the matinee audiences go for it. Evening performances I'm not worried about."

"They're not such fools any more," said Marc. "When I did—"

The waitress was with them. "Be twenty minutes on your chops, ma'am. I shoulda told you."

"Give her mine and bring me hers," said Ellis. "Mine must be almost done."

"No, just give me a steak sandwich. Rare. And an order of sliced tomatoes. And a cup of coffee with the meal. Bring me the coffee whenever his chops are ready."

"You wouldn't want a filet mignon?" said Ellis.

"No thanks. A steak sandwich," said Zena. "Ellis, is this where we're going to rehearse till we go to Boston?"

"Yes, why?"

"I just wondered," she said.

"Getting back to those Wednesday matinees," said Marc. He then chattered until he had consumed his yogurt, whereupon he said, "I'm going to leave you two kids. I have some phone calls."

Ellis watched him go. "I hope I made the right choice there," he said. "What's on *your* mind, Zena?"

"Can you get me a room here?" she said.

"In the hotel? You mean a place you can lie down? Sure, I guess so."

"Nobody else knows about it except you and I?" she said.

"I don't get it. You mean that includes Barry?"

"We had a fight," she said. "Just now, a few minutes ago. I'm going back to the apartment, don't think I'm not. But I want to have a room here that he won't know about. Will you get it for me?"

"Sure. Anything else you want to tell me? I better know."

"When there's something to know, I'll tell you," she said.

"Oh. I ought to warn you, Zena, as a friend I ought to caution you. Barry can be mean."

"Ho-ho, you're telling me."

"You signed the contracts, but did you read them?"

"No."

"Then I'll tell you. As long as you and Barry stay together, the contracts are very beneficial. But if you and Barry break up you don't stand to get all you should. You personally don't own a piece of the show. You could be working for your salary, but that's all, and even there he takes ten percent. Who's the guy? Not Scott Aubrey?"

"No."

"I'm glad to hear that, anyway," said Ellis. "I could tell you a few things about him."

"Barry saved you the trouble," she said. "He even told me things about old Joe Grossman. Barry doesn't go around giving people the big build-up."

"No, I wouldn't guess he did. Why did you marry him, Zena?"

"You want to know something? He's the only guy that ever asked me to marry him. The absolutely only one. I know why he wanted to marry *me*. I always did know. Listen, it wasn't such a bad deal. You get to a certain age and you begin thinking, Christ sakes, I made out a list of guys I went to bed with and I left out two. Is that a life? You ought to have something to show for it. All I had to show for it was a couple scars where they took out my appendix and damn near everything else. I was getting to be such a tart that the fairies and the lezzes were going for me. I was getting to be a clown for a bunch of queers. 'Here comes Zena! Hyuh, Zeen!' And end up with some dike chewing away at you. Well, he got me out of that, Barry. I had a girl tell me one time that once the dikes get you, you never go for a man again. Well, that's dike propaganda. Or else Barry rescued me before it was too late. He's great in the hay, you know. I couldn't have stayed married to him that long if he wasn't. Oh, I give the son of a bitch a lot of credit, but the time has come. The time has come."

"It isn't another guy?"

"It is, and it isn't," she said.

"Aw, then I know who it is," he said.

"You probably do, Ellis."

"A certain party that's out getting a haircut, may I ask?"

"I don't even know if he *likes* girls. I never had five minutes' conversation with him. But all the same I'm on the make for him, with or without but preferably with."

"It'll be with," said Ellis.

"Does he have a girl?"

"That I don't know. But he was married, and he's one of those fellows that it doesn't seem to bother him but he gets it. Some guys they advertise it that they're continuously on the make. They come in a café and give their tie a little pull, take hold of the coat lapels, fix the little handkerchief in the coat pocket."

"Oh, yes."

"Not this fellow, though," said Ellis.

"No, not this fellow."

"His mind is occupied with other things. He's what I call a very introspective individual. Very. You ought to hear him tell me about when he used to wash dishes, a dishwasher in a cafeteria. I think it was one of the Horn and Hardart chain. Very philosophical, you know what I mean? All he wanted was enough to eat and a place to sleep—and work in. There's the crux of the matter. In those sordid surroundings he rose above the surrounding atmosphere because he was imbued with the creative spirit. Positively imbued with it."

"Imbued with it, huh? Imbued—that's—well *I* know what it means."

"Positively imbued. And I'll be absolutely frank with you, Zena. I'm positively convinced that this young fellow is probably going to turn out to be one of the authentic geniuses of our time. But wait a minute, girl. In the creative world, mind you, all is not a bed of roses. Permit me if I may, but this word of caution may not go amiss. Heartaches and headaches may lie ahead."

"Quite a few of them lie behind, though, too," she said.

"That is for you to decide. Be it one way or the other, that is for you to decide. I'm speaking to you as a friend, perhaps a trifle conventional and old hat. But in a situation such as this, I owe it to our friendship to give you the benefit of— well, I'm your senior by more than a decade. And sometimes the old tried-and-true clichés seem trite, but there's a lot of truth contained therein."

"I wish I had your education," she said.

"I only graduated from Evander and took evening courses at N.Y.U. I didn't have the benefit of the classical education, Zena. But I did probe rather deeply into the classics every opportunity I got."

"I went to Evander, too, but I quit. As soon as I got my per*mit*."

"It may interest you to know that the gentleman we're speaking of does not possess a college degree. Actually, your husband, Barry Payne, is better educated than Lucas. Barry holds a B.A. from City."

"I wasn't thinking about degrees. Degrees or not, Lucas is more intellectual than Barry."

"Yes, a person would be more apt to call Lucas an intellectual type than Barry Payne, although we shouldn't denigrate Barry in that department. Jasper Hill has a college degree. Wilberforce. Joe Grossman, a Fordham Law grad before entering the theater. Shirley Dick attended Barnard. Quite an intellectual company we've assembled. But none of them hold a candle to you, dear girl."

"You can bet your sweet ass I don't hold a candle to myself," she said. "Seriously, Ellis, I'm not going to give you any trouble. This thing is between me and Barry. All I'm asking you for is to get me a room here in the hotel, and make like you don't know a thing. Which you don't. There's nothing to know. But another thing, come to think of it—Sid Margoll. He's a stooge for every columnist in town."

"Oh, not a word to Sid, of course."

"That little shitheel could ruin everything. If he does anything to embarrass Lucas, I swear I'll walk out of your fucking play."

"To embarrass Lucas," repeated Ellis. "Is this amour toujours? You're the strangest girl I ever met."

"You can say that again, but don't," said Zena.

T he company was a company now. When they came back from lunch they did not reassemble; they reunited; and it made no difference that they had been separated from each other and from the play for less than two hours. They had talked about the play, or they had not, but that they had been thinking about it, feeling it, there could be no doubt. They greeted each other with smiles and quiet cordiality, and returned to the bandstand and to the chairs they had occupied in the morning reading.

Marc DuBois, in slacks and dark blue pullover, held the playscript to his belly as he addressed them. "All here, and all on time," he said. "Most of you are unfamiliar with the way I work, so just a word about that. Well, I work differently in every play, and this one I decided we want to stay close together. Some plays you can rehearse piecemeal, but not this one. No taking time off to do radio commercials or anything like that. Everybody has to be here all the time, not just for the scenes you happen to be in. This is what they call a *mood* play, and I want everybody here so that you'll not only get the mood of the scenes you're in, but the mood of the scenes you're not in. If there's anybody has any radio commitments that I don't know about, please get out of them. Or modeling jobs. Or anything that distracts you from the mood of this play or makes it impossible for you to be here all the time. Anybody that has any such commitments, please speak to me later this afternoon. O.K. Now, we're going to read again, but this time I want every one of you to give it the reading you think belongs there. If you want to shout, shout. If you want to hesitate, hesitate. I don't promise you that your way is the way we'll eventually do it when we freeze. But as a director I'm not so high and mighty that I reject everybody's ideas that aren't mine." He put on his glasses and sat down. "Act One, Scene One. At Rise..."

This reading took much longer as the actors availed themselves of the freedom to act. The individual personalities and eccentricities came out, and there were hints of conflicts between the personalities. The actors were no longer dominated by the play, and the contrast with the morning reading was all too apparent. At the end of the reading Marc DuBois said, "Thank you. That'll be all today. See you here at ten-thirty tomorrow morning." He came down from the bandstand and seated himself beside Yank Lucas and Ellis Walton. "Well," said Marc DuBois, "they certainly did stink up the joint this afternoon."

"Oh, well," said Ellis Walton.

"And they know it," said Marc. "They'll know it tonight,

[81]

too. They'll all be blaming each other, but they're pros, and they'll secretly admit that they were as much to blame as the other fellow."

"You don't seem very unhappy," said Yank Lucas.

"I'm not. I just showed them that this play needs a director. I hope I showed you, too," said Marc.

"I never said it didn't," said Yank.

Zena Gollum had been chatting with, listening to, Shirley Dick but with an eye on Ellis, Marc, and Yank. The moment Marc left the others she went to Ellis. "Did you take care of that?" she said.

"Oh, yes," said Ellis. "In my name." He reached in his pocket and took out a room key and slipped it to her by pretending to take an affectionate grasp of her hand.

"Goodnight, everybody," said Ellis. He left, and the others drifted out. Zena Gollum and Yank Lucas were alone.

"Don't be discouraged," she said. "We tried to louse up your play, but we didn't."

"You didn't louse up my play. You just proved that good actors can be bad actors," said Yank.

"I thought you were discouraged. You certainly had a discouraged look."

"How would you know? Maybe this is my natural, every-day look."

"That's true, maybe it is. Is it?"

"No. I was discouraged."

She laughed. "You're a tough man to figure," she said. A man opened the ballroom door and looked at them, and immediately closed it. "I suppose they want us to get out of here. They use this place for banquets, Ellis said."

"Where do you want to go?" she said.

"Well, would you like to go someplace for a drink or something?"

She held up the room key and let it dangle from the heavy metal tag. "Or something," she said. "I had to wait till you invited me. I didn't want you to think I was forward."

"Where is that for?" he said.

She read the tag. "Room eight one nine, Judson Arms. Return postage guaranteed. I'll bet it's the best offer you've had all day."

"It *is* an *offer?* What about Payne?"

"I don't know about Payne, frankly."

"You don't know about me, either. But you want to find out," said Yank.

"Well, as far as that goes, you can be finding out about me, too," she said.

"What'd you say it was? Eight one nine? That just happens to be my lucky number," said Yank.

She smiled. "Luck has nothing to do with it," she said. "Maybe you ought to go up first."

"Yes, they may be having a banquet there," he said. He bent down and kissed her softly on the mouth. It had a very sobering effect.

"Thank you for that," she said. "That was exactly the right thing to do. I was beginning to lose my nerve."

"The wrong time for that. I'll see you in three minutes?" he said.

"Pretty slow elevators. Maybe four," she said. "What's the number?"

He looked at the key tag again. "Eight one nine. My lucky number. Eight-nineteen."

Eight-nineteen was a two-room suite. It even contained a piano. Yank struck a C-chord, and the piano was out of tune. He tossed his reversible coat on a plush armchair. One dead match lay in a glass ashtray; a single dead yellow paper match. "Reconstructing the crime," he said aloud. "I am inclined to believe that a lazy chambermaid lit a cigarette in this room, then went out, carrying her vacuum and dustrags. Inspector, I suggest that you find out which chambermaid is in the habit of smoking cigarettes without removing them from her mouth. You will then, I feel sure, have your murderess. Good day, Inspector, I shall be just in time for the concert in Albert Hall."

There was a double bed, brass, with a single thin blanket under the rose-studded counterpane, and a pair of soft pillows. The enamel in the bathtub and washbasin looked like the veins in a traveling salesman's nose. He almost did not hear the rap on the door. He swung it open and closed it quickly, and she stopped dead. "For God's sake. A parlor? Yes, that would be Ellis. He got the room for me." She took off her sable coat and laid it carefully on the chair with his reversible. She ran her fingers through her hair and came to him slowly, stood against him and put up her mouth to be kissed. "Take charge," she said.

"Take charge?"

She nodded vigorously. "Take complete charge," she said. "I'm losing my nerve again."

"If everything comes off right away?" he said.

"Yes," she said. She kissed him and then got rid of her suit and sweater. "I don't see you in any hurry."

"I'm skinny."

"I never thought you were fat," she said. "Go on, I'm not going to be the first one naked."

"Why not?"

"What if there's a fire? You're all dressed and they have to cover me up with a raincoat." She shivered. "Goo. Just the thought of one of those firemen's raincoats." She undid his necktie and unbuttoned his shirt. "Shall I?"

"What?"

"Unzip you? You want me to. All right." She reached inside and felt him. "You're not so skinny."

"Not now," he said. "I just fattened up a little bit."

"I should hope so."

"I better get undressed."

"Both of us," she said.

In a minute they were sitting on the bed, and then she knelt to him.

"Zena!"

She got up and lay on the bed. "Quick," she said. "Hurry!"

"Is it?"

"Oh, yes. Ooh, Jesus yes."

"You ready?"

"I did," she said. "But I am again. Lucas! Odarling. Odarling. I want to cry."

"You all right?"

"Uh-huh. I want to cry. But I can't cry."

He put his arm under her neck and gently squeezed her breast. Suddenly and violently she put both arms around him and held him so tight that she hurt his ribs. Almost as suddenly she released him. There was a little sweat between her breasts. She ran a finger across his lips and smiled. "Who'da thunk it?" she said.

"Who'da thunk it," he said.

"You. You'da thunk it. I wouldn't. I'm not that smart. But you would. Did you?"

"I wonder. I guess so."

"Yes, you knew. I didn't, but you did. I give you credit for knowing everything."

"Not quite," he said.

"If you don't know it, it isn't worth knowing," she said.

"That may be true," he said.

"Do you have to go anyplace? Do you have some bitch waiting for you?"

"No."

"Can we just stay here?"

"Yes."

"We can just stay here till the money runs out, and then I'll go out and hustle for you. I could make a hundred dollars during the lunch hour. All I have to do is go in the coffee shoppe. It's full of men. Men with money. Jews. A few goyim, but not many. I'd come back every day with a hundred bucks and throw it at your feet."

"A very distasteful thought," he said.

"To me, too. I don't want anybody but you. The next question is, how did I get rid of Barry Payne?"

"Are you planning to get rid of him?"

"I just did, in a way."

"Yes, I'd be inclined to think so," he said. "But not really."

"For me as really as if I hired a mobster to knock him off. And he knows that. But it isn't the same as getting rid of him. He'll want to hang on."

"Leave him."

"Leave him? You mean walk out on him?"

"From what I know about you and him, he will make it tough for you. But you don't have to live with him."

"It's funny, I've gotten so used to it, it didn't occur to me I could leave him. No. He'll screw up your play."

"How can he?"

"I don't know, but if it's humanly possible, he will. No. I'll go back tonight and tell him some lies. He's a little shaky now, and he'll believe them because he wants to believe them. He's supposed to be full of con, but I got news for him. I con eight hundred people eight times a week including matinees. I can con him, too."

"What happened to you and him?"

"You happened to me, that's really what happened. But I'll

give you the whole schmeer." She related the episode from the end of the morning reading to her impulse to have lunch without Barry Payne.

"Can you depend on Ellis Walton?" he said.

"He wants me to work for him. He can't put Barry Payne in your play. That much I can depend on him. That's the angle with Ellis Walton."

"Why does there have to be an angle? With Ellis or anyone else?"

"Well, there just has to be," she said.

"No, that's where you're wrong. Is he home now?"

"Who? Barry? You can bet on it. Walking up and down the apartment, figuring all the angles. What to say when I get home. Sure, he's home."

"Then let's get dressed and go and have it out with him."

"You mean tell him we've been screwing?"

"Yes. No angles. No con. That's the trouble, you see. You people are so used to the angles and conning each other, you lose sight of the best angle of all. The truth."

"Oh, sure. And where do I spend the night?"

"In the apartment that you paid for. With me."

"What?"

"When bedtime comes, we say goodnight to him, and go to bed. You and I."

"You're a crazy man. Meshuga Lucas. I don't mean when meshuga walks down the street."

"I know what it means," he said. "And I'm not crazy."

"He has a bad temper. Terrible."

"As long as he hasn't got a gun," said Yank.

"Oh, he doesn't have a gun. He has some friends are gunsels, but a revolver he'd never have in the house."

"Then what can he do? He can't blackmail you."

"Why not?"

"And tell the whole world that we slept together with him in the same apartment? How does that make him look?"

"Oh, don't you ever be my enemy," she said.

"He's not my enemy."

"I guarantee you he isn't your friend," she said. She reflected for a moment. "What can we lose? Let's try it. I want to see his ratty little face, the little rat."

"Right."

"I'd do anything you asked me. Ask me to do something. If we stay here much longer I'll do it without you asking." She put her hand on his cheek. "Do you like me?"

"Yes," he said.

"That's all I have to know," she said.

They went down in the elevator together and took a taxi to her apartment. At the door she said, "Naturally this'd be the time I don't have a key with me." She rang the doorbell, and Barry Payne opened the door. The total lack of surprise that he showed on seeing Yank Lucas was, for him, an expression of astonishment. To be impassive was not his way.

"Hello," he said. "How'd it go?"

"You mean the reading?" she said.

"What else would I mean?" he said.

"You'll see," said Zena.

He looked at Yank. "Why, you miserable son of a bitch."

"Miserable? Not me," said Yank.

"You, you tramp, what'd you bring him here for? Protection?"

"I wasn't thinking of that," said Zena. "But I guess it must have been somewhere in the back of my mind."

"I asked her if you had a gun, but she said you didn't," said Yank.

"I don't need a gun. I'll take care of her later."

"When?" said Yank.

"When I get you out of here."

"But I'm staying. That was the whole idea," said Yank.

"Listen, Buddy, a fast piece of tail with this tramp, that figured. She laid so many guys in this town, she can't even remember how many. For her that was like shaking hands. And I'll tell you the God's honest truth I couldn't care less. But we got other things going for us, and you're not in that picture. Every trick in the book she has to pull to get me in the hay with her."

"I didn't know there were that many," said Yank.

"I didn't either, but she knows them all. If I wanted to take the time I could tell you things about this tramp'd make you throw up."

"Let him find out for himself," said Zena. "What I want *you* to do, Barry, is find someplace else to live."

"Why should I? The apartment's in my name. I own the thing. I could call the cops and have him thrown out for trespassing."

"But we all know you're not going to do that," said Yank.

"You can't ruin my reputation, because I don't have any," said Zena. "You just said so yourself. I'm a tramp."

"And you can't ruin my reputation, because I haven't got one either. As an ex-newspaper man I can tell you that any disturbance you make isn't going to hurt me. On the contrary, you can ask Sid Margoll. The only one that suffers any damage will be you, the cuckold. And as far as public sympathy's concerned, I haven't met anyone that doesn't think you're a shitheel. You yourself are rather proud of that."

"Do we have to stand here in the foyer? Let's sit down," said Zena. "I'll be with you in a minute. I have to go to the ladies'."

The men moved to the sitting-room, which was two stories high, unmistakably the work of an interior decorator and completely devoid of any other character. The price tags on everything had been removed, but they still belonged on the chairs, the tables, the rugs, the lamps and the non-representational paintings. Glass was everywhere, glass, glass, glass. Yank Lucas sat down, Barry Payne remained standing.

"I'm not out to deprive you of an honest living," said Yank.

"You? You couldn't. You're not used to money yet, so you don't know the first thing about business matters. All you're interested now is screwing my wife. All she's interested is screwing a playwright. I knew this was going to happen. I know that broad inside and out, because I made a careful study. If you had any dough I'd sell her to you, but you don't have any dough and you never will have *that* kind of dough."

"Just out of curiosity, what price would you put on her?"

"About five hundred big ones. Five hundred thousand dollars I figure she's worth to me. But to you she isn't worth a nickel. She'll go to bed with you any time you want to, but I guarantee you, you'll get tired of her. I made a little study of you, too. As a playwright, you may be great. So I'll give you that, you are. But that very same fact is gonna get in your way as a human being. In other words, Lucas, all you care about is your writing. That worries me."

"*Worries* you?"

"Worries me. Not that I give a shit about you. But I got this tramp up to the top dollar in the theater, and I been keeping her out of pictures. She don't photograph so good, so if I let her take those Hollywood offers they might put her in a dog and that would be it. One picture. On the other hand, what I been doing with this dame, every play she's in the picture people offer more money. Sooner or later they'll talk the kind of numbers I want to hear. We start with something basic, like fifty thousand a year for her and the same for me for the next twenty years. Then comes the schlag. A piece of the producer's gross, so much after the picture makes X million. All them things. So you think I care if she's copping your joint? Ridiculous. Utterly ridiculous, my friend."

"You do think things out, don't you?"

"I ain't finished. Sit down, Zena, you might as well hear this. I been telling your gentleman friend the financial details, why I kept you out of pictures."

"Because I don't photograph well," said Zena.

"But if you cost them enough money, they'll invent a new camera for you. And they'll put you in pictures where you don't have to look like Grace Kelly. But what I was coming to, I told this guy I didn't care if you were copping his joint—"

"I heard you say that," she said. "Nice."

"But what I *do* care. Supposing this guy gives you a bad time? Supposing he gets bored with you before you get bored with him? He walks out on you. You're still in love with him. It begins to show in your work. Pretty soon you start getting the laryngitis. Your understudy has to go on two-three times a week. You begin working on the sauce. The next thing you know, they have to close a play because you got nothing but laryngitis all the time. And so forth and so on. You blow the whole bit. Maybe we're within a couple weeks of signing the kind of a contract I been working for, and you blow it. All because this guy here is giving you a bad time. I could of got you a hundred and a quarter, a hundred and a half, plenty of times these last couple of years. But I've been nursing you along, and then this jerk has to show up. You know, Lucas, she doesn't need your play. Any play I'd let her go in will bring us that much closer to the big deal. The last two plays she made big hits in, one was written by a woman and the other was written by a fag. I think there's a little mouse in you, too, but the way she looked when she came home just now, whatever you do, she likes."

"That's right. Whatever he does, I like," said Zena.

"I was trying to explain to Mr. Payne that I had no desire to deprive him of his hard-earned cash."

"Desire or not, right now you're a God damn pest. A nuisance," said Barry.

"Not to me, he isn't, and you are. So what do we do?" said Zena. "I mean like right now, tonight?"

"Just a second, Zena. I have something I want to say to Mr. Payne."

"You can call me Barry."

"I'd rather not," said Yank. "Here is what I want to say to you. You've been going on at a great rate about the terrible things that will happen to Zena when I get tired of her. She becomes unhappy, and consequently this big deal you've been working on blows sky-high. That may be true. But what makes you think she's going to be happy with you? After the things you've said to her, and after what happened to her and to me this afternoon, is she going to be very happy to have you hanging around? I somehow doubt it. If you make a God damn pest of *your*self, our play may never get to Boston. So why don't you get the hell out?"

Barry Payne saw the happy smile on Zena's face. He pointed a finger at Yank. "Lucas, I underrated you. I'll be out of here in a half an hour. I hate your fucking guts, but you made a valid point. Absolutely valid." He looked at his wristwatch, a narrow band of gold mesh with a timepiece the size of a postage stamp. "She gave me this. I practically have to put on my glasses to see what time it is."

"Ten after seven," said Yank.

"You want me later, I'll be at the Copa. Little Irish doll there is crazy about me." He pointed to Zena. "She makes *you* look like a traffic accident."

A situation was known to exist in the married life of Zena Gollum and Barry Payne. More accurately, a new situation was known to exist, and neither the old nor the new situation was unique in the world of show business. On Broadway and in Hollywood it was almost conventional for the female star to have a husband who got his living off her, and in time he was classified as a son of a bitch or a slob. Zena and her son of a bitch had been together long enough to be a fixture, subject, as were all such fixtures, to adjustment. Fixtures that remained fixed became a bore, but no one had seriously believed that Zena Gollum, with *her* record, and Barry Payne, with his, would become an institution. The people of show business and the people outside the business who followed their activities in the press assumed that when Zena's son of a bitch had stashed away a suitable sum, the marriage would arrive at Situation II. Situation II was invariably followed by Situation III, in which the parties of the first part communicated with each other through their lawyers, and by Situation IV, in which the principals and their attorneys fought it out in the courts and in the press until they became bores. Actually, when a show business marriage reached Situation II (for whatever reason) the element of suspense disappeared; the form was quite rigid, and only the details varied from case to case. The star might complain through her lawyers that her son of a bitch had robbed her deaf, dumb and blind, and his lawyers might reply with charges that on five separate occasions the star had committed an unnatural act with five different men, among them an advertising executive, a restaurant owner, a car-hire chauffeur, the young son of a Negro actor, and an airline pilot. Soon even the details ceased to fascinate, unless, of course, the star and her lawyers chose to entertain the public with a list of counter-charges. If, for example, the star wished to make it known that her son of a bitch, not she, had committed an unnatural act with the Negro actor's son, the adroit rewrite men on the newspapers could put it into publishable language without depriving the public of its five cents' worth. But in every case a saturation point of lubricity was reached. Nothing that the principals could say or do, or say that each other had done, could maintain or revive interest in their case. The press and the public demanded new faces, and always got them.

The earliest printed rumor, which had the status of a confirmation, of the Gollum-Payne Situation II appeared in the *Daily News*. The *News* man said, "The Barry Paynes (Zena Gollum) acting silly?" Only one line in a gossip column, but it was quickly followed by other lines in other papers. The woman on the *Journal-American* did not mention names, but wrote that the latest ménage à trois was that of a star, her husband, and a new playwright. A man on the *Post* did not mention the marital difficulty, but said that Barry Payne had threatened to belt that new playwright for his anti-racial slurs. One of the Hollywood trade papers took the position that

Broadway, and not picture business, would supply the next sin-sational scandal now brewing. Sid Margoll clipped the columns and ringed the items with red crayon, and when he had enough of them, placed a pile on Ellis Walton's desk. Ellis was expected to infer that Sid Margoll was earning his keep, that he had planted the items that were not too disgusting, and that the worst ones would have been worse if Sid Margoll had not been able to persuade the columnists to go easy. Sid Margoll would have been proud to claim credit for having engineered the romance between Zena Gollum and Yank Lucas, but Ellis Walton gave him no such opportunity.

"You get a load of Ed Sullivan's column?" said Sid Margoll.

"I saw it last night," said Ellis.

"You don't seem surprised," said Sid.

"I'm surprised he got hold of it so quickly."

"You knew about it?" said Sid.

"I could tell you the first day she laid him," said Ellis.

"Ellis, you ought to let me in on these things. It don't make me look so good. Eddie called me, and I said there was absolutely nothing to it. Absolutely nothing. I as much as took my oath. I guess maybe I did take my oath."

"Don't start upbraiding me, Sid. If I told you what I knew it would have been printed sooner, only you'd have given it to Kilgallen."

"So now what happens next?"

"What happens next? We open in Boston the twenty-fourth of next month," said Ellis.

"Oh, come on, Ellis. What happens with Zena and Lucas?" said Sid. "I gotta have something to feed the columns with. If *you* hold out on me."

"Talk to Zena. Talk to Lucas."

"They won't talk to me."

"Talk to Barry."

"Even he won't talk to me. You got a publicity thing going here and it sounds as if you engineered it. I know you didn't, but it sounds that way."

"And you want the credit," said Ellis. "All right, take it. I'll say you engineered it."

"I want to ask you something. Is that right about the menadge a troy? Are they three-high?"

"You know better than that. Zena would go for anything, but Lucas and Barry hate one another's guts. You shouldn't believe what you read in those columns."

"Why not? A lot of times I put it there."

"All the more reason for not believing it," said Ellis.

"Well, you got a point. So next question, Ellis. Knowing how Barry operates, Zena is the meal-ticket. Is that why he's acting so civilized?"

"As long as he keeps on acting civilized, I don't care why he does it."

"But he is acting civilized? You'll tell me that much."

"So far," said Ellis.

"All right. Now I got a question for you, you gotta give me a straight answer."

"Do I?"

"Yes," said Sid. "When we go to Boston, did you reserve a room for Barry or what?"

"You son of a bitch," said Ellis.

"All the papers'll find out. You might as well level with me on that."

"Zena has a sitting-room and a bedroom by herself, in her name. Lucas has a bedroom on the same floor."

"And Barry?"

"Barry will be on the Coast."

"That tips it then."

"Not necessarily. He can have business on the Coast."

"Sure, but who believes that?" said Sid.

"Nobody," said Ellis.

"Well, I wangled that much information out of you."

"Yes, but before you give it to Kilgallen or anybody, just remember that Barry is liable to cross us up."

"He could at that," said Sid. "Where is he living now?"

"That I honestly don't know."

"But not at the apartment?"

"No, you know who's at the apartment."

"He still keeps his room at the Algonquin."

"He does, but they're saving a lot of money on sheets."

"You know something, Ellis. That guy'll never marry Zena."

"Maybe not, but look who did."

"I guess so," said Sid.

"And look how many didn't," said Ellis. "Let's not worry about who's gonna marry who. We got a play, we got the for the play, and we got a theater to open in. And we ⎯ ig advance. We got mail orders coming in from as far away as Sheboygan, Wisconsin. I didn't know they ever heard of Zena in Sheboygan, but somebody did."

"I'll put out a release on that," said Sid Margoll. "The amazing response to our announcement. Mail orders flocking in from all over the country. Maybe I'll get my guy to write a feature and you sign it. By Ellis Walton. How the theater-going public are getting hep, as witness the fact that over twenty-eight thousand dollars came in forty-eight hours after our first announcement, despite the fact that Zena Gollum has never appeared in a motion picture. I could develop that idea into something pretty big. We could fake some letters from the out-of-town people, how they're starved for good theater, et cetera. Like if the theater will not go to the people, the people will still go to the theater. You can say in the piece that on the strength of this big response you are planning to send out two road companies after the play opens in New York."

"You get carried away, don't you?"

"Always. Give me a germ of an idea and I'll milk it for every last drop you can get out of it. I have to. I had that idea of Lucas doing a Garbo, and it blew right up in my face. I had him refusing interviews before anybody asked for an interview. Now they're all clamoring for interviews and he won't even talk to me. Zena won't talk to me. So I'm forced to steal space by having my fellow ghost pieces by you. And let's face it, Ellis, the public interest in you, you can put under your eyelid and it won't cause an irritation. When you see Lucas you might suggest to him to wear dark glasses."

"Why?"

"More of the Garbo act. The papers don't have any photographs of him and nobody'll recognize him if he don't wear dark glasses."

"He won't go for it," said Ellis.

"He will if you put it to him the right way. Don't say what *I* said, for God's sake. Don't tell him to wear dark glasses to attract attention. Tell him he ought to wear dark glasses so there won't be any good pictures of him around, and then he can come and go unmolested. What else can we do with the son of a bitch? He doesn't come over very strong, you know. Personality-wise, he's one of the dullest bastards I ever saw. He looks like an economics professor at some cow college, and he dresses the part. You wouldn't give him a second look if you saw him anywhere, unless you saw him coming out of the ladies' toilet. Then you could get him arrested. I'm trying to figure out some ways and means whereby he can avoid the press but the press don't avoid him. I know a dame on one of the Boston papers, one of your oldtime sob sisters. If I could get her in to see him she'd trap him into making some controversial statements."

"Don't fool around with this guy, Sid."

"Why not? Are you afraid of him?"

"Am I afraid of him? No. What's to be afraid of? Oh, he could louse up Zena and Zena could louse up the play. But I don't want you fooling around with this guy just for the sake of a few lousy lines in the newspapers."

"How dya mean fooling around?"

"Tricking him into making foolish statements, things like that," said Ellis. "I'll tell you what I really mean. I don't want to ruin a first-class talent."

"You're kidding," said Sid.

"I'm not kidding, Sid. Who knows but that I'll go down in history as the first one to recognize that talent."

"Oh, Ellis, please. This I don't believe."

"No, I don't expect you to believe. Nevertheless I got that side of me. I'm not all commercial, Sid. Commercial, but not all commercial."

"Was your mother ever frightened by Herman Shumlin? The next thing you'll start thinking you're Eddie Dowling. Shumlin and Hellman, Dowling and Saroyan. You want to be Walton and Lucas."

"I can think of worse," said Ellis.

"You never saw Hellman and Saroyan ducking any publicity. In fact, Hellman was a press agent herself. Ellis, I'm willing to go along with you in any direction, be it commercial, artistic, or I don't care what it is. But let's be commercial first and then when we got the money in the till, that'll be time for the artistic. If this guy *is* a first-class talent, two or three plays from now, not just this one play—it'll take more than a few lousy lines in a newspaper to roon him."

"But if you ruin him now we may never get those other plays."

"Then he's easily rooned, and you don't roon a first-class talent that easily."

"How would you know?" said Ellis.

"You don't have to get personal, Ellis. If you wish to have my resignation, I'll have it on your desk inside of a half an hour."

"Cut the crap, Sid."

"You're a great one to talk. Cut the crap."

"If the shoe was on the other foot, me working for you instead of you working for me, you'd see it my way. So see it my way, please. One day perhaps you will be sitting here and I will be sitting over there where you are, but in the meanwhile kindly leave to me the policy decisions, Sidney."

The subjects of the policy decisions were making and postponing decisions of their own, beginning with the basic one of who was to live where. Barry Payne got out of the apartment, and went to an East Side apartment-hotel, but left behind two closetfuls of clothes and various other possessions. Yank Lucas left his small wardrobe at the Algonquin, but put in a supply of shirts, underwear, and pajamas at Zena's apartment. In a practical sense she and Yank were now living together; he stayed with her every night, they ate nearly all their meals together. They hardly ever went out, and when they did they avoided the restaurants that employed press agents. After a week Zena told Ellis she would no longer require the suite at the Judson Arms, a problem which had solved itself. Somewhat more complicated was the problem of money, and here Barry Payne could have been difficult.

Zena had gone on salary—$1500 a week—the moment she signed her contract with Ellis Walton, but it was stipulated that her salary was to be paid to her agent, who, of course, was Barry Payne. Over the telephone Barry agreed to deposit her salary, less commission, in her personal checking account. He pointed out to her that she was living in an apartment which he owned. For the time being, he said, he was not going to slap her with the cost of the upkeep, but if she intended to go on living in the apartment after the play opened in New York, she or Lucas or both of them together would have to straighten that out, preferably by Lucas's sub-letting the apartment. As the annual upkeep came to about $10,000 it was obviously impossible for Lucas to assume such a commitment until he was making more money, but Barry was not going to let Lucas get away with a free ride after the Broadway opening. "He could have been a lot tougher," said Zena.

"I suppose he could," said Yank. "He's probably talked it over with a lawyer. I don't know how these cooperative apartments work. They never had them in Spring Valley, P A, and the only cooperation we ever had in the places I've lived in was not to make too much noise after eleven o'clock at night. If you were going to beat up your wife or your girl friend, do it before eleven P.M. They didn't *always* cooperate, but most of the time."

"Would you ever beat me?" said Zena.

"I don't think I'd ever beat you. I might take a crack at you, under provocation."

"What provocation?"

"I don't know. Not for kicks, though. Not even if you wanted me to for kicks. I knew a girl like that when I first came to New York. In fact, that's one of the first things I remember about New York. She didn't want me to beat her, exactly. She wanted me to nick her with a razor blade. Then I knew I'd left Spring Valley and was out in the great, wide world."

"Did you do it?"

"Yes. Once."

"Where?"

"In her room."

"I mean, where on her?"

"On her belly. It didn't do anything for me, but it did for her. Actually it frightened me. It wasn't a deep cut. I've cut myself worse shaving. But it frightened me because it didn't have more effect on me. I should have been horrified and I wasn't. I was worried because if I could do that, I probably could do a lot more. So I stopped seeing her. Not literally seeing her. I still see her in the Algonquin lobby."

"You must have her up to your room sometime and tell her you're going to take out her appendix," said Zena. "The poor kid is starved for affection."

"Kid about it if you like, but it wasn't funny to me. It was myself I was worried about."

"If you want to get it out of your system, go get a razor blade and cut me," said Zena.

"The hell I will. Don't tell me *you* go for that."

"I'd probably faint, but I told you I'd do anything you want to do. That's how much I love you."

"I don't think that has much to do with love."

"I don't either, but you've never been in love. You thought you were, with your wife, but she knew you weren't."

"Do you think she did?"

"Yes. Because I've seen that same look on boys when they saw me naked the first time. The same look that was on your face when you saw her naked the first time. 'Oh, boy! How long has this been going on?' And that has nothing to do with love, either."

"All right, what *is* love?"

"You want me to give you a definition of love?" she said.

"I certainly do."

"All right. Love is what I feel for you, that I never felt for anyone else, and no woman ever felt for any other man. And no man ever felt for any woman."

"You call that a definition?"

"It's my definition. Can you top it?" she said.

"I wouldn't try. That's not a definition of love. It's a description of how you feel. It doesn't cover the whole subject as a good definition should."

"Yes it does. I've never heard a better definition in all my life. Do you want me to give you a definition of life? Life is just a bowl of cherries," she said.

"Oh, it is?"

"Absolutely. Life is just a bowl of cherries."

"Well, there I'm inclined to agree with you. The eminent

philosopher Rudy Vallée used to claim that life was just a bowl of goldfish. I'll accept either definition. But when you talk about life you're dealing with something tangible. Concrete. Love is not. Life endures. Love is a passing fancy. We are trying to define the undefinable, which is undefinable because it does not exist. A man can go on thinking he loves the same woman for fifty years, or another man gets an erection because he saw a couple of inches of thigh in a subway train. In both cases a passing fancy. Undefinable and non-existent. Cogito, ergo sum. Nonsense. Thinking has nothing to do with being. Being is sufficient, and doesn't need any confirmation by thought. Life *is* just a bowl of cherries. Or, conversely, a bowl of cherries is life. A bowl of thoughts, on the other hand, is not life at all. Show me a bowl of thought."

"Your play," she said. "Your play is a bowl of thought."

"If I took a playscript and put it in a bowl, you could call that a bowl of thought. But it wouldn't be. It would be a bowl of paper with some markings on it, that's all. Cogito, ergo sum—"

"That's the second time you said that. What does it mean?"

"It means 'I think, therefore I am. Therefore I exist.' A philosopher named Descartes—well, we won't go into that. I was just getting into it in college when I quit. But anyway his argument was that if you could think, you existed. I don't go along with that. My argument is 'Cogito, ergo cogito.' I think, therefore I think. That's as far as I'll go."

"Are you saying that if you can't see it, it doesn't exist?"

"It doesn't."

"There's no such thing as love, or thought?"

"No such thing," he said.

"How can you say such a silly thing? Go turn on the light. Electricity. Think of the thought that went into that, discovering electricity. Just that one thing alone. This apartment house. The Chrysler Building. Look out there, all those buildings across the Park. Look down at those cars."

"They all exist."

"You'd know that all right, if one of them hit you. But before they could manufacture a single one of those cars they had to think about it. And you say thought doesn't exist. That's silly. And you're silly."

"I could probably prove to you that what you call thinking, or thought, is part of each of those cars. A form of energy that produced the car, and disappeared after the car went into production."

"Ah, energy! Can you see energy?"

"Of course not. It disappeared, like smoke. It burned up and disappeared. Energy. Thought. Love. If they exist they only exist as part of the tangible things."

"You don't make sense, and you know you don't make sense. Tomorrow night you'll be arguing that nothing you see exists. That only the things you don't see exist. You just like to argue. Such a chochem, Mr. Yank Lucas. You throw your Latin at me, I'll throw you a little Yiddish."

"Vot means it, kokum?" he said.

"Is meaning you are such a wise guy," she said. "Well, anyway I like it better than what I had before. It's conversation. Before it used to be, with Barry it was how much money he was gonna make for me. Not how much I was gonna make for him, but how much he was gonna make for me. And before Barry it was, 'Okay, baby, when do we screw?' You don't like that when I talk about my past."

"You bring it up an awful lot," he said.

"You know why?"

"I'm not sure," he said.

"Because you're trying to change me, you're starting to pretend I wasn't what I was. But I was what I was, and most of the time I liked it, or else I wouldn't have done it. I don't say I loved any of them. Not the way I love you. But don't you start making me feel guilty. Maybe you did some dirty things, mean things, before I ever met you, but did I ask you that the first afternoon in the hotel?"

"I've made a point of not asking you what you did before then," he said.

"Made such a *big* point that it isn't natural. Everybody wants to know what the other person did. That's only natural. But you have to keep it under control, your curiosity. I'll tell you everything I ever did, with everybody I did it with, any time you want to know." She smiled. "If I can remember. Don't call me a liar if I forget one or two."

"I don't want to deny you the pleasure of reminiscence, but I really don't want to hear about it. At least I don't want to sit here and listen while you relive all those tender moments."

"Okay, but don't try to change what happened. And if I'm

gonna change myself, let me do it because I want to change. You're a great writer, Yank, but I'm pretty good too. I'm damn good. It isn't only my ass that gets people into the theater. I never would of got anywhere without it, but I had to have a lot else besides. Like thought, and energy, and love."

"Are we having a little quarrel?" he said.

"So all right, we are having a little quarrel. A kind of a peaceful quarrel. Just getting rid of a few things that ought to be gotten rid of. It's probably around the time I should be getting the curse. I don't get it any more, but I still get cranky every four or five weeks. Or feel sorry for myself. This will be followed by such hot pants that I won't be able to keep my hands off you. So look out at rehearsal tomorrow. You know what love is? Love is that you're my preference."

"Now you've really said something. *You* are *my* preference."

"We're getting somewhere," she said.

T hey were in Boston. Amidst all the confusion of even this small company on the day of an opening, a fatalistic optimism prevailed. At three o'clock in the afternoon Marc DuBois sent the actors to their hotels to get some rest. No one believed for a moment that anyone would get any rest. "You might as well have kept them here," said Ellis Walton.

"Is that what you think, Ellis?" said Marc.

"Well, they're only human. They'll go back to the hotel and start fidgeting."

"That's exactly why I sent them home," said Marc. "I want them to fidget. I want them keyed up by seven o'clock. God deliver me from an actor that isn't keyed up on opening night. I know I'm taking a little chance with Scott Aubrey. He's liable to take one too many and get a little spifflicated. But by eight o'clock he'll be puking in his dressing-room, and by curtain-time he'll be ready to go on and give a good perform-ance. It's taking a chance, but he's not going to let his under-study go on tonight. As to the others, I'm not worried. I'd adore it if you could keep our author away from Zena, but I don't imagine that's possible."

"Keep her away from him? This is when she needs him," said Ellis.

"She may need him, but I'd give a lot to keep her out of bed with him between now and curtain-time. If I had my way I'd keep a chastity belt on her till she's ready to make her entrance. Is there any word of Mr. Payne?"

"She got a couple bushels of flowers from him," said Ellis.

"I wouldn't mind if the son of a bitch showed up. The only thing I'm afraid of tonight is everybody being too sure of themselves. If they play it wooden, the actors'll get bad notices. Overconfidence could hurt them. I don't think they can hurt the play. But I don't want my actors to get bad notices. I don't want to have to get new actors."

"Well, you come to Boston to get rid of the bugs."

"Oh, piss on that, Ellis," said Marc. "I'll take good notices wherever I can get them, and so will everybody else. Don't think Kerr and Atkinson don't read Norton. If Norton goes to work on a play, those New York characters know what to expect. If you get a good, respectful review from Norton, you'll get a good respectful review from Atkinson. You'll get a long-winded essay from Kerr, but it'll be respectful."

"I want good reviews from Atkinson and Chapman," said Ellis.

"Chapman? Who cares about Chapman? You get it all in the headline and that saves you the bother of trying to read him. I want good reviews from Atkinson, Kerr, and Gibbs. But I'll *take* good reviews from anybody anywhere . . . Did you ever see *anybody* as calm as our author? I'll never understand how such a cold fish wrote such a gutsy play. If I didn't know better I'd suspect that someone else wrote it. Irving Berlin's little colored boy."

"Outwardly he don't seem to have much fire, but inwardly it must be there," said Ellis.

"Yes, and don't you go telling him I said he was a cold fish. I want to direct his next play—good, bad or indifferent."

"Ah, somebody else making plans. You talk about Hellman and Shumlin. Now you want to be Gadge and Tennessee."

"Nothing wrong with that. Has he said anything to you about another play?"

Ellis hesitated.

"Oh, he has, you bitch!" screamed Marc. "Tell me!"

"All he said was the next play he wrote, I'd get first look at it."

"And that'll be the last look any other manager gets at it. You better sew him up quick."

"I wanted to, but I got Peg McInerney to contend with."

"That's a lot to contend with, I must say," said Marc. "I told her—politely, but I told her—I said I didn't want any outsiders coming to rehearsals. Only members of the company and staff. She looked around and saw my secretary, and your secretary, and Sid Margoll's writer, and Scott Aubrey's dresser, and Doc Bender, and Jesus-to-Jesus I don't know who all. She pointed to one young fellow and said, 'Who is *that*, for instance?' and I had to tell her it was your nephew, down from Dartmouth. And she pointed to someone else and asked the same question and I had to say I didn't know."

"My other nephew, from Harvard," said Ellis.

"It couldn't have been, unless he was in drag. This was a woman. About forty-five, fat and Jewish-looking."

"Oh, that was my sister, from Brockton, Mass. I told her she could come and watch a rehearsal if she kept out of the way. It's too bad she happened to come that particular day. Where was I all this time?"

"How should I know where you were? I have enough trouble keeping track of my people."

"So what happened with McInerney?"

"Oh, she left quietly, and then came back later with Lucas. I didn't say anything. What could I say? *She* didn't say anything. She didn't *have* to. She as much as dared me to put her out."

"You should have. That would have showed real character," said Ellis.

"I don't have any," said Marc.

"Anybody that says that about themselves has character," said Ellis. "You got character all right, Marc."

"Oh, don't start giving me compliments. The state I'm in I'm liable to burst out crying. The day after we open in New York I'm going to absolutely let go. You don't know how good I've been—"

"Yes I do, and I appreciate—"

"Oh, I don't mean my work. I mean goody-good. I didn't get arrested, you didn't have to bail me out. These Boston cops arrested me three years ago, so I had to watch my step. The least sign of *anything* and they'd have arrested me and I'd have been in no fit condition to go on with rehearsals. You don't know these Boston cops, but believe me I do. Especially if you're from out-of-town. But am I ever going to have a time after New York! Right straight to Key West for me."

"Key West? Florida?"

"Only the gayest place there is. We have a ball in Key West. It's positively wild, all that Navy and Cubans. You can't imagine. Every bitch I know wants to go to Key West."

"Well, I guess you're entitled," said Ellis. "I didn't know you were arrested in Boston."

"They can't prevent me from coming here, but if I stop to tie my shoe in that park, they'll run me in. Even if I was only stopping to tie my shoe. Of course I wear loafers all the time, so I'd have to have a better excuse than that. Look. Genuine alligator. Seventy dollars, handmade."

"Give me the name of the maker. I want to make you a present of a couple pairs."

"I'd rather have the money if it's all the same to you. I *told* you, I'm going haywire in Key."

"Stay out of the park till we open in New York, and I'll show you my appreciation."

"I don't say it was all unselfish, Ellis. I had to do this play."

"Everybody connected with it had to do this play," said Ellis. "You. Me. Zena. My nephew that goes to Dartmouth, you know what he said to me that just expresses it? I'll see if I can remember his exact words. Well, I can't remember his *exact* words, but he said there was a whole aura about it. And he's a very intellectual kid, one of the most intellectual kids I ever met."

"Yes, and he's fruit, too. But he's right. There is an aura about it. Spooky. Beginning with that spooky author, and Zena is kind of spooky if you stop to think about her. And everything's gone so well. Too well, maybe. I always fight with the people that do the lighting, but this time I didn't. The sets were rights, we hung the scenery on time. I'd be very happy to settle for some little thing going wrong tonight. Like if one of the stagehands broke a leg or something. To use the old expression, I never had it so good, and it makes me wonder."

"Don't *talk* that way, Marc. We got till eleven o'clock for plenty to happen," said Ellis.

But disaster did not come; none of the thousand calamities of an opening night occurred. Scott Aubrey's cigarette lighter worked. Joe Grossman was not too loud. Shirley Dick got over her case of the trots. Rick Burtyne remembered to count five before answering the telephone. Ada-Anne Allen's teeth stayed in place. Jasper Hill did not lech for Zena. Barry Payne stayed in California. Ellis Walton's wife stayed in New York. No sandbags fell, no lighting cues were missed. The audience did not cough. No nervous man guffawed at the bedroom scene. The critics stayed to the end, and there were eight curtain calls.

And then, backstage, there was activity but it was carried on in an atmosphere of quiet. "I think we're in," the actors said to each other. They stood together in the third-act set while Ellis Walton made a little speech, which he began by saying, "I think we're in." The author followed with his little speech. "I finally know what it means to love the theater," he said. "For that I have each of you, and Marc, and Ellis, to thank. I do thank you." They applauded him, and unknowingly in the Russian style, he applauded them back.

"I forgot to say," said Ellis. "There'll be drinks and sandwiches in my sitting-room at the hotel. Eight-twelve is the number. Not a real party. Just us here and anyone you care to bring. Small and informal while we wait for the papers. I promise you a real party in New York, but this is just for us."

"And now if I may say a word," said Marc DuBois. "I love every one of you, and I want every one of you here at two o'clock tomorrow afternoon. Nobody fluffed, nobody did anything wrong. But I have a few things of my own I wish to correct. And if any of you are going to catch cold, please catch it here in Boston and be over it by New York. But regardless, no son of a bitch in the world can ever take tonight away from us. I don't think even the author knows how proud we all are. It'll always be his play, but tonight it was ours. Tomorrow night it'll be his again. But tonight, the first performance before an audience, this play belonged to us. We brought it to life, and if you think I wasn't up there with you, with each and every one of you, everything you said and did—why am I more exhausted than any one of you? No, this was the experience that makes you forget all the crap. Joe Grossman. Ada-Anne. Both of them in show business over forty years. They'll tell you what tonight was. Only they don't have to tell you. You already know. Ellis, anything more you want to say?"

"No, you said it all, Marc," said Ellis.

"All right, cream your faces," said Marc to the actors, and they went to their dressing-rooms.

Zena, whose dressing-room was on stage level, stood waiting for Yank, who had been detained by Ellis and Marc and their personal congratulations. Now he appeared. He took her in his arms. "Don't kiss me till I take the guck off," she said, but held on to him. "How was I? I know I was good, but tell me."

"You were. You were good," he said.

"Really good," she said. "I know I was. I can feel it. But I want to hear it from you."

"You were really good."

"Did you hear them call for the author?" she said.

"Sure," he said. "Didn't I go onstage and take a bow?"

"Yes, but I wanted to be sure you heard it yourself and weren't just pushed on by Marc or somebody. It's important for you to hear them."

"Do you think so? Why?"

"Sometimes you're so strange that you're creepy." She sat at her mirrors and began pulling a long stream of Kleenex out of the box. "We don't only get paid off in money in this business," she said. "You should understand that better than anyone else."

"I do. I understand it perfectly."

"That's why it was important that you should hear them call for the author."

"Maybe. But I'm inclined to agree with Marc. This was the actors' night."

"Oh, you'll take your bows in New York?"

"I didn't *say* that," he said. "I didn't need to hear them or take a bow. In fact, I don't approve of it. I wish I hadn't. I enjoyed it, but I'm against it. The author has no business going onstage. If he goes on the first night, he ought to go on after every performance or not at all."

"Oh, relax. That's one of the little things that make show business what it is."

"I enjoyed it, but I think it was wrong. I don't want to get that kind of stagestruck. I want to write plays, but I don't want to read *Variety,* and have dinner at Sardi's. I don't want people to recognize me in the lobby of the Algonquin."

"Well, God damn it, I do," said Zena, rubbing her face with cold cream. "They may say, 'Look at that little tramp.' But by Christ they're compelled to look at me, no matter what they say."

"You're getting even with them," said Yank.

"You're damn fucking right I am," she said. "All of them. Every son of a bitch that was ever nasty to me, or looked down their noses at me, or wouldn't let me read for them when I needed a job, or wouldn't lend me a few bucks unless I got in the hay with them."

"Very interesting. Then you're not quite a star," he said.

"Oh, I'm not, eh? Go out and look on the marquee."

"That way you're a star, but you still have to get even with people. A real star has got over that stuff."

"You go fuck yourself. And you keep talking like that and you're going to have to. Unless you want to settle for Shirley Dick. She'd accommodate you."

"I know she would. But I don't want to be accommodated. Do we *have* to go and wait for the papers in Ellis's room?"

"We don't have to do anything. I'm the star—and you're the author. We can do as we please, together or separately. You can go lay Shirley Dick, and I can go to a party with some society dikes, and believe me this is the town for them. If you'd rather not go to Ellis's, we can skip it. But on the other hand, if I don't go—it's just the cast—they'll think I'm snoot-

ing them. And if you don't go, and I do, they'll think you're
snooting me. We can go for a minute."

Every member of the cast brought someone to Ellis's
party, and so did the lighting man and the set man and everyone else closely connected with the production. As a con-
sequence the party was larger than Yank had anticipated;
thirty people, more or less, and they were all equipped with
newspapers to read from. Ellis handed a paper to Zena and
one to Yank. "Not gonna say a word. Just feast your eyes,"
said Ellis. The concentration was intense; some of the people
were rereading the reviews for the second time. It was a small
enough cast to allow some critical mention of each actor, and
the compliments went through the positive, comparative, and
superlative degrees, in the same order as the importance of the
actors' roles. Shirley Dick was "good," and Zena Gollum was
"superb." Marc DuBois's direction was "sympathetic" and
Yank Lucas's play was "on the evidence, the arrival of a major
new writing talent in the American theater." The knocks were
delivered half-apologetically. The first act needed some trim-
ming; the veteran Joseph W. Grossman had a slight tendency
to mutter his lines; the pace of Mr. DuBois's direction was
somewhat uneven. But it was easy to overlook these minor
faults in a production whose impact was as powerful as the
early work of Clifford Odets and the Group Theatre. Mr.
Lucas obviously had been influenced by Odets and by Maxwell Anderson, but his play was reminiscent of neither. This
was a talent that possessed originality, sensitivity, and instinc-

tive stagecraft. A spellbound audience demanded eight curtain calls.

"Well?" said Ellis Walton.

Yank smiled. "I'm satisfied, if you are," he said.

"Satisfied? Name it and you can have it, Yank. This takes me out of the hoi polloi. Never again will my friends call me the poor man's Gilbert Miller, not after this." He slapped the paper with his fingertips. "I'm taking another full-page ad in the Sunday *Times*. Another half a page in the *Tribune*. I was on the phone to Lew Weissinger just before you came in, and I told him to start hiring girls to handle the mail orders."

"Who is Lew Weissinger?" said Yank.

"Well, he's more in the business end. You never met him."

"He's the fellow that arranges for the buy with the ticket brokers and so on?"

"Oh, you heard about buys? I didn't think you were inarrested."

"I'm not, really, but Peg McInerney is," said Yank.

"Yeah, uh-huh. Well, you got nothing to worry about with Peg taking care of you. I have tremenduous respect for Peg. Tremenduous. I want to have a talk with her tomorrow. I notice you didn't bring her here."

"She said that if you had wanted to invite her, you knew where she was staying."

"I don't like the sound of that. Did she take umbrage because she wasn't invited? Maybe I ought to call her. At the Copley she's at. I'll phone her."

"She won't be there now, Ellis."

"Well, will you explain to her that it wasn't intentional? I wouldn't do anything to annoy Peg. I've known her for years. I want to offer her a proposition on your next two plays."

"She knows that. Only she thought it would be one play."

"When did you talk to her?"

"About a half an hour ago. She rode back with Zena and me."

"God damn it, there's always something. Why didn't you *make* her come?"

"Ellis, you really mustn't expect me to cover up for your mistakes."

"No, but I hope you won't let Peg talk you out of making a deal with me."

"I'll do anything she says. Maybe she'll talk me into making a deal with you."

"Do you like to see me suffer? Yank, I treated you right, didn't I?"

"As far as I know you did. But I don't know about buys and those things, and Peg does."

"Well, all I can do is offer her a proposition she can't refuse. And this one Barry Payne won't be in on it. But she knows I had to do business with Barry or else I didn't get Zena. Peg knows that."

"I'm sure she does," said Yank.

"Did she say anything?"

"She's said a lot, but you have to discuss that with her."

"Yank, you're torturing me. Do you consider that nice?" He put down his glass and it missed the table and fell to the floor. "I have a heart condition with the hypertension. Both of my two brothers died of a heart condition, and I'm supposed to be careful."

"Well, be careful, Ellis."

"How can I be careful when you're torturing me? Here, I'll give you a cheque for five thousand dollars, no strings attached. Just you give me your word of honor as a gentleman that you won't sign with anybody else till I had a chance to meet their offer. You can cash the cheque downstairs, tonight, and I'm out five gees if you don't keep your word. My personal cheque, not the Elbar Corporation."

"What the hell is the Elbar Corporation?"

"El for Ellis, Bar for Barry. That's the corporation we formed to put on your play. Nothing funny about it, it's done all the time. But this'd be between you and I, my personal cheque as man to man. One gentleman to another."

"No thanks," said Yank. "By the way, Ellis. I paid Peg the fifty-dollar commission that time you lent me five hundred."

"Hell, I figured you would. I wish I could figure you as easily on other things. But talk about the inscrutable Chinese. You take the cake. Go on, she's trying to catch your eye, Zena."

"I knew that."

"But you were having a good time torturing me?"

"Not torturing you, Ellis. Just studying you," said Yank. "This may make you feel better."

"Tell me quick, I need it."

"Well, I know you've been giving me a screwing, but Peg

tells me it's not as bad a screwing as I could have got from some other managers."

"This I'm supposed to feel better from?" said Ellis.

"It's the best I can do tonight," said Yank. "Thanks for the drink. Goodnight."

He and Zena went to her rooms. "I'm tired. Are you?" she said.

"Yes. Very," he said. "Do you want me to sleep in my own room?"

"No, I couldn't stand it to be alone. Not tonight. I wouldn't sleep unless I took a pill, and I don't want to take a pill because I want to think about everything. And I want to think about everything so it'll make me go to sleep. I'm silly-tired. I get that way."

"So I've noticed," he said.

"When you finally get down to it, the trouble with Boston is it isn't New York," she said. "It's just as bad as New York. Worse, in some ways. You have to get through Boston knowing that no matter what happens here, you still have New York to go through. This is your first time here, so—"

"No it isn't," he said.

"You never told me you were here before," she said.

"When I was an atomic scientist," he said.

"You? An atomic scientist?" she said. "This I *don't* believe. Some things you tell me I take with a grain of salt, but this one I don't believe at all."

He told her of his earlier visit. The recital amused her, but did not make her laugh. "You don't like that story," he said.

"I guess I don't. Women aren't supposed to like anything they don't understand. If you were one of those practical jokers—but you're not. It's out of character with what I know about you—but then what *do* I know about you? I wonder if I really love you. It'd be awful if I didn't."

"But of course you don't, Zena," he said.

"If I don't, I never loved anybody, and maybe I can't. I used to say to myself, 'Watch out, kid. Every time you sleep with a different man you use up that much of the supply.' The supply of love, I meant. Maybe what I had left wasn't enough for you. You need a lot, whether you know it or not. Actually you need it more than I do. But the God damn hell of it is that while I was giving away my supply, you've held on to yours. Some bitch will come along and get it all, all that you've been holding out on me, and the girl you were married to, and everybody else. I thought we were going to have such a good time tonight, but I feel empty and low and God knows what all."

"I think you'd be better off if I went to my own room," he said.

"Don't! If you leave me now I'm liable to jump out that window."

"But I'm the one that's depressing you," he said.

"Yes, but you're the only one that—I wouldn't have any trouble getting someone else to sleep with me. I could get Marc to sleep with me, and no sex. Or Scott Aubrey and plenty of sex. Or one of those Boston dikes and that kind of sex. But whether I love you or not, you're the only one I want to be

with. Tonight, anyway. Please don't leave me. I really think I
would jump out the window."

He was silent.

"What are you thinking?" she said.

"I was thinking that this was the first time in my life anybody ever needed me."

"And you don't like it," she said.

"I'm not used to it," he said.

"You don't have to get used to it," she said. "I'll be all right
tomorrow. I'm just afraid to be alone tonight."

"Ah, now I'm beginning to understand it. I should have
realized before that you're used to having Mr. Payne. I wonder if *he* knows that."

"Maybe he does, but I doubt it. No, I don't think he does.
Once you're washed up with Barry, he's washed up with
you. From that day at the apartment on we were strictly
business."

"You gave me the impression that you always were," he
said.

"Oh, no we weren't. That's an animal, that man. He made
me an animal, too. He made me feel like an animal. He made
me *want* to be an animal. And I was. That's where the hold
was. I was, uh, promiscuous, as they say. But as long as I was
with him I wasn't. I was his donkey, and he called me that."

"What if he came in this room now, this minute?" he said.

"Now? This very minute? Nothing. Because I've been
talking about him and I remembered how I hated it when he
called me his donkey. But ten minutes ago, before I started

talking about him and I was so depressed, I guess I would have been his donkey again. That's all I ever was. His donkey, and his meal-ticket. But that was before I met you, before I read your play, before we all read your play."

"I think you're beginning to feel better," he said.

"I am," she said. "And that's where you have it on Barry Payne. He'd have never noticed that, but you *did*. You *do*. You know, it must be absolute hell to be as sensitive as you are and not be able to love anybody."

"Did you ever stop to think that sensitivity may have nothing to do with love? What you call sensitivity, and what *I* call sensitivity when I'm not being overheard—may very well be so far removed from love that they're not even opposites. My inability to fall in love with anybody could very well be blamed on that sensitivity."

"Horrible," she said.

"Is it? I wonder. If I had the chance to trade my sensitivity for the ability to fall in love, I don't think I would. I've never known love to last. Sex gets into it. What two people hate each other more than a man and woman who've been in love and one of them is sexually attracted to someone else? But sensitivity—I wish we could call it something else. Acute perception, maybe, but that's just as bad. Anyway, sensitivity does last, at least as long as the brain lasts. Even old people retain acute perception if they had it in the first place. But how many of them retain love? When I was working on a newspaper I used to be fascinated by old people. I wasn't very wise, but it seemed to me that the crankiest, sourest old people were those that had lost the power to love. Whereas the old ones that seemed to be enjoying life, in spite of aches and pains, were the ones that look at life as a big joke. As you say in the theater, they exit laughing."

"Oh, you want to be a jolly old man, is that it?" she said.

"I didn't say that, but maybe I do. I'd rather be a jolly old man than a cranky old man."

"How would you like to be a jolly *young* man?"

"God forbid," he said. "Life is a big joke, but you don't get many laughs out of it when you're young. Look at you, Zena. You're young, very successful, always believed in love, and a few minutes ago you were ready to jump out the window."

"If you don't shut up, I still may," she said.

"No, you won't now, although I believed you would have then. You're all right now."

"Maybe I am, but just for safety's sake I want you to stay. You will stay, won't you?"

"Of course I'll stay. I got news for you, kid. If I'd had to go back to my room tonight—*my* room has windows, too. I might have met you on the way down."

"Ah, sweetheart. Come here. Put your head on my shoulder," she said. "Did you have a let-down too?"

"I must have," he said.

They made love with tenderness—and with reservations that were created by their unadmitted, unresolved crisis. But he stayed the night and they slept well. They were younger than they were old.

The New York opening was an ordeal and a delight, for which none of Yank's experience had prepared him. He had never been to an opening night in New York, and though he thought he knew the company rather well, he was disturbed and amused by the frenetic solemnity of the actors. Their return to Broadway had been preceded by newspaper and word-of-mouth publicity that conveyed, among other effects, a warning that this was an opening not to be missed. The day before the opening he was sitting in Ellis Walton's office. As Ellis sat down he spoke to his secretary on the inter-com. "I'm not in to anybody. Nobody." But a moment later the secretary's voice could be heard. Yank did not get the name, but *somebody* wanted to speak to Ellis. "All right, put him on," said Ellis, then, to the telephone caller, "This is Ellis Walton speaking . . . Well, I can't stay no to him, can I? That's one I can't say no to. I don't know where I'm going to get them, but I'll get them." He hung up. "That was the mayor's secretary. The mayor's on our regular list, but he wants two more for your opening." In the course of the conversation between Ellis and Yank they were interrupted several times, and each time it was a request for opening night tickets by a V. I. P. "I guess you saw in the paper, tickets are going for a hundred bucks a pair—and they'll go higher," said Ellis.

"At that price I'll sell them mine," said Yank.

"I suppose Peg McInerney told you, if you wanted to make

a nice little piece of change, you could turn over your house seats for the run of the play. Any ticket broker will be glad to do business with you."

"I've turned them over to her," said Yank.

"You're learning fast. That way, when people ask you for them you just tell them to get in touch with Peg. Save you a lot of headaches. Did Peg speak to you about my conversation with her?"

"Yes."

"Do I get your next two plays?"

"I don't know. And I'm not trying to torture you. I've left that up to Peg."

"Yes, but I thought if I made a personal pitch—"

"I wish you wouldn't," said Yank. "Peg was sure you would, and for the last time, Ellis, I have to tell you that all that stuff is in Peg's hands."

"All right. I give up. Next question. Who is a guy named Jiggs Muldowney?"

"You got me," said Yank.

"You sure? This guy was here yesterday and the day before. A personal friend of yours, he said. Yesterday he pushed my secretary out of the way and barged right in here. I was having my hair cut, and he barged in and demanded to know your address and phone number. Jiggs Muldowney. He seemed to know—"

"Oh, God, yes," said Yank. "He saved my life once. And not too long ago."

"How could you forget a man that saved your life?"

"I hardly knew his name. What did he want? My address and phone number. Is that all?"

"That's all he wanted from me. From you—I would hazard the guess that from you he wants more. I'm glad it wasn't my life he saved. I wouldn't want to be indebted to him."

"Indirectly, you are. But don't worry about it."

"There's all kinds of blackmail, and that could be one of the worst. If he was a Chinaman *he'd* have to take care of *you* the rest of your life."

"So I've heard. But he's not a Chinaman, and neither am I. So, what he wants, I'll give him—within reason."

"Whose reason? Yours, or his? This guy won't let go of you that easily."

"Whatever I give him, it'll be the last."

"My advice to you, Yank, is don't give him money. Give him a gift, but not money."

"A brilliant idea," said Yank. "I shall discharge my debt with a token of my gratitude, other than cash." He paused. "All kinds of blackmail, you said. Have you ever been blackmailed?"

"Not the usual way. But I got a couple of actors that blackmail me in a different way. They know I pity them, feel sorry for them. So they come in here looking for a part, only they're not looking for a part. They know I wouldn't give them a part if they'd work for free. So they come in and sit out there in my outer office till I finally tell them I don't have anything for them. And then I give them a couple of bucks. They work on my pity, the bloodsuckers. You know, you hear a lot nowadays about lonely people. We're all supposed to feel sorry for lonely people. All they have to do is be lonely, and we're all supposed to burst out crying. It doesn't make the slightest difference why they're lonely, how they got lonely. Some of them are lonely because they stink from never taking a bath. Some of them have halitosis. Some of them are the meanest sons of bitches you can imagine. But if they get the reputation for being lonely, we're all supposed to be nice to them. Even if they hate you. We got a neighbor in the same building that calls me a Jew bastard, and you know what my wife said? She said, make allowances, he's lonely. He wanted a pair for your opening—free, yet! You know what I told him? I said if I was a Jew bastard last October, I'm a Jew bastard now, and he could go fuck himself. Wait'll my wife hears about that, but I had the pleasure."

"Revenge is sweet, to coin a phrase," said Yank.

"It's not supposed to be, but it is. Who do you hate, Yank?"

"I don't know. Why?"

"I got a theory you don't hate anybody. But I got another theory you don't love anybody," said Ellis.

"Were you thinking about anyone in particular?"

"I guess I could pin it down," said Ellis. "But I don't have to pin it down. A man saves your life, and you have a hard time recollecting him. You see a sexy broad in the Algonquin that you laid, but she's nothing. I don't know, Yank. You didn't get any excitement out of Boston. The notices. Tomorrow night they're paying a hundred dollars a pair for your play. The mayor wants two extras. The society people. Picture people. But you could be having an appointment with the dentist."

"As a matter of fact, I have one tomorrow morning," said Yank.

"See what I mean? I bet you don't even get drunk. Do me a favor. Get a little load on at my party. Let me see you enjoy yourself."

"I'm sorry, Ellis, but I won't be at your party."

"Not at my party? You gotta be at my party. The party is *for* you, and Zena. I got everybody coming. Prince Obolensky. Dietrich. Mr. and Mrs. Gilbert Miller. Gypsy Rose Lee. Every name in town. Gregory Peck. Elsa Maxwell. Bernie Baruch. The mayor, I guess. I hate to tell you what this shindig is going to cost me. Where are you going? Zena's coming, and you *have* to be her escort."

"Those are just names I see in the papers, Ellis."

"What's wrong with that? They had to do something to get their names in the papers."

"Well, so did—Bruno Richard Hauptmann."

"Who? Oh, the Lindbergh kidnaper. Come on, Yank. You can't disappoint Zena."

"I'll bet I can."

"God, don't tell me you and Zena had a hassle. You wouldn't get her all wrought up the day before her opening. For her this is going to be the biggest night of her career."

"I'm immodest enough to think that it probably is. And I wouldn't do anything to spoil it for her."

"Listen, she wants to make an entrance at that party, with you. I know that, because I know that little girl, Yank."

"I'm just a skinny guy with glasses. She can make her entrance with Scott Aubrey."

"Did you tell her this?"

"No, but I'm telling you."

"You didn't answer me where you'll be?"

"Probably at Peg McInerney's."

"You're kidding. You must be kidding."

"I don't know where I'll be."

"How does Zena get to the party?"

"On her own power."

"There *is* something wrong with you and Zena."

"Not in the way you think, Ellis."

"Torturing me again. You love to torture. You don't love anybody, you don't hate anybody."

"I'm going away, Ellis. I'd swear you to secrecy, but I don't think that'll be necessary. Tomorrow night, after the curtain goes up for the third act, I'm taking Peg's car and driving till I get tired."

"Where to?"

"Not where to. What from," said Yank.

"I get it. The whole mishmash," said Ellis.

"The whole mishmash," said Yank. "I won't be getting away from myself, but maybe if I got back to myself I'd start doing what I want to do. That I haven't been doing for quite a while."

"Which is writing," said Ellis.

"Yes."

"Well, I wouldn't be smart to keep you from that, even if you don't make me any promises. But what happens to Zena? She got rid of Barry Payne so she could latch on to you. Now she won't have anybody."

"But is that true, Ellis?"

"Oh, I don't say she won't have anybody to go to bed with. But Zena got used to being taken care of, speaking other than sexually. Even you took care of her, or at least you were with her all the time. You know, for a girl that was the next thing to a hooker, she has a lot of wife in her. She never cheated on you."

"No, I don't think she did. I know she didn't," said Yank. "I could probably be useful to her for a while. I could probably get in the habit of being useful to her, meanwhile getting nowhere myself, not doing what I want to do. Then the day would surely come when I was no longer useful to her, and I'd have wasted a year, two years, and gotten into the habit of postponing work. That's why I am getting out tomorrow."

"You don't have a guilty conscience about ditching her?"

"No."

"She wasn't just a piece of tail to you, Yank. That I know. I caught you looking at her a couple times, and she wasn't just a lay in the hay. You cared for her."

"The most I ever have for anyone."

"Marc—Marc DuBois—said to me one time you had a positive instinct for the drama. You're certainly showing that by walking out on Zena tomorrow night."

"Balls, Ellis. Balls. I'm doing it out of self-preservation and nothing else. There's nothing dramatic about it."

"Well, it's good timing, and that's dramatic," said Ellis. "Or bad timing, the way she'll look at it."

"Yes, it's good timing."

"Tell me—you don't have to if you don't want to—but say tonight. Will you get in bed with her tonight and give her a good screw? Just like there was nothing out of the ordinary?"

"I intend to, if she's in the mood."

"And she won't catch on?"

"I doubt it. She'll have tomorrow night on her mind, don't forget."

"And that will be the last time you ever screw her?"

"Oh, hell. You know better than to ask me that. How do I know what'll happen a year from now, ten years from now? Or were you thinking of moving in? Is that why you asked?"

"I had in my mind can you get in bed with her for the last time and not let on it'll be the last time. This I could never do. If it was me, the woman would know there was something funny. In the hay I'm a talker. I say anything comes into my head. To your question, was I thinking of moving in. Once I wouldn't of touched her with a ten-foot pole. Now is different. This ex-nympho is very, very close to being one of the great ladies of the theater. Slowly but surely, she is acquiring that indefinable something called class. The Zena Gollum I used to hire for one-seventy-five a week isn't the same Zena Gollum I open with tomorrow night. Looking ahead to when I'm in my sixties and seventies, I would like to think back and have intimate memories of her. Like Peg McInerney and those famous authors. Like those rich guys and their opera singers."

"Then my departure will be very convenient for you. Good timing on my part."

"If she doesn't go back to that semi-gangster."

"She won't," said Yank. "And what if she does? You're not planning to marry her."

"Who says I'm not? If, God forbid, my present wife should take up horseback riding in Central Park, like she did some years ago, and she got hold of a spirited mount that tossed her into the Reservoir, why shouldn't a successful manager offer matrimony to a big star? It would be too costly to get a divorce from my present wife. But if conditions made it possible, I'd marry Zena. We're of the same religion, and that's nice."

"Oh, balls again, Ellis. You want to lay her, and you probably will."

"You won't give me credit for higher motives?"

"No."

"Well—maybe you're right. I won't argue the point. I must say you'd make a lousy shadchan, if you know that word."

"Marriage broker."

"You have a remarkable ear, Yank. I noticed before how you picked up so many Yiddish expressions in the short time you lived in New York."

"New York my ass. Living next door to us in Spring Valley was a professor of political science, Morton Sperry, and his wife and three kids. So I don't even owe New York my few words of Yiddish."

"Did they have a daughter, Professor and Mrs. Sperry?"

"They had two daughters."

"Close to you in age?"

"Ask what's on your mind, Ellis."

"Well, did you?"

"One of them. She wouldn't let me screw her, but anything else was okay. Why?"

"Then Zena was no novelty to you?"

"Because she was Jewish? Zena doesn't even eat kosher. But if you want to know any more about her, you'll have to find out for yourself."

"The code of the gentleman," said Ellis.

"The gentleman dishwasher," said Yank. "I've got to go now, Ellis. I hope you're taking care of that heart condition. All this excitement."

"So I lied about a heart condition. Does that make me a felon, guilty of a felony?"

"No, you're actually a pretty nice guy, Ellis."

"Coming from you, I take that as a high compliment."

"And well you may. But don't let it go to your head."

"Do I say goodbye to you now, or tomorrow night? To wish you a pleasant journey."

"If you let a peep out of you about my going away, you can be sure you'll never see another play of mine. And I'll tell Peg that if you're one penny out of line, she's to take it up with the Dramatists Guild. So long, Ellis. See you tomorrow night. Briefly."

✦ II ✦

The house was at the edge of the village of East Hammond, population 482, among whom there seemed to be few early risers. There was a filling station in the center of the village, but it was not open; the night light inside the station was still burning. The night lights were still on in the post office and the branch bank. An arrow-shaped road sign at the filling station read, Georgetown 8 M. Beneath it was a similar sign, pointed in the opposite direction, which read, Cooperstown 9 M. Yank Lucas knew about Cooperstown; he had just come from there, and Cooperstown had shown no more signs of life than East Hammond. In Cooperstown the fuel gauge needle in Peg McInerney's coupe had first touched E for empty. In East Hammond the needle left no doubt that the extra eight miles to Georgetown would be impossible.

He parked the car near the filling station and got out. It was not yet six o'clock, but what about all those legends of early rising in New England? He heard a rooster and then another, and while he was wondering what to do next a twelve-wheeler tractor-trailer rumbled past him. It was a milk-tanker. He waved to the driver, but the driver paid no attention to him. There was, of course, no place to get something to eat. He had been driving aimlessly most of the night, and in a town called Hoosick Falls he had stopped and eaten two thin little hamburgers, but he was hungry again. Worse than hungry, he was sleepy. He went behind the filling station and took a leak, and momentarily the sleepiness vanished, but here he was in a Vermont village, with all the money in the world, and he could not buy a cup of coffee or a night's lodging. He could take a nap in the car while waiting for the filling station to open—an hour, two hours, perhaps—but he wanted to get undressed, put on pajamas, and get between some clean sheets and sleep, sleep, sleep. Then he remembered that the house on the edge of town had an austere sign on the lawn that said Tourists. It was two short blocks to the house, and there he went.

Approaching it from a different angle he saw that the light was on in the kitchen. A small dog inside the house barked the moment he stepped on the driveway, and when he reached the kitchen door it was open. A woman's voice called, "Come in, Ed."

"It isn't Ed," said Yank Lucas. "I'm a tourist, and I saw your sign."

The dog, a mixture of fox terrier and another small breed, was only more articulately suspicious than the woman. "You come by car?" she said.

"I ran out of gas. I'm parked at the filling station."

"He's usually open between seven, seven-thirty. You by yourself?"

"All by myself. I've been driving all night, all the way from New York—"

"New York City?"

"Yes. And I was wondering if I could have some breakfast and then make up for lost sleep."

"Most people have breakfast and go out and do a day's work. Could I see your auto license? Some identification? I don't ordinarily take guests traveling by themselves. Mostly it's couples. Man and wife."

"Oh, hell, I left the registration in the car."

"Well, your driver's license," said the woman.

"That cooks it. I don't have one."

"You don't have a driver's license? You could get into trouble."

"I know."

"Here especially. They're having a campaign on to check up on people driving without a license."

"The car is owned by a friend of mine. I haven't had any use for a car in recent years."

"Pays to keep up your driver's license, though. I do, and I don't own a car."

"Then I'll make a deal with you. I'll take a room here, pay

for it in advance, and stay till I can get a Vermont driver's license."

"All rooms are payable in advance, there's no exception to that rule," said the woman. "Don't you have any other credentials?"

"Social Security, and draft card. And I have this." He handed her a folder of traveler's cheques worth $1,000.

"Lucas. I don't suppose you're related to the Lucas family over in Cooperstown? Warren Lucas?"

"Not that I know of. I'm originally from the western part of Pennsylvania, but the last few years I've been living in New York."

"Well, I guess you look all right. Room is five dollars a night, in advance. I don't usually serve but breakfast. A dollar for that. Don't many tourists hang around much after nine or ten o'clock in the morning. They like to be on their way. Were you thinking of board and room for a week?"

"Maybe even longer. It'd take that long to get a driver's license, wouldn't it?"

"I don't know, I had mine so long I don't know the rules and regulations for a new person. But a week anyhow, I should think."

"Then we'll say a week," he said.

"Seven nights'd be thirty-five, and say four dollars a day board, is twenty-eight and thirty-five is sixty-three dollars. I cook the meals, it's nothing fancy but it's good plain food. Everything fresh in season, although there's some canned goods such as spaghetti I happen to like myself. Do my own baking, bread and pastries. You didn't bring your suitcase with you?"

"Left it in the back of the car."

"Well, while you're getting it I'll start on your breakfast. How do you like your eggs? And would you care for hot cereal?"

"The works. Oatmeal. Fried eggs over. Bacon. Toast. Coffee."

"And you can make out the cheque payable to me, Anna B. Phelps."

"Sixty-three dollars? I'll give you the cash."

"Very well, I'll always take cash," she said. She laughed. "I pulled a fast one on you, Mr. Lucas."

"How was that?"

"There's nobody named Lucas in Cooperstown. Nor for that matter in East Hammond or Georgetown, or in the whole township. I know just about every name in this vicinity the past two hundred years. I used to be president of the Historical Society, so *I know*."

"I'll just bet you do," said Yank.

The dog got up and made quietly joyful sounds, and a man appeared at the kitchen door. "Come in, Ed," said Mrs. Phelps.

The man, dressed in a checked jacket called a car-coat, plaid shirt with no necktie, Marine Corps surplus pants, and paratrooper's surplus jump-boots, seemed not to be surprised at the presence of a stranger in Anna Phelps's kitchen. "Morning," he said. "Morning, Anna." He placed his black leather cap on a chair and seated himself at the kitchen table. He surrounded a cup and saucer with his fingers and assumed a waiting attitude.

"Well, I'll be right back," said Yank.

When he returned with his suitcase Ed was gone.

"That was Ed Cross," said Anna Phelps. "Stops in here every morning for a cup of coffee, on his way to work. He's batching it. Has his sister living with him, but he gets up too early for her."

"I had an idea that everybody in this part of the world got up at the crack of dawn."

"Some do. The dairymen. The poultrymen. But here in town there's not much use in getting up much before ha' past six or seven."

"What does a man like Mr. Cross do?"

"What does Ed do? What would you say he did?" said Anna Phelps. She placed his oatmeal on the table and pointed to a pitcher filled with top cream.

"Well, I'd say he did some work with his hands. They looked strong. Fingernails broken. A carpenter, maybe?"

"On that order. He's a slateworker, or was. Now he has a township job. Drives the school bus, and in between he runs the grader and the tractor. He would have been the one to ask about getting a driver's license. I should have thought, but I had three separate breakfasts on my mind. Ed's and yours and my own. How's your oatmeal?"

"Just right. I like it to have a salty taste."

"That's why I put a lump of butter on it. It makes a big

difference. A man of your build doesn't have to worry about putting on weight. Ed has to watch his. He gave up taking cream in his coffee. *Thick* cream. I give him about half and half. The doctor told him he ought to take off about twenty pounds. That was two years ago. He didn't take off any, but he didn't put any on. A man like that, out in all kinds of weather, he needs a certain amount of fat. You never saw a skinny Eskimo."

"I never saw an Eskimo, period."

"Well, you saw pictures of them. You wouldn't make a very good Eskimo."

"So far I haven't been tempted," said Yank.

"Tempted?"

"To turn Eskimo," said Yank.

"Oh. Oh, I see. More toast?"

"I guess not, thanks. Is Mr. Cross a widower?"

"What makes you ask that? Yes, he is. But what made you think of it?"

"Oh, people interest me. Lately I've been thinking about how people take care of other people. The way you, for instance, give Cross his breakfast in the morning while his sister lies in bed."

"Ed could get his own breakfast if he wanted to. He's a first-rate cook in certain things. But his wife was a great friend of mine and that's the least I can do. And he earns it. We get a lot of snow up here, you know. If it wasn't for Ed bringing his shovel in the morning, I'd have to get out there and dig myself out some mornings. Many a time I've seen it as high as that windowsill, the snow. If it wasn't for him Prince wouldn't get out for his morning constitutional."

"Prince being that ferocious animal that wanted to chew my leg off," said Yank.

"Mm-hmm. Well, if you're ready, I'll show you your room. I'm putting you in the attic, because that way you'll be quiet and you have a bathroom all to yourself. There didn't used to be a bathroom up there, but I put one in the summer before last. Everything brand-new. I'll be in and out all day, but in case you wake up hungry, you can help yourself to the icebox."

"I imagine I'll sleep most of the day. I might even sleep around the clock."

"That'd be a good idea. You won't find much to occupy you in the evening. Picture show in Cooperstown, but I got so sick of Gene Autry, Gene Autry, Gene Autry, I stopped going. Ed tolerates him, but he likes the singing and I don't."

"Thank you very much, Mrs. Phelps," said Yank.

They renewed acquaintance again late in the afternoon. Yank, in pajamas and bathrobe, was having coffee and toast in the kitchen when Mrs. Phelps and Prince returned. "I see you helped yourself," she said. "Did you get enough sleep?"

"For the time being, thanks," he said.

She smiled. "I notice you made your toast over the flame. That's the way Ed likes it too. Can you cook?"

"Not very well. But I'm a very good dishwasher."

"A lot of young fellows learned that in the army."

"I learned it in restaurants. I *was* a dishwasher."

"What can I get you? It's getting close to supper, if you

care to wait that long. Or else it might be a good idea if you went and got your car before the filling station closes. It'd look funny if it stayed there all night. Matt Lewis is the man at the filling station. You can tell him you're staying at my house and then he won't start asking you a lot of questions. He's a kind of a special policeman. Constable. I don't exactly know what, but he can arrest people. He'd be sure to ask a lot of questions if you left the car there overnight, and then they'd find out you don't have a driver's license."

"By God, you think of everything," said Yank.

He dressed and got the car. He had a vague suspicion that during his absence Anna Phelps had taken a look at his effects. "I made your bed, in case you didn't have enough sleep. I tidied up and aired the room. Did it go all right with Matt?"

"As soon as I told him I was staying here," said Yank.

"You look as if you could sleep some more. Nothing to how you looked this morning, but why don't you let me give you some milk toast and then you go back and sleep it out."

"Will you tuck me in?"

"Will I what? Don't step over the bounds, Mr. Lucas. Don't step over the bounds."

"You must know I was joking," he said.

"Not in the best of taste," she said.

"No, and I apologize. I won't abuse your hospitality again."

"Just remember, there're certain bounds. I may be old enough to be your mother, just about, but I'm not your mother. I'll bring you your milk toast when it's ready."

Once or twice during the night he was awakened by sounds and by the absence of sound; otherwise he slept even more deeply than he had during the daylight hours. The long sleep told him something of the degree of his physical and nervous exhaustion, and the sleep, rather than the journey, was the method, the bridge, by which he had achieved the passage from the world he had deserted to the world that was ahead. He lay in the calm of the clean white sheets with his head on the clean white pillowcase, his hands clasped behind his neck and his eyes wide open and cool. He was refreshed, restored, reinvigorated—and released. He recognized the rumble of the milk-tanker passing the house, and already it was a familiar sound that fitted into his new life. He got up and shaved, put on his bathrobe and went downstairs. The terrier offered a token growl and was quiet.

"Good morning, Mrs. Phelps."

She handed him a cup of coffee. "Good morning. Heard the water running. Now you're beginning to look like something."

"Feel like something, too," said Yank. "Mr. Cross been here yet?"

"Not quite his time. But he'll be along, never fear. One of us ought to be sure and remember to speak to him about your license. If not one of us, the other ought to remember."

"Yes. And I have to ask you, would you be disturbed if I used a typewriter? It's a portable, it doesn't make too much noise."

"*That's* it? You're a *writer?* No, it wouldn't bother me a bit. I never did have a writer staying here, but I used to have a traveling man spend the night here once a month, and he wrote out his reports on the machine. Sometimes till well into past midnight, but it never interfered with my sleep. Should I have heard of your writings?"

"Afraid not."

"In other words, it wouldn't do me any good to ask for them at the library?"

"Not so far."

"Well, you go right ahead. The trucks going by may bother you some, but after New York City—dear me, how they can put up with that noise? I've been there five times in my life, and every time the noise got worse."

"You get used to it if you have to."

"Like anything else," she said.

Now, as was not the case yesterday, he scrutinized her as a woman and not as a landlady. Her hair was parted in the middle and tied in a bun at the back of her neck. The skin was drawn so tightly across her cheekbones and along her jawline that it was unwrinkled and slightly glossy. Her nose was hooked, the nostrils prominent, the lips thin, the teeth regular. The color of her hair was a nondescript brown-and-grey, but in his present viewing he discovered that her eyes were a brown that was startling, and were her best feature. She was inclined to be round-shouldered, with an ample bust and a waist that was no longer slender but once had been. Her calves and ankles were slender, her feet not small, her hands useful and not ornamental. Her age was past fifty—beyond that he could not guess. He wondered what she would do if he put his hand under her skirt. He thought he knew: she would hold still and let his fingers explore, and then she would say to him something like, "You can stop that now, Mr. Lucas. I don't care for it." And then of course in a few minutes she would give him a precise financial accounting, return the unused portion of his money, and tell him to pack up and go. On the other hand, if he got into bed with her at three o'clock in the morning, with her breasts loose and the uncaring world asleep, she might lead him inside her and keep him with her till daylight. She was surely not devoted to Ed Cross to the exclusion of all other pleasure with all other men. It might only be for that one night, and she would send him away in the morning, but she would have had that one extra night to reassure her when, as was inevitable, she was married to Cross. There was another possibility: that some night she would come to him; but he thought that extremely unlikely unless he went to her first.

"Is there any place in town that sells the New York papers?"

"Not in East Hammond, except during the summer. You could try Bostwick's, over in Cooperstown. They may have them. Or if you just wanted to look at one, I believe they take a New York paper at the Cooperstown library. I'm not sure. Now I think of it I'm under the impression that Seymour Atterbury has the New York papers sent to him by mail. He's our gentleman-farmer owns some twelve-hundred acres to your right on the Cooperstown Road. You can just barely see the top of his house as you go by. Set back maybe a quarter of a mile. But you can't miss the property, whitewashed fences and I don't know how many head of Ayrshires in pasture. I could call up his superintendent, Adam Phelps, my husband's cousin. He'd know for sure. Was there something particular you wanted to look up?"

"Yes, but it wouldn't be worth the trouble. I can have it sent to me from New York."

"A visit to Seymour Atterbury's place is worthwhile. I could phone Adam. This hour of the morning he'll be in his office, and it'd give you something to do."

"I'm not much for dairy farms," said Yank.

"Oh, that's only an excuse. They have a regular castle. Seymour's mother was a local girl. Married Atterbury and moved to New York, then when old Atterbury passed on she bought back the Seymour farm and added to it. They have visiting hours from two to five. People come from all over to see the place, and I doubt if most of them would know an Ayrshire from a Guernsey. Worth a visit."

"All right," said Yank.

Anna Phelps telephoned her husband's cousin. Yes, the Atterburys still took the New York papers, although they arrived a day late. He would leave them on his desk for Mr. Lucas, in case he was out in the field when Lucas got there. Lucas could feel free to walk around the place. Seymour and his wife were in New York and not expected back till evening. No, he could not have a look inside the big house. The Atterburys had put a stop to that; too much pilferage and cigarette burns. Visitors were restricted to the barns and the pasture land. Even there some son of a bitch had stolen a halter right off a cow, a halter worth twelve dollars. Nowadays they'd steal anything wasn't nailed down. The Atterbury butler could let Lucas in to see the house, but Adam was on the outs with the butler and wouldn't ask him for the time of day. What kind of a looking fellow was Lucas?

"Well, I guess you gathered from the conversation, I wasn't altogether successful. But you *can* get your New York papers," said Anna Phelps. "Go see the place, just to have a look at it. They tell me there's only about two or three like it left in the whole of New England. Taxes."

Ed Cross came in and put his fingers around a cup of coffee, and there was something about the position of the fingers that reminded Yank of the grip he would get on Anna Phelps's buttocks if he were to pay a successful visit to her room. It would be a good idea to get such ideas out of his head, and keep them out. The energy that had been restored to him was not to be dissipated in the seduction of the first woman he saw. If this strange, unprecedented desire for a woman in her fifties persisted, he would have to go away, and he did not want to go away. He liked the house, he liked the village, and he knew why: the house and the village reminded him of the two hamlets he had known all his life that were nestled in the eastern slope of the Spring Valley Mountain. He had run away from New York, and accidentally found himself in a familiar scene that he had never seen before. The area in and about Spring Valley had been founded by New Englanders, and they had kept their memories of New England alive in the kind of houses they built. There were even Phelpses and Crosses in Spring Valley, along with the Everetts and the Appletons and the Framinghams. The Framinghams of Spring Valley were probably the Atterburys of East Hammond, whom he had no wish to see, and already the pattern of the town, the village, was as familiar and recognizable as New York had been foreign and harsh. Here he could listen atingle to the silence, gathering the strength that would soon impel him to work again. He knew what he wanted to do. He knew what he had to do. And he had not abandoned the ready excitements of Zena Gollum for the uncertain frustrations of Anna Phelps.

He permitted himself no lubricious thoughts of Zena. She was still too close—as close as the telephone. Closer than the telephone, she was as near as the presence of Anna Phelps. A woman would be necessary, indispensable to his balance as food and sleep were necessary when he began work. But he would discipline himself, deny himself a woman for casual pleasure until the need of one went beyond pleasure. And then he knew that in another week, two weeks, the woman would be Anna Phelps. He knew how it would happen. In a week, two weeks, whenever, she would have begun to wonder about him. She would make his bed every day, and she would wonder how long he could go without a woman. Thinking such things, she would think more often of him until he was constantly on her mind as a womanless man. And the nature of her thoughts would be of the nature of sexual curiosity, stimulating her into a condition of excitement. She would make his bed, fold his pajamas under his pillow, hear the water running in his tub, feed him, talk to him, do small favors for him, and finally make an excuse to come to him. "Are you all right?" she would say. "I thought I heard a noise up here."

"I was having a nightmare," he would lie to her lie.

"Do you want me to turn the light on?" she would say.

"No, I'll be all right in a minute," he would say. She would not want him to turn the light on.

"Was it a bad nightmare?" she would say.

"Yes, I get them, sometimes. Stay awhile," he would say. He would reach out his hand and she would sit on the edge of his bed, and he would not speak. She would be facing him in the dark, holding his hand until he took it away and felt her breasts. He would fondle them until they demanded to be sucked. "Is that what you want?" she would say.

"Very much," he would say, and for a little while they would pretend that that was all there was to be. But she would be unable to leave him and he would take her hand and put it between his legs. She would try to cover her nervousness with a joke. "Might as well be hung for a sheep as a goat," or something like that, she would say. "Put it in. Put it way in. As far in as you can go."

Then she would say, "Well, we did it."

"Aren't you glad we did it?"

"I am now. It was enjoyable," she would say. "But we know it's not right, both of us."

"Why not?"

"For me and you? No, that's not right. But it *was* enjoyable, I don't say for a minute it wasn't enjoyable."

She would be half-smiling all the next day, and she would come to him the next night. Beyond that his fantasy would not go, because he had no proof of the extent of her relationship with Ed Cross.

"Anna was saying something about you wanting to get a driver's license," said Ed Cross. "You have to be eighteen in Vermont, but I guess you're all of that . . . Maybe I can hurry it up a little for you."

"Thank you very much," said Yank.

"Till he gets his license, what would you think of him driving his car?"

"Well, you know some folks and so do I that've been driving automobiles since Hector was a pup, and they never took the trouble to get one."

"They're having a drive on."

"So they are."

"And Mr. Lucas's car has York State plates on it," said Anna Phelps.

"Then you might say he'd be tempting fate. Why? Does he want to go somewheres?"

"Out to Seymour Atterbury's place."

"Mm. Supposing I give him the loan of my car. Naturally I have Vermont plates on mine, and I do have a driver's license. He's lacking in a driver's license, but they're not apt to stop him if he's driving my jalopy. Everybody around here knows my car, and they'll presume that he has my permission. One nice thing about keeping up a good reputation, you never know when it'll come in handy."

Everybody in East Hammond knew Ed Cross's car, and well they might have. It was a Ford V-8 coupe, a veteran of many Vermont winters and a victim of Ed's neglect. "But she still runs," said Ed. Yank drove it out to the Atterbury farm, which he had no difficulty finding.

"I see you come in Ed Cross's car," said the man in the superintendent's office. "Adam Phelps is my name. Anna seemed particularly anxious to let you have a look inside the owner's house, but that's not my territory. You'd have to speak to the butler. *I don't*, if I can help it. Here's the New York papers since Monday. They pile up when the owner's away, but I don't dare throw them out. He likes to do the crossword puzzles. He hasn't been stumped on a one of them since quite a while back."

"I'll try not to rumple them up. I only want to look up two items," said Yank.

"Well, if you got everything, I'll just leave you be," said Adam Phelps. He was a tall, big-boned man in a plaid shirt, surplus Marine Corps green pants, tucked into half-length tan rubber boots. He put on an Eisenhower jacket and a bright red felt hat and took a double-barrel shotgun out of a closet. "Unwelcome chore," he said. "Have to put an old setter out of his misery before *they* get home. 'Have it done before we get back,' *she* said."

"Too bad," said Yank.

"Ah, well, he's sixteen years old and that's plenty old for a setter. He's ready to go. Don't take any interest any more, and he smells so bad the other animals shy away from him."

Adam Phelps went out to kill the dog and Yank Lucas sat in his swivel chair and read the New York reviews. He read them once quickly to classify them, favorable or otherwise, and they were extremely favorable. He was in the midst of a second reading of Atkinson when he heard the shot. He waited for a second shot but there was none. A man like Adam Phelps would do the job right. The instantaneous picture of the ugliness that lay on the ground at Adam Phelps's feet made the review and the theater and even life itself seem trivial, and Yank had no wish to go on reading, but he reread what the two critics had to say about Zena Gollum. In both cases they were so complimentary that he was grateful to them; with such notices she would be a pig to ask anything more, and now he was free. He began to feel less badly about the dog.

He refolded the newspapers and put them on the desk. As he was doing so Adam Phelps returned, put the shotgun back in the closet, put the unused shell back in a box, hung his hat and jacket on wall pegs.

"Get it over with?" said Yank.

Adam Phelps nodded. "I passed the buck on burying him. This time of year we do a lot of burying, this part of the country. Humans. Anybody passes on after the ground freezes, they have to wait for spring for burial. These past few weeks I attended no less than four interments. Two friends, two relatives. So I let one of the hired men do the honors for the dog. No use being the boss if you can't pass some of the buck. You find what you wanted?"

"I did, and thank you."

A young woman swung the door open. "Mr. Phelps, can I borrow the jeep? Oh, excuse me. I didn't know you were busy."

"That's all right. Yes, you can have it if you'll bring it back by late afternoon, around four-thirty. I won't need it before then. What have you got wrong now?"

"My battery went dead. William said I left the parking lights on all night. I don't see how I could have, but try and argue with William. And I have a hair appointment in Cooperstown. I *have* to look my best tonight. So I'd really appreciate it."

"The keys are in it."

"Thanks ever so," said the young woman, and closed the door behind her.

"Who was that? Does she work here?" said Yank.

"Work? That's her daughter, the owner's daughter by her first marriage. Her name is Sheila Dunham."

"A breath of spring," said Yank. "She doesn't live here all the time, does she?"

"I should say not," said Adam Phelps. "She's staying here now while she's getting a divorce. Married to some fellow down in Boston, but I guess she was too much for him. She'd be too much for me, I'll say that."

"Seems very young to be getting divorced."

"Twenty-three or -four. Could be twenty-five by now."

"Seems younger."

"Well, she has a mental age of fifteen at the most," said Adam Phelps.

"In her case that probably doesn't matter."

"Exactly. Born rich, married rich, and I guess she's divorcing rich."

"I wasn't only thinking of money," said Yank.

"Oh, that goes without saying. She runs around here in those riding pants and that sweater, those boobies bouncing up and down, and every man on the place gets a hard on. One of these days there'll be a gang fuck, and maybe it'll teach her a lesson."

"Here? In Vermont?"

"Huh. I got thirty-four men working for me, and out of that over half of them only been here a year or so. You take what you can get. French Canucks. Irish. Two niggers. Somebody has to shovel the cow-shit, you know. They're not exactly itinerants, but a year is about as long as most of them'll stay, and then they pull out. The single ones, which is most of them, we have living in the bunkhouse. Supposed to call it the dormitory, but bunkhouse is the name it goes by. You care to take a look at it?"

"I'd like to come back some other time, if that's all right. I have to write some letters."

"Anna said you were some kind of a writer. There's plenty to write about right here. I'd never attempt to do it myself, not a very good speller, and I use the old Hunt & Peck System on the machine. All the same, somebody ought to write a kind of a history of this place from the days it used to be the old Seymour farm right down to the present. At that I don't suppose anybody'll ever know the amount of money was spent on the place, mostly because the owner's mother was born here and never really wanted to live anywheres else. She could have lived anywhere in the world, and did spend some time in England and California. But this was it for her. Oh, you could write a whole book about this farm—leaving out some of the things that happened here, to be sure." He made a sweeping gesture that indicated the steel, wood, and cardboard filing systems. "There's a record of every cow we ever had, the butter-fat content of her milk, health record and so on. The bulls and their breeding records. I could pull out a drawer and tell you how much a cultivator cost in 1916, when we put in our first tractor and so on. One of those son of a bitches in the Income Tax Bureau decided the farm was just a rich man's hobby. But when we showed them how this place is run he had another think coming. Maybe it started as a hobby, but nearly every year we show a profit. A place like this, you have to show a profit every so often or the tax people come down on you like a ton of brick and disallow everything. I put in over forty years here, including summer jobs during high school and college, but at that we have two men were here before I was."

"You ought to be writing the story. You're a college man. Where did you go?"

"Oh, I graduated over at Burlington. Where did you go?"

"A small college in Pennsylvania called Spring Valley."

"Spring Valley? Yes, we have a chapter there. I'm a Phi Doodle. Phi Delta Theta. What were you?"

"Phi Gamma Delta. But I wasn't much of a fraternity man. I lived at home. My father was on the faculty, and he was a Phi Gam, so I was a legacy."

"We didn't have Phi Gam at the University of Vermont. I don't know why. I was a legacy myself, but I guess I would have made it anyway, through football. I scored a touchdown against Yale."

"You must have been pretty good."

"Not bad. And always in good condition, working summers on the farm. Clumsy, but strong. The owner and his father were there the day I scored the touchdown, and I guess they were almost as pleased as I was. Not quite, maybe. But they both came to the dressing-room afterwards, and I always thought that was pretty nice. Of course Yale won, so they didn't have to be too upset about my touchdown. We lost forty-two to six."

"Fortunately I was too light for football," said Yank. "Do you live here on the property?"

"Yes indeed I do. We have our own cottage down at the other end of the lane. I say our own cottage, but it isn't. It goes with the job. However, we're the only ones ever occupied it, and I got a promise we can live there when I'm retired. The owner and his wife never go there unless we ask them."

"I would say that you have it made," said Yank.

"Well, it works both ways, you know," said Adam Phelps.

"The wife and I take a trip every second year, but she says after one week I'm ready to come home. Start fidgeting and wondering if a cow came fresh when it was supposed to. There's more than enough to occupy me on a place this size."

"And I'll use that thought to make my exit," said Yank.

"Come again whenever you feel like it," said Adam Phelps.

On the way back to Anna Phelps's house Yank saw Sheila Dunham, easily recognizable in her jodhpurs and sweater, coming out of the post office. She might very well be the means of diverting him from an awkwardness with Anna Phelps.

For he was now determined to stay awhile in East Hammond. The reviews of his play implemented his decision. As far as money was concerned, he could live in East Hammond for a year or more without having to return to dishwashing— or shoveling cow-shit for Adam Phelps. Literally no one in New York knew where to find him at the moment, and he had warned Peg McInerney that it might be weeks before she heard from him. The accident that terminated his journey at East Hammond could have occurred in Hoosick Falls, N.Y., or Cooperstown or Georgetown, Vt., but it had happened at East Hammond, and already he had admitted into his life Anna Phelps and Ed Cross and Adam Phelps and the Atterbury family, whom he had not seen, and Sheila Dunham, whom he had. He knew a dog called Prince, and he had heard the shot that ended the life of another dog. He was getting a driver's license, and he had a place for his typewriter. At a certain time in the morning he could count on the sound of the milk-tanker. It all might have been just the same if he had run out of gas in Hoosick Falls or Cooperstown or George-town—but he did not think so. He could not believe in love, but he could believe in a centrifugal force that had spun him off and landed him precisely where he was. It was all he needed to believe; he was unconvinced of God's mercy and therefore of God. On the other hand he could put faith of a kind in a couple of talky Yankees who had put faith of a kind in him—Anna Phelps, who had made love to him in a day-dream; Adam Phelps, who had proudly displayed his touch-down against Yale. Best of all, he had not had to buy their faith with a sample of his work. They were not being nice to him because he had come up with a great third act.

It was easy to get back to work. It had been hard not to. The valuable things he had learned about the theater in the months just past could have been learned in a week; the rest was a waste of time. Zena was not a waste of time, even Ellis Walton was not a waste of time. Barry Payne, Sid Margoll, Peg McInerney, Scott Aubrey, Marc DuBois—they were not a waste of time any more than Jiggs Muldowney was a waste of time. But he had wasted time in their company, and he would never do that again. His play, written before he had ever learned that a tormentor was a piece of canvas and that ice was a term for the money in a devious transaction, had given him the entree. It was all right to know such things; it was all right to know all such things. But he did not have to know them to write a good play. He did not even have to know Zena Gollum or Ellis Walton or Marc DuBois. During the writing of the play he had known a girl who was thrilled to be cut with a razor blade. The predecessor of Ellis Walton, if there was one, was a Greek who ran a hole-in-the-wall on Twenty-third Street, whom Yank knew only as George. When his money was down to pennies he could go to George and drink the watered milk and eat the greying pie. George never gave him any money, but the emergency rations were there. It was against the law to employ Yank in a restaurant without putting him on the payroll, but it was against the law to dilute the milk, to take bets on the races, to sell policy slips, or, for that matter, to consort with the known criminals who operated the neighborhood shylocking business in George's place. Pederasty, for which George was finally sent away, was certainly against the law, but prison would not be as tough for him, George said, as for some people. He was every bit as much a philosopher as Ellis Walton, though of a different school. "How come you never made a pass at me, George?" said Yank at their final meeting.

"You ain't built right," said George. "Also, I like them younger. That's the trouble. No young ones where I'm going."

George was going to be a character in the new play. George, and the mother of one of his young boys, a woman who would leave George alone with the kid whenever she needed a fix. The girl who liked to be cut with razor blades was to be another character. The Catholic priest who was a lush. The fairy hack-driver who could not stay away from the waterfront saloons. The tweedy poet who could not pass a trash can without examining the contents, never finding anything he wanted. Jiggs Muldowney, who saved a man's life. An artist's model whose boy friend called her a donkey. The Cuban bus boy who acted in dirty movies. The hundred-dollar call girl who fell in love with the Cuban bus boy after seeing one of his movies. The aged waterfront whore who was known as Nancy the Snatch. The bail bondsman–politician who was known as Harry the Queen. The undertaker's twenty-year-old daughter who was known as Miss Innocence.

Yank had a good feeling about the new play. As with the one that was now established on Broadway—"in for a run"—he was starting with nearly fifty characters, many more than he would need or could ever use. But they would be, as it were, waiting in the wings if he wanted them to go on. Some of them he had cut out of the earlier play, but they would not go away. They were old friends by now, and some of them deserved a play of their own. They *all* deserved a play of their own; there was no character who did not. But you followed your instinct for selectivity; you stayed with some girls for one night only, you married others. Everybody could not be President of the United States. But Yank knew he was rich again, he had riches inexhaustible so long as he spent them— characters that dominated him by refusing to go away. Here, if nowhere else, was his love; his love of the men and women he had seen and then imagined, his love of the men and women he had imagined and then seen. How too God damn bad that he could not love a woman as a bank cashier in Grand Rapids, Michigan, loved his wife! How too God damn bad that he could not love a cunt like Zena Gollum! Love? He loved

Nancy the Snatch, not when she was cadging boilermakers in a Twelfth Avenue saloon, but here in a spotless Yankee bedroom in East Hammond, Vermont. Here in this spotless Yankee bedroom he could hear her fart, and the men at the bar laughing and saying, "You sure ripped off a good one that time, Nance." And her saying, "Oh, ixcuzay mwah, you mother-fuckers."

Now, once again, there were two kinds of time for him: the immeasurable and unnoticed time that passed while he was working, and formal time, the kind that is measured in seconds, minutes, and hours. He created a schedule of sorts that began with the noise and vibrations of the milk-tanker in the morning, through breakfast with Anna Phelps and Ed Cross, and upstairs again to his bedroom and his typewriter. He volunteered for the chore of getting the noon mail at the post office—none of it so far for him—so that he could stretch his legs and get some fresh air. After lunch he read the newspapers and magazines, fell asleep, washed his face and went back to work. He visited Cooperstown and Georgetown for supplies—typing paper and typewriter ribbons. After supper he was often alone in the house; Anna Phelps, it appeared, was a great one for meetings of committees related to the planning of the small philanthropies of small towns. When they were held in East Hammond, she walked; to the meetings in Cooperstown and Georgetown she was driven by Ed Cross in his car. On non-meeting nights she sewed, knitted, and listened to the radio. From his years in Spring Valley he should have known that a woman like Anna Phelps led a busier life than a city woman who lives in an apartment and an urban shell. She had many little things to do besides sitting idly in her house while waiting to be seduced by her boarder.

The first piece of mail addressed to Yank contained his driver's license, and it was handed him by Anna. "Here's something for you," she said. "Don't you even look at the mail?"

"I wasn't expecting any," he said.

"Well, you'll be getting it now. You'll be on all the mailing lists. R. Y. Lucas, 215 Cooperstown Road, East Hammond, Vermont."

"Speaking of which, are you willing to have me go on living here? I believe our original understanding was for a week, but we're well past that now."

"I'm agreeable if you are," she said. "It's still early for the tourists, and I'm not even sure but that I won't take the sign down this season. It's extra money, but it's extra work as well. Not that I'm afraid of work, I never have been. But it interferes. If you were thinking of staying on through the summer, I'd take the sign down. You'd about pay my taxes, and I'd have much more time to myself."

"And you obviously aren't dependent on tourists."

"Well, I always managed to keep body and soul together before I took any. During the war I had some very nice young people staying here. Air Force people that came and went. We had a baby born in the back bedroom on the second story, and they named her Anna after me. Now living in Charleroi, Michigan. I hear from them once in a while. But they weren't exactly tourists. This was their first home for a lot of those young people, and one of these days I'll show you my scrapbook of the young couples. Two of the flyers lost their lives during the war, and I felt just as bad as if they'd been my own relatives. But after the war it was a different class of people. I don't know as I care very much for some of the visitors that are attracted to Vermont. Not that they ever get a room here, but you see them over in Cooperstown, women walking barefooted and wearing shorts that shouldn't call attention to that part of their anatomy. The minute I see a young man with a guitar getting out of his automobile, I'm full up, even if I don't have anybody staying here. . . . Well, that's neither here nor there. You think you might stay all summer?"

"I'd certainly like to."

"Then that's settled. I'll take the sign down. That's not saying I won't ever rent out one of the rooms in case one of my Air Force couples wants to spend a night or two."

"Mrs. Phelps, you've never told me anything about your husband."

"What do you want to know about him?"

"Anything and everything you want to tell me."

"Well—Daniel Brewster Phelps was born right here in town, just like all the Phelpses. Went to school here. Married me and went overseas in 1918 with the 26th Division. Got wounded in August that year and had to have a silver plate put in his knee. Returned home in spring 1919 and went to work in one of the quarries. On the second day of June, 1927, he went to work as usual. I filled his lunch can and his vacuum bottle right here in this kitchen, though I had a different table then and didn't have all these modern improvements. He said good-bye and opened the door to leave, and then walked into the screendoor. We made some joke about it. He'd only put it up a couple days earlier, and forgot it was there. We made some joke about him drinking Canadian ale at the Legion the night before. It was Prohibition, and the men at the Legion used to get in a supply of Canadian ale. He was never a steady drinker, Dan, but any time they had Canadian ale at the Legion post he got his share. Developed a taste for it myself in those days. But it was only a joke, you understand. Dan wasn't hung over. He just forgot about the screendoor. So off he went, and then around eleven o'clock in the morning they phoned me from the quarry. Dan. Carrying a heavy drill up the face of the quarry, he fell backwards and landed down at the bottom. Only a fall of seventy-eight feet—they measured it —but it was enough to break his neck. I got a friend of mine to drive me over to the hospital, but Dan was dead when we got there. Never regained consciousness. Personally I always thought and still think that it was his knee, from the war. With that knee he shouldn't have been carrying a heavy drill up a narrow path only a couple feet wide. But I never said any-thing. I got compensation and lodge insurance, and then for some years I taught school, always had work of some kind and I had this house free and clear. Then first my father and then my mother died, leaving me a little. Considered getting mar-ried again, but pretty soon I got used to living alone and both men that proposed to me had young children and I didn't want that responsibility. Dan and I never had any of our own, and I guess I saw enough of them teaching school. My own I would have been all right with, but not other women's. Young children take advantage of you every chance they get, and if you're their mother that's one thing. It's a different story when you're not their mother."

"Did you not want children of your own?"

"With Dan I did. At least I never tried to prevent them. However, when he got killed I didn't have a child to think of when I went looking for work. I'd have had to have someone else to take care of it. Women are supposed to have children, so they say, but not all of them do. And men are supposed to have children, but they don't. I'm pretty sure you've been married, but I'll bet a dollar you don't have children."

"Divorced. No children."

"Dan would have liked a boy, to go gunning with and so forth. But there I'd have had a boy and I couldn't even go gunning with him. I'd have spoiled him till he grew up to be a mama's boy or else one of those ne'er-do-wells that try to prove they're not mama's boys. If Dan'd lived he'd have been strict with his son. If the boy didn't like to go gunning that wouldn't have made any difference to Dan. He liked to give orders. His cousin Adam said to him one time, 'Dan, you're not a sergeant any more, and even if you were, I was a lieutenant.' Then they had it out hot and heavy because Adam was a lieutenant but never got over there, and Dan had a medal from the United States and one from France. No, Dan Phelps wasn't the easiest man to get along with, but that didn't apply to me. I always understood men better than women. Yet here I am, getting up in years and spending most of my time with women."

"I have a sneaking feeling that there's a lot more to your story than you'll ever tell me."

"You do, do you?" she laughed. "Well, as they say, what you don't know won't hurt you."

"What I do know doesn't hurt me, either."

"Maybe so, but I'd advise you to keep your guessing to yourself, the same way I do."

"Have you been guessing about me?" said Yank. "What have you guessed? Besides the fact that I was married."

"Any number of things, living in such close quarters. But I don't bank too much on things I only know from guesswork."

"Any time you care to ascertain the facts, just say the word."

"The trouble there is I don't care to be obligated. You trading your secrets for mine."

"Why not? What was the worst thing you ever did?"

"No, I won't join in any such trade. Anyway, I couldn't say what the worst thing was. And what I judge was the worst maybe you wouldn't think was bad at all. I go by different standards. The worst thing I hate is a liar, but I had to tell a few lies in my time. Yet I don't hate myself."

"Now that's interesting, because I feel the same way. I hate a liar, but I never hesitate to tell a lie when necessary, or convenient. And here you are, a self-confessed liar, and I couldn't possibly hate you. Here *I* am, a self-confessed liar, and I doubt if you will ever hate me."

"Don't get in too deep. I'm not going to pull you out."

"Mrs. Phelps, I'm in so deep that I can't pull myself out, and I have been for a long time. But I don't want to be pulled out, by you, by myself, or by anyone else."

"Something you got yourself into."

"Yes indeed. Not any scrape or anything like that. Nothing more or less important than a way of life. Not even a way of life. An occupation."

"You mean writing?"

"I mean writing, or being a writer. It isn't my religion. I have no religion. But the way a priest is supposed to be about being a priest, I am about being a writer."

"I don't see you as a priest, but I guess I only knew a few of them. One was a nice elderly father over in Cooperstown. He finally died during the flu epidemic, back in 1918. The other was a wishy-washy namby-pamby that got transferred. I don't know the one they have at present. You're not Catholic, though, are you?"

"Good God, no."

"No, I didn't think so. I can usually pick them out. The only thing that made me think you might be ... No."

"Well come on, don't stop there."

"You don't seem to care much for women."

"When a woman says that, it's a serious accusation, but not as serious as when a man says it. I like women, but I don't like women to—"

[174]

"Go ahead, say it."

"All right. I don't like to be dominated from the bed. I hope you appreciate how much trouble I went to not to shock you."

"Maybe you're too smart-alecky with them."

"No, it isn't really that, Mrs. Phelps. It's because I don't believe in love. Permanent, romantic love. Most women don't really believe in it either, but they have some notion that we ought to. Don't you agree with me that women devour men?"

"If they do, they must have strong stomachs, some of the men I've seen."

"Well, if you want to take that attitude, consider the women that some men have to resort to to have their needs satisfied."

"If everybody had to wait for beautiful and handsome people, the human race would soon die out. But fortunately some men like ugly women and some women like ugly men."

"Very fortunately. Not that I care whether the race dies out or not. But I'd be in a bad way if I had to depend on my manly beauty. They used to call me Skinny and Four-Eyes."

"Dan Phelps reminded you of a horse."

"But you were pretty."

"There were others prettier, but I didn't have to take a back seat to many here in East Hammond. Around thirty I was at my best, for looks, till I started putting on weight."

"Your legs are pretty."

"Never mind about my legs, Mr. Lucas. Never mind about

this conversation, either. How we got into it I don't know, but it's gone far enough."

"Yes, it probably has," said Yank. "We got into it by my asking you about Mr. Phelps."

"Oh, my goodness, you're so smart-alecky. But the next time I'll be just as smart as you," she said. It was plain that the thought rather entertained her.

"It's a go," said Yank.

Several times at the post office he had seen Sheila Dunham, and she had seen him. If anything was to be done about her, it would be more auspiciously begun at the Atterbury farm than on a village sidewalk in front of sharp-eyed villagers. That something must be done, if not about Sheila Dunham about *some*body, there was no doubt. He was well aware that he had been half-seducing Anna Phelps in his conversation with her, preparing the way for a possible seduction by her. But the aftermath of a night in bed with her was not desirable at this point. He had inferred from their conversation that she had had several men in her life besides Dan Phelps, and one of them certainly was the current Ed Cross. If, then, he allowed a seduction to take place, it was inevitable that Ed Cross, an uncomplicated individual, would catch on, and awkwardness and even trouble would ensue. Yank was afraid of the kind of trouble that would ensue for Anna Phelps. He liked her too much to cause her that kind of trouble, the downward revision of her standing among her friends. With Sheila Dunham there would be no such problem; people like Sheila Dunham were expected to be immoral.

Yank had never known any society types. In college a few, a very few, turned up at the Deke, Alpha Delt, and Psi U houses, often with their fathers after football games. The fathers were sending their sons to Yale and Princeton and the social prestige of Spring Valley College had dwindled. Consequently the recognizable society types among the girls from Pittsburgh, Cleveland, and Fort Penn were rare, and the Dekes and Psi U's seldom brought them to Phi Gamma Delta. There was no use pretending that they were not different from the others. A girl whose stepfather was as rich as Seymour Atterbury had come under environmental influences that were different from those of, say, the publisher of a newspaper in Spring Valley, Pennsylvania. Not to mention the environmental influences that had produced Zena Gollum, the last girl he had slept with.

Yank drove his—Peg McInerney's—car out to the Atterbury farm and knocked on the door of Adam Phelps's office. He could see Adam Phelps at his desk, but it was important to give an impression of diffidence. "I hope I'm not disturbing you," he said.

"Come right in, nobody ever knocks," said Adam Phelps. "Take a chair."

"When I was here before you said I could come back."

"I did, that's right."

"I'm still not a fancier of Ayrshires, but you said something about keeping records. Specifically, the price of a tractor in 1920, things like that. I'm writing something now that goes back to those times. This comes under the head of research."

"Well, I hope I have what you want. I've even got a file of old catalogs, all kinds of farm equipment."

"You have? That's exactly what I want. Illustrated?"

"In color. And prices and detailed specifications. You said 1920? That was a good year. They'd just started manufacturing a lot of new stuff after World War One. Here, let me show you a few."

For the next hour Yank simulated an interest in harrows and cultivators, milkers and separators, trucks and tractors. Phelps did the talking, and obviously enjoyed the picture books. He looked at his watch. "Holy Moses! I have to get to the bank before it closes," said Phelps. "You stay as long as you like."

"I was wondering if I could come back again. Will you tell your secretary it's all right for me to look at your catalogs?"

"Any time at all. You can borrow them if you promise to bring them back."

"I wouldn't think of it. They're too valuable."

"Yes, I guess they are. Some of those manufacturers went out of business. *I* have to be *going*. I'll leave a note for Miss Wilson. She's up at the big house taking dictation for the owner, Mr. Atterbury."

Phelps departed, and Yank sat alone in the office with a Fordson catalog in his lap. A workman came in and laid a printed form on Phelps's desk and went out without a word. A few minutes later a woman who could only be Mrs. Atterbury came in. She wore a blue cashmere sweater, blue tweed skirt, muddy golf shoes with fringed tongues, and a necklace of tiny pearls. She was hatless, and her snow-white hair was just enough rumpled by the mild breezes to humanize her austerity. She was fiftyish. "Good afternoon," she said. "Did I just miss Mr. Phelps?"

Yank stood up. "By about fifteen minutes. He had to hurry to the bank before it closed."

"Yes, I was hoping to catch him before he left." She waved a long envelope on which were many stamps and a strip of red, white, and blue Air Mail tape.

"Can I mail that for you? Is that the difficulty?" said Yank.

She hesitated, barely noticeably, but noticeably.

"I'm going past the post office, and I'm thoroughly reliable. At least in such matters," said Yank.

"Will you *promise* not to put it in your pocket and forget it?"

"I'll put it between my teeth," said Yank.

"That won't be necessary, but I do want to get it off this afternoon. I'm Mrs. Atterbury. I don't believe we've met."

"My name is Lucas. I'm staying in East Hammond, at Mrs. Phelps's, boarding there."

"I thought that's who you might be," said Mrs. Atterbury. She studied him carefully.

"I promise you, I'm absolutely dependable on small matters."

"That's not why I was staring—forgive me," she said. "Your name *is* Lucas, you did say that, didn't you?"

"Yes."

"Then you are *Yank* Lucas, are you not?"

[179]

"Why, yes. How did you know?"

"Because I've seen your picture several times, and I heard that Anna Phelps had a new boarder named Lucas, *and* I've seen your *play*. How on earth did you ever happen to come to East Hammond? We've never had a celebrity before, at least not a literary celebrity. How did you happen to land here?"

"Just by luck. I ran out of gas, and I stayed."

"I don't believe anyone knows who you are. Am I right? Someone said that Anna Phelps had a young writer staying there, but no mention of the fact that you were the author of the biggest hit on Broadway."

"There are lots of Lucases. When did you see my play?"

"About a week ago, a little longer than that. Actually we were taken to see it the night after it opened. Friends of ours, terribly interested in the theater. They pay unbelievable prices for tickets, but it's such fun to be able to say you've seen the big hits. I thought your play was terribly interesting."

"In other words, you didn't like it," said Yank.

"Well—that depends on what you mean by liking it. You certainly didn't intend to entertain your audience in the usual way. It isn't—forgive me—but it isn't exactly an elevating play. But the girl *is* marvelous. Marvelously acted, and I suppose honestly written. I haven't known any girls like that, so I couldn't say. I'm probably saying all the wrong things. I've only met two playwrights. Philip Barry, we've seen at Hobe Sound, couldn't be more charming. And of course Noel Coward, in London before the war. And now you, on of all places our ridiculous old farm that we love so. The contrast. The most sophisticated playwright we have, and Cow Heaven, as my husband calls it."

"The contrast isn't really so great. I'm a small-town boy."

"Not any more, I'm afraid. Every magazine I pick up has articles about you."

"I've only seen two, and they were nonsense. *Time*, and *Newsweek*."

"Well, Harry Luce is such a strange man, those eyebrows and carrying the weight of the world on his shoulders," she said. "Are you here to get away from it all? Working? Relaxing?"

"Working," he said. "That relaxes me more than anything."

"Come to lunch on Sunday. Just family. One o'clock. If you like, that is."

"I'd like very much."

"Good. And here's my letter. You won't forget it, will you? The person it's addressed to—there's a cheque inside, and she needs the money quite desperately."

"I've had that experience myself," said Yank.

She left him, and as he watched her striding up to the big house he saw where her daughter got her figure and her gait.

On Sunday he said nothing to Anna Phelps about his luncheon engagement. She would subtly resent his being invited, as she would less subtly resent later his not telling her where he had gone. But he would deal with those crises when they arose. He timed his arrival at the Atterbury house for five past one. The butler let him in and led him to a glassed-in side porch. Mrs. Atterbury and her husband were reading the papers. "Mr. Lucas," said the butler.

"Oh, there you are," said Mrs. Atterbury, removing her reading glasses. "Like you to meet my husband."

Atterbury rose, removing *his* reading glasses. He was a large man, with thinning brown hair plastered down, a rather large nose. He wore a loud tan and white houndstooth jacket, tan slacks, highly polished brown loafers, and a striped blue and yellow tie. "How do you do, Mr. Lucas. I'm so glad you could come. What can I offer you to drink? We're about to have a daiquiri, if that interests you."

"A daiquiri would be fine," said Yank.

"Sit over there, where the sun won't get in your eyes," said Atterbury. The butler vanished to get the drinks.

"My daughter will be here later. She hasn't met you, but she's seen you at the post office."

"I think I've seen her, too. Wearing riding breeches?"

"Jodhpurs, actually," said Atterbury. "She lives in them up here. Jodhpurs and blue jeans."

"She's wearing a skirt today, though, Sy. She went to church this morning, which is more than we did."

"Yes," said Atterbury. "Well, Mr. Lucas, you're a long way from your regular stamping-ground. Not so much a matter of mileage as, uh, tempo. My wife said you ran out of gas and decided to linger on. Good."

"Yes, I've even taken out a Vermont driver's license."

"Have you really? That's a hopeful sign," said Mrs. Atterbury.

"That's not an undiluted compliment. My wife's become interested in politics, and her reasoning is that if you've taken out a driver's license, the next step is to register to vote, and she's hopeful of enrolling you in the Democratic Party."

"In Vermont?" said Yank.

"Hope springs eternal, as they say," said Atterbury.

"I've never voted," said Yank.

"Never? Not even in Spring Valley, Pennsylvania?" said Mrs. Atterbury.

"You amaze me. How did you know about Spring Valley?" said Yank.

"It was in one of those things I read about you, and we have, or at least my husband has a friend who lives there."

"Give me one guess?" said Yank. "Is it Porter Ditson?"

"Yes," said Atterbury. "The old scalawag."

"*Scalawag?*" said Mrs. Atterbury. "I haven't heard that word—"

"It fits Porter, though," said Atterbury. "Don't you agree, Mr. Lucas?"

"Yes, I think I do. He's unique in Spring Valley. We had other scalawags, but Porter Ditson's the only one there that wears golf knickers to go skating."

"Oh, he would indeed," said Atterbury. "He's one of the last of the old school, and I understand he has a brother that's a real stuffed shirt. Brice?"

"That's right. Brice Ditson, and you've characterized him. A real stuffed shirt."

"*He* wouldn't enroll in the Democratic Party," said Mrs. Atterbury.

"No, but neither would Porter Ditson," said Yank.

"I'm so glad you like Porter," said Atterbury.

"I do. I've never known anyone like him," said Yank.

"Well, you never will again, either, unless you go to England. This country never did produce many like Porter Ditson. A few here and there. But not many of our fellows have the strength of character to go through life doing absolutely nothing. It *takes* strength of character to hold out against those pressures. Do you agree?"

"Emphatically, and especially in a place like Spring Valley," said Yank.

"Because a man doesn't do anything, is that an indication of strength of character?" said Mrs. Atterbury.

Atterbury and Yank looked at each other. "It's the way, the manner," said Atterbury.

"But Mr. Lucas—"

The butler entered with the tray of drinks. "Mrs. *Dun*ham telephoned, ma'am, to say she'd be late and to go ahead without her."

"How late, I wonder. Did she say?" said Atterbury.

"No sir."

"And of course she didn't say where she is," said Atterbury.

"No sir."

"In about ten minutes, William," said Mrs. Atterbury. She was not very successful at covering the uneasiness that was being caused by Atterbury's annoyance. There was much more to Atterbury's irritability than his displeasure at Sheila Dunham's lateness. "I imagine her battery ran down again," she said.

"It usually does if you leave the lights on," said Atterbury. "Tell me, Mr. Lucas, is this your first play on Broadway?"

"Yes it is."

"Isn't it quite remarkable to have such a great success with a first play? I should think you'd be enormously pleased."

"I am."

"How can you resist going to the theater every night and watching those crowds?" said Mrs. Atterbury.

"Not to mention the line at the boxoffice," said Atterbury.

"Well, I had a little of that in Boston. It isn't what I want."

"Ah, what *do* you want?" said Mrs. Atterbury. "I suppose that's a very difficult question to answer."

"Well, I don't want the razz-ma-tazz. The excitement and glamour. That's why I got away. I left the theater at the end of the second act on opening night."

"And vanished into thin air. I read that," said Mrs. Atterbury. "Now that *did* take strength of character, when you knew you had a hit."

"In a way it did. On the other hand, a complete lack of character. A playwright ought to be able to take those things in stride, but I was afraid to put myself to the test. So I lit out."

"And you're at work here in East Hammond?" said Mrs. Atterbury. "Anna Phelps is a terribly nice woman—"

"You're damn right she is," said Atterbury.

"But can you set yourself down in such different surroundings and go right to work? You wrote this play in Greenwich Village—"

"Chelsea."

"Uh-huh. And had to take all sorts of odd jobs while you were writing it. I understand you've had fabulous offers from the movies—and they don't even know where to find you. Our secret. But now that you don't have to do outside work, and you're up here in a far-off Vermont village, it must take strength of character to settle down to writing something brand-new."

"I love my work."

"Yes, you must," she said.

"Mr. Atterbury loves his work," said Yank.

Atterbury chuckled. "I'm what they call a gentleman-farmer. Nobody believes there's any work to that. I just pay the bills."

"It isn't that way at all, Mr. Lucas. He's up at six-thirty every morning. Adam Phelps brings him a Thermos of coffee—"

"Damn good coffee."

"And the two of them go over everything together. He's done a day's work by the time he comes back for lunch. You know that's true, Sy. Why do you depreciate it?"

"I think he loves what he's doing, and what other people think doesn't matter," said Yank.

"That's very nice of you to say so," said Atterbury. "I do love *this place,* and getting up at six A.M. is a damn nuisance, but it's part of the whole set-up. A *real* gentleman-farmer wouldn't get up that early. Your real gentleman-farmer is a dilettante. I'm a dairy farmer, and I've got this place making a little money, thanks to a great deal of help from Adam Phelps."

"Luncheon is served, ma'am," said the butler.

They took about a dozen minutes to consume the oxtail soup, a little longer on the lamb and asparagus Hollandaise, not more than five minutes on the mixed greens, and five minutes on the strawberry mousse. Mrs. Atterbury was more skillful in directing the table talk away from her daughter, and Atterbury unconsciously assisted her by his concentration on the food. She drew out her guest, who was perfectly willing to be drawn out. As they got up from the table Atterbury heaved a great sigh. "Ah, that was a good lunch," he said. "Do you smoke cigars, Mr. Lucas?"

"When they're offered me," said Yank.

"Then let's have one."

"I'll be waiting for you on the porch," said Mrs. Atterbury. "In other words, don't take forever with your cigars."

Atterbury was leading the way to his study when Sheila Dunham came in. The four met in the hall. "Sorry I was late. I had to be pushed," she said.

"Sheila, this is Mr. Lucas," said her mother.

"It couldn't be anyone else, could it? How do you do?"

"How do you do," said Yank.

"My daughter, Mrs. Dunham," her mother continued.

"Couldn't be anyone else, could it?" said Yank.

"Oh, I'm going to like—him," said Sheila. "Hello, Seymour. I'm sorry I was late. But I see you struggled along without me."

"Managed to, just barely," said Atterbury. "Is it true that you've been to church?"

"Yes. You support it, so I thought I'd get some of your money's worth for you."

"If that isn't one of the strangest reasons I ever heard for going to church," said Atterbury. "Actually, I don't support it. I contribute, but the people themselves support it. I make up the deficit, and I assure you it's never very large."

"The house wasn't exactly packed today," said Sheila. "God hasn't got as big a hit as Mr. Lucas. Congratulations. I haven't seen your play, but I'm going to the first chance I get."

"Be, as they say, my guest."

"No. My stepfather backs God Almighty. I'll support you. In a nice way, of course. Have you all had your coffee yet?"

"Mr. Lucas and I were just about—"

"Cigars," said Sheila. "All right. "I'll have coffee with Mother."

"Oh, why don't we all just sit on the porch? The cigar smoke doesn't really bother me when the windows are open," said Mrs. Atterbury.

"I'll smoke one," said Sheila.

"Bravado. You've never finished one," said Atterbury.

"Of course it's bravado," said Sheila.

"And it's also a waste of good cigars," said Atterbury.

On the porch they made an uncongenial foursome, and after a few minutes Atterbury rose and said, "I have to see a man about a cow. Sit still, Mr. Lucas. Very nice to have seen you. Come again, will you?" He left the porch, went inside the house and in a few minutes they could see him, with a shooting stick and arctics over his loafers, walking toward the cow barns. He did not look back.

"Pissed off at me again," said Sheila.

"Sheila!"

"My language isn't going to shock Mr. Lucas, not according to the reviews I've read."

"That's different. The sort of people that use that language in Mr. Lucas's play—that's the sort of language they use. Am I right, Mr. Lucas?"

"So it seems to me," said Yank.

"Whereas, you've been here since one o'clock and you haven't uttered a single damn," said Mrs. Atterbury.

"Utter a couple of damns for Mother," said Sheila. "Throw in a couple of God-damns."

"I must say going to church didn't have much effect on you," said her mother. "Not just your language, Sheila, but your disposition."

"I was sweetness and light when I came out, but I couldn't get anyone to push me for the longest while, and I knew Seymour would be annoyed. Finally Ed Cross came along and gave me a push. He doesn't think it's the battery. When Billy Dunham finally comes through, the first thing I'm going to do is buy a new car. I'm going to get an XK-120, painted white for purity. Somehow I expected you to have something like the XK, Mr. Lucas."

"I don't own any car. That belongs to my agent."

"Oh, well, when you do buy one you can go all out. Start with a Ferrari."

"You know a lot more about cars than I do. I've never even heard of a Ferrari, and I doubt very much that I'll ever get one."

"Not everybody cares that much for fancy cars," said Mrs. Atterbury.

"Seymour used to. When you were first married I can remember a Cord, pipes running out of the hood. And before that a real antique, a big old Lagonda."

"Oh, do you remember that Lagonda? It wasn't so terribly long ago, really, but you were only a little girl. Still, you were always mad about cars."

This was what they talked about? Yank asked himself. Was it this easy? "I don't suppose you remember the Pierce-Arrow?" said Yank.

"Hearing about," said Sheila.

"Oho, I remember it very well," said Mrs. Atterbury. "My uncle never had anything else."

"The town I grew up in, there were supposed to be more Pierce-Arrows in proportion to the population than any other town in the country," said Yank.

"I know where that was. Gibbsville, Pennsylvania," said Sheila. "A boy I know—"

"No. Spring Valley, Pennsylvania. Gibbsville is at the other end of the State."

"But this boy said they had more Pierce-Arrows in Gibbsville, proportionately," said Sheila.

"Then he was a big liar, and you must never believe anything else he ever tells you," said Yank.

"He was a liar, all right, but not about things like that. And how do I know you're not as big a liar?"

"Shei-la!" said Mrs. Atterbury.

"Well, don't writers live in a world of their own imagination? Mr. Lucas is a, uh, professional liar. He may not like the word, but he didn't hesitate to apply it to a friend of mine that he never even saw."

"A foe worthy of my steel," said Yank.

"Me? I'm not your foe. But you were awfully quick to call a friend of mine a liar, even in kidding. So, if you dish it out, you have to take it."

"Which naturally leads to the question, do you take it as well as you dish it out?" said Yank.

"I can answer that. No," said Mrs. Atterbury.

"How do you know, Mother? How do you know what I have to take?"

"Well, maybe I don't know. But I do know when someone is being disagreeable, Sheila, and Mr. Lucas is our guest."

"Then let's pretend he's our host. In fact, didn't he say just a minute ago, 'Be my guest'? When he offered me tickets for his show? He did. He said, 'Be my guest.' Therefore it's very easy for him to switch from guest to host, host to guest, guest to host, host to guest. I embarrass my mother, but that's because she doesn't understand people like you and me. Which is only fair, because we don't understand people like her. Or do you? A writer couldn't possibly admit that he doesn't understand everybody."

"You're wrong there," said Yank. "There are millions of people I don't understand, because I haven't taken the trouble to. But I think I can understand anyone I give some time to. I'm not having any trouble understanding you, for instance."

"Why should you? There's nothing terribly mysterious about me, and I'm more or less your generation. But I think you might have a little trouble understanding Mother, and Seymour, and other people like them."

"Why?" said Yank.

"Well, when I say people like them I don't only mean their age. I mean the way they were brought up. I read all about you, so I *know* how *you* were brought up. You haven't spent very much time in houses like this, have you?"

"No, of course not."

"Or with people like Mother and Seymour Atterbury?"

"No."

"*You* didn't have an uncle that wouldn't own anything but Pierce-Arrows."

"No," said Yank.

"You came from good, honest people that always had to

work for a living. Your father was a college professor in a hick college that I never heard of."

"Really, Sheila, I—"

"Mother, he knows I'm leading up to something," said Sheila. "And I'll get there if you'll let me. The point is, Mr. Lucas, my mother, this attractive, pretty, well-mannered woman—what would you say her life has been? Pretty soft?"

"You're tipping your mitt. It probably wasn't," said Yank. "But all right, I'd be inclined to think it has been pretty soft."

"Well, it hasn't been. She's gone through several kinds of hell that you'd never in a million years know about unless you were told. Our generation, you and I, we don't hold it in. We let ding, splash it all over. Not my mother, though. And not Seymour Atterbury. He and I rub each other the wrong way and always have. But that doesn't alter the fact that I know the several kinds of hell *he's* been through. But I'm sure your opinion of him is that he's a rich, rather stuffy, immature person. And I really don't believe you'd understand him any better if you took the time to. Because they'd never tell you. They'd never tell you, Mr. Lucas. They'll have you here for lunch, and you'll go away thinking what nice, dull, friendly people they are. Which they are. But that's as much as you'd ever know about them. Today, or five years from now. They would never open up to you."

"Maybe they wouldn't have to. I have certain instincts, intuitions. I really don't think I'd have much trouble understanding them."

"Mr. Lucas is right," said Mrs. Atterbury. "He knew instinctively how much Sy loves his work."

"That's fairly obvious, I should say. A man as rich as Seymour wouldn't be here if he didn't like what he was doing."

"Love, not like," said Mrs. Atterbury. "Mr. Lucas knew that Sy *loves* his work."

"I think Mrs. Dunham is getting back to the old argument that only the rich can understand the rich."

"Not at all. Butlers can understand the rich. Adam Phelps understands Seymour. But Mr. Lucas is a complete outsider. Seymour would never unbend with Mr. Lucas. He doesn't much with Adam Phelps, either, but they have a sort of friendship based on mutual respect and working together."

"And Phelps scored a touchdown against Yale," said Yank.

"You think you're kidding, but he's that much closer to Seymour than you'll ever be. Even so, Seymour would never, never talk to Adam about the intimate, personal things. He just wouldn't. He wouldn't know how to begin."

"Well, why should they understand each other, more than they do? Adam Phelps has his life, Sy has his," said Mrs. Atterbury.

"Not my point at all, Mother. My point was that Mr. Lucas would never really understand people like you and Seymour. He was trying to say that he could if he took the time, and I say he's dead, dead wrong."

"Mrs. Dunham is giving me a lesson in humility," said Yank.

"You probably need it," said Sheila. "Do you play tennis?"

"I haven't for a long time."

"Neither have I. Would you be up to playing this afternoon? We have shoes and socks and even jock straps that you can borrow. In fact, you can keep the jock strap."

"Thanks, but it's too soon after lunch," said Yank.

"Well, let's do something. I hate to see you go to waste."

"You haven't had any lunch, Sheila. It might improve your disposition," said Mrs. Atterbury.

"That's a thought. There's a diner over in Cooperstown. Would you like to take me to lunch there?"

"Mr. Lucas may have other plans—and I wouldn't blame him."

"Mother, Mr. Lucas understands me perfectly, and I understand him. That's not to say we have an understanding, but a little flirtation's been going here under your very eyes."

"One-sided," said Mrs. Atterbury.

"Not entirely," said Sheila.

"I didn't bring any money with me," said Yank.

"That's something we don't often mention in this house," said Sheila. "We think about it, but not out loud. It's supposed to embarrass my stepfather. It doesn't at all, of course, but people think it does . . . Unless you really have got other plans?"

"None," said Yank.

"Let's take the station-wagon. My car's on the blink, and your agent's car has no style at all."

Sheila drove. She did not speak until they had passed through the gate posts and entered the Cooperstown Road. "Believe it or not I love this place, but sometimes when I leave it it's like being sprung. It's terrible to have nothing to do. If I could write, or paint, I'd be happy here."

"Even with your stepfather?"

"Oh, come on, Lucas. You know the trouble there."

"Do I?"

"Of course you do. He loves my mother. He really does. But he wants to get in the hay with me. I would. But then I could never come here again. As long as we snap at each other the way we do, Mother knows that Seymour and I haven't gotten anywhere. But if I ever do get in the hay with him, I can never come back."

"Why do you call him Seymour?"

"Because he asked me to. I called him Father till the year I came out, and it was always awkward because my real father was still alive till I was fourteen. He was in the drunk tank or the looney bin most of the time. He must have been a real prick, from all I've heard, and I never saw much of him. Then when I was eighteen Seymour suggested that I call him Seymour, and stop calling him Father. It took me a little while to realize—as I'm sure he didn't—that he was changing the relationship by changing the name. In other words, he wasn't my father, and it wouldn't be incest."

"Doesn't he make passes, ever?"

"Never. Sometimes he suggests that my sweaters are too

tight, when I go for a walk in the pastureland. Arouses the men on the place. Well, he's one of the men on the place, and I'm in as much danger from him as I am from the workmen. But for Christ's sake, I'm not going to wear a Mother Hubbard to go to the post office, either."

"Don't you get a little steamed up when men stare at you?"

"Not really. One man, yes. A lot of men, no. A lot of men with the same thought are just a bunch of apes, and they look like apes. How do actresses feel about that?"

"Pretty much as you do, I think."

"What happened with you and Zena Gollum? I read the gossip columns, and you were screwing her. Then you suddenly disappeared on the opening night. That's quite a dish."

"I had to get away."

"From her, or from everything?"

"From her and everything."

"I did too. It was a different rat-race, but it was a rat-race just the same. I want to be like my mother. She married a bum and he gave her a bad time, but then she married a terribly decent guy, and they've been happy together. The trouble is, I keep looking for a man like Seymour Atterbury. Is that crazy, or isn't it?"

"Pretty crazy, but perfectly understandable. The thing you forget, of course, is that your mother didn't go looking for Atterbury. He was there, wasn't he?"

"Yes."

"And she didn't have to go looking for him. Another thing

is, you want to be like your mother but you're not and you're not going to be. Therefore, you may be asking for trouble by wanting to be like her."

"Trouble is something I've never had to ask for. You were divorced. What for?"

"My wife was a slut."

"And what were you?"

"Me? I was a chump."

"Were you an idealist that you now call a chump?"

"Exactly. Exactly."

"That's what happens to our ideals. I married my ideal, too. Attractive. Wonderful sense of humor. Terribly well liked. But a shitheel."

"How?"

"Well, other girls, of course. Right away. No kidding around about that. 'Now listen, Sheila, don't expect me to stop having fun out of life. I'm not made that way.' Well, I wasn't made that way either, but he thought he was something special. I liked boys, but I got married thinking I'd at least give it a try. Not him. Five weeks we were away on our wedding trip. The second day after we were back in New York he had a cinq-à-sept with one of my bridesmaids."

"A what?"

"The sophisticated playwright. An afternoon lay," she said.

"Oh, French. I took Spanish. How long before you began stepping out?"

"Oh, not long. I shed a few tears, all by myself. Tears of anger as much as anything else, I guess. I'd been a chump, as you say. After that I played it his way, till one day he said to me that I was getting a perfectly rotten reputation, and I had to watch my step and that was all there was to it. So there. Oh, I hauled off and whacked him *so* hard. That *son* of a *bitch*, im*agine?* I gave him the knee, I scratched his face. And do you know that he never knew why I flew into such a temper. We had to go out to dinner that night, and he had to wear a Band-Aid where I gouged him. He was a hypochondriac, among other things, and when we got home he stayed up all night, putting peroxide on his wound. He didn't want to shave the next morning, so he didn't go to the office. He was on the phone all day, trying to get an appointment with a famous skin specialist, who just happened to be doing an operation in Baltimore. Lover-Boy flew down to Baltimore, made a complete horse's ass of himself, and then I didn't see him for two weeks. He pretended to be in the hospital in Baltimore, but actually he was having a perfectly lovely time in Middleburg, Virginia. Which I found out the second day he was there. Oh, hell, it was ridiculous. The whole thing was ridiculous, and I was ridiculous. We went back together for a while, but then we separated and last February I told him I wanted a divorce. The lawyers are haggling over the financial settlement."

"Why do you care about a financial settlement? Aren't you loaded with the stuff?"

"No. Naturally I'll inherit some day. Mother has the income from her father and mother's two estates, and eventually I get the principal. But now I have nothing, so Lover-Boy Dunham is going to have to shell out."

"Why?"

"*Why?* Why shouldn't he? Revenge is a good enough reason. It isn't the best reason, or the only one, but it's good enough."

"You had no children," said Yank.

"No wee ones. The time I stabbed him with my fingernails I was pregnant, but I wasn't sure who Daddy was, so I had an abortion. I didn't want to wait for two or three or five or ten years, when I'd be able to identify the father through the kid. A friend of mine is going through that right now. She has a two-year-old boy that so far has all the characteristics of her husband and two of his pals."

"Whither are we drifting?"

"Oh, come off it, Lucas. Come—*off*—it."

She stopped the station-wagon at the Cooperstown diner. Before they got out of the car she handed him a five-dollar bill. "Whither are we drifting?" she said. "You'd be mortified if I paid the check. Some truck driver might think you were my gigolo."

"Bad casting. I don't look the part," said Yank. "But thanks."

She ordered the minute steak *without* potato chips and *without* the cole slaw. A cup of black coffee for him. Just a cup of black coffee. She ate quickly, pleasurably, and when they got back in the car Yank said, "Tell me about you and the counterman. He obviously knows you, but he's a surly son of a bitch."

"Russ Tanner, his name is. He used to work on the farm. When I was about fifteen we rubbed noses together—"

"You mean he screwed you?"

"No I don't. He didn't even get to kiss me. We were sitting on a fence, talking, and he put his arm around me and I struggled. He had the great misfortune of being seen by his father, who worked on the farm and still does. Mr. Tanner came down and beat the hell out of Russ, right in front of me. He told Russ to go home, where I imagine he beat him again. In any case, Russ has always been surly with me ever since. I didn't tattle. It was as though Mr. Tanner and I had some kind of an agreement that if he punished Russ then and there, my end of the bargain was to keep my mouth shut. Which I did. So I have a lifelong enemy and a lifelong friend, both in the same family. Actually I have two lifelong enemies. Mrs. Tanner, Russ's mother, is absolutely convinced that I was to blame. She doesn't speak to me either. She, by the way, is a great friend of your landlady, Anna Phelps, so I doubt if you'll get a very good report on me there."

"Where are we headed now?"

"Whither are we drifting? Back to the house. Too soon after my lunch now, to play tennis. So whatever you'd like to do."

"I was invited for lunch. They didn't say anything about spending the afternoon," said Yank. "By the way, here's your change."

"Keep it and owe me five dollars," said Sheila. "Visit *me* for the rest of the afternoon, will you?"

"And then what?"

"Then what? Then go back to Mrs. Phelps's and put me in your next play."

"I can't put you in my next play. It's already overcrowded. However, I'll certainly think about you for the one after that."

"Don't know if I can wait that long."

"Two years? Three years? Sure you can," he said.

"Two years is an eternity. Three years, I'll probably be *in* eternity."

"Why do you talk that way?"

"Because I've had it," she said. "Something terribly good has got to happen to me soon, or I've really had it. Do you hear me, God? That's a threat. As if God cared."

"What are you complaining about? You haven't had it so tough. Earlier you were so proud of your mother for the courage she showed through her various hells. Then you told me you wanted to be like her. Now you're bellyaching, making vague threats about suicide."

"I didn't say anything about suicide."

"Don't quibble. It was a suicidal threat. People that say, 'I've had it,' are announcing that they're giving up, and giving up is suicidal. What else could you mean?"

"I could mean that I was going into a convent."

"But you don't."

"Then what do I mean?"

"I don't know what you mean, but what you're saying is that you're bored. Well, why shouldn't you be bored? You're leading a healthy life here, storing up surplus energy that you don't know what to do with. One solution would be for you to line up the workmen on your stepfather's farm and let them all get a whack at you."

"You've been listening to Adam Phelps."

"No."

"You're a liar. That's what he's afraid'll happen. You didn't think that up yourself."

"All right, I'm a liar," said Yank. "He *is* afraid of just that."

"Well, it won't happen, I'll see to that. It would only happen on a Saturday night, when some of them get drunk. Unless, of course, I went down to the bunkhouse and said, 'Here it is, boys, come and get it.' You know what chance there is of that. So what other suggestions have you got for using up my surplus energy? Chopping wood? Painting barns? You won't play tennis with me, and Seymour isn't allowed to play tennis. Shall I become a social worker? The trouble is, there's nothing you could think of that I haven't thought of myself, and I've had more time to think about this particular problem than you have." They were at the house. "Are you coming in?"

"I don't think so."

"You want to be coaxed a little."

"Hell, no. I'll come in," said Yank.

"It won't do you any harm. You can stay for tea. That'll give you an opportunity to study Seymour and my mother. In the light of what I've told you about them. Then you can go back to your boardinghouse and think solemn thoughts about the lives of the rich. You'll never be that rich yourself, so whatever you think, you won't have to worry. It just occurred to me, Lucas. No matter how much money you make writing plays, alongside Seymour Atterbury you'll be comparatively poor."

"True. But alongside what I have been, I'll be enormously rich. Therein lies the danger."

"Then give me your money. I'll know how to spend it. I'm used to it. It won't be a corrupting influence on me."

"Suppose I did give you my money? What do I get in return?"

"Nothing. A big fat nothing. Not even thanks. If you got anything in return, you'd be corrupting yourself. You should thank me for taking it off your hands. Is it a deal?"

"I'll think about it."

"We'd have to keep it pure, you know. If we so much as rubbed noses you'd be corrupting yourself with your money. You see that, don't you?"

"Yes, I do."

"So perhaps it would be better, really, if you kept your money. We may want to rub noses sometime. Or hadn't you thought of that?"

"More or less constantly since the day you barged in at Adam Phelps's office."

"Ah, that's very reassuring. Suddenly I'm not as bored as I have been. I have a new suggestion. Instead of coming in for tea, you go home now and decide whether you want to get involved with me or not. Think about it till Wednesday, and meanwhile I'll be thinking about it too."

"Why Wednesday?"

"They're going to a dinner party and spending the night in Manchester. I wasn't invited. I promise not to entertain the boys in the bunkhouse between now and Wednesday."

"Promise me something else."

"What?"

"Cut your fingernails," said Yank.

She laughed. "I *said* I'd like you," she said. "Call me Wednesday afternoon, yes?"

That was their beginning. The tentative nature of their affair was confined to their thoughts of each other and of themselves; in a few weeks their frequent appearances together, and particularly his visits to the Atterbury place, created a conversational topic, a somewhat insipid scandal, and a disturbance. Inevitably the East Hammond natives found out that the young fellow staying at Anna Phelps's was the Yank Lucas who had a play on Broadway, a revelation that would have made him stareworthy without the Atterbury-step-daughter association. He certainly didn't look like much, they said, but the back numbers of the news magazines provided the information that he had turned down $150,000 for the movie rights to his play before it opened and that $500,000 would probably be paid this former dishwasher by Metro or Warner's. He had taken out a Vermont driver's license and had told several East Hammond folk that he intended to become a permanent resident. And thus and so. It was not easy to get anything out of Adam Phelps, but that was who had introduced Lucas to the Atterbury stepdaughter, and they had hit it off right away. She was in the midst of getting a divorce, but a little thing like that would not stop *her*. Nobody was quite sure where they *went;* Anna Phelps would not countenance any funny business in her house, and the Atterburys —although *she* was making noises like a Democrat—were just about as conservative as that other Vermonter from Plymouth. Some said Lucas had another room over in Cooperstown, and there was another report to the effect that he was the secret owner of the motel that had just opened up east of Georgetown. Still others said that if you were going to do it, you did it, and those two were sure as hell doing it, even if they had to do it on a blanket. So much for the conversational topic and the insipid scandal.

The disturbance was not a public matter. It was a matter between Seymour Atterbury and his wife, who discussed Sheila and Yank so little and in such guarded terms that they accomplished the thing they were trying to avoid: acknowledgment of the existence of a major situation. Seymour Atterbury and his wife were accustomed to candor between themselves, and when candor was absent they created polite animosity to take its place. Since there was no reason for animosity, there was no reason for a discussion that would clear the air, and the air continued uncleared. "Where do you suppose those two are till this hour?" said Seymour.

"Till this hour of twenty past eleven?" said his wife. "I'm sure I haven't the faintest idea, but it's still a bit early to call the police."

"Who said anything about calling the police?"

"They're probably at a movie."

"You don't believe that, and neither do I."

"All right. They're in bed together."

"I *am* prepared to believe *that*," said Atterbury. "But I must say you're taking it very calmly."

"Not because I want to, and not because I approve of it. But worse things could happen to Sheila—and have. At least she's got someone, even if it's only temporary. And if it's more than temporary, thank God."

"Would you want her to marry this fellow?"

"At this stage of her life I'd be glad if she married Ed Cross. I have to face the unpleasant fact that Sheila doesn't do things by halves. If she hasn't got one man to be in love with, her alternative is several at a time. *I* know that, only too well, and it's not nice knowing that about your only daughter. I'd much rather not talk about her if you don't mind."

"Very well. Sweep it under the rug."

"That's exactly what I will do, and I must ask you to do the same. No useful purpose is going to be served by treating them like adolescents."

"Under the rug it goes," said Atterbury, and no more was said then or at any other time. It was tacitly assumed that Sheila and Yank were having an affair that would more than likely lead to marriage.

No such assumption was made by the principals of the affair. They were on a meeting-to-meeting basis. They would meet as often as three times in a day—and not at all. Sheila was discovering that a lover could be unfaithful to her with people who did not exist, that on some days her rival was

someone called Nancy the Snatch or someone else called
Miss Innocence. He would not permit her to see his manuscript until the first draft was finished, and he did not expect
to be so far advanced until late September, early October. One
day he telephoned her and was told she had gone to New
York. "This is Mr. Lucas. Did she leave any message for me?"
No, she had left no message. He telephoned the next day with
the same result. He could have asked to speak to her mother,
but he was unwilling to proclaim such a degree of concern.
But the concern was there: on the second day he did no work.
His imagination was too actively engaged in the invention of
the details of Sheila's disappearance. None of them proved to
be accurate. On the afternoon of the third day she telephoned
him. "Where are you?" he demanded.

"In the library," she said.

"*What* library?" he said.

"The library, here in the house. Where did you think I
was?"

"The last I heard of you, you were off on some trip to New
York. You might have told me you were going."

"I'll tell you all about it when I see you. Which should be in
about fifteen minutes, if you're free. Are you?"

"No, I have to umpire a ball game between the married
men and the single men at the Methodist church picnic."

"Whose side are you on? I'll be there in fifteen minutes."

She arrived in the Atterbury station-wagon and they drove
away immediately. "Where are we going?" she said. "We're
going someplace where we can be private. I love that expres-

sion. Someplace where we can be private. I want to be private with you. It sounds so dirty, to be private with somebody. Do you want to be private with me?"

"I don't know. I want to find out about your trip to New York, first."

"I wasn't private with anyone there, if that's what's eating you."

"Well, it is," he said.

"Actually I just want you to kiss me and tell me you missed me. I don't want to get too private till later. Tonight maybe we can be so private that—let's just stop here and have a cigarette."

He kissed her.

"That was brotherly," she said.

"You said you didn't want to be private."

"You're right," she said. She lit a cigarette, took a very long drag and a long time exhaling, and sat herself back in the corner of the seat. "Well, why did I go to New York? And why didn't I tell you I was going? I wanted to go see your play without telling you, because if I didn't like it, or *hated* it, I could always pretend I hadn't been anywhere near it. But I saw it, and obviously I think it's great. For me, at least, it's the most wonderful play I ever saw."

"You're a very sensitive and very sensible dame. I don't mean because you liked my play, but the way you went about seeing it."

"Eventually, I suppose, it would have slipped out, if I'd seen it and hadn't liked it. But then it wouldn't have mattered. I don't give a damn about the reviews, you know. The critics have misled me so often that I don't take anyone's word for it. Actually, if I hadn't met you I wouldn't have been in any great hurry to see your play. I might even have missed it entirely. You know, I'm the girl that doesn't like Mickey Mouse. Bores the ass off me. But in this case you came first, you before your play. However, the more important you became in my life, the more important it was for me to see your play—and like it. If I didn't like your play—your work being so important to you—you and I could never be more than what we have been. A friendship sprinkled with sex. Now I've seen your play, I love it, and if you want me to, I'll love you. I know you better now."

"Don't love me, Sheila," he said. "I can't reciprocate."

"No, after seeing your play I don't suppose you can. You were so *fair*, so honest with those characters, that you didn't seem to have any prejudices. And if you can't have prejudices you can't have love. Love is one of the worst prejudices there is. In fact, it's the worst. You love people at the same time you hate them, so I can easily understand why love is impossible for you. But fortunately I'm all full of prejudices, so I can love you, and I do. I was wondering if we ought not to get married. The other thing I did in New York was to see various lawyers, and Lover-Boy Dunham wants me to go to Reno. He has a new chick that he actually wants to marry, and he's stopped being difficult about money and stuff. My lawyer thinks the chick may be knocked up and they want to have the child, so time is of the essence—although I don't know why it should be in our set. So I have another announcement to make, and I haven't even told my mother. I'm leaving for Reno in two weeks."

"You certainly are full of news today," he said.

"Just bursting with it, aren't I?" she said. "As soon as I spoke to the lawyers the thought occurred to me—is there any reason why you can't go to Reno with me?"

"I don't suppose there is, except that I don't particularly want to leave here."

"I'll have to be gone six weeks, you know," she said. "We haven't even known each other six weeks. Or just about. I'm a little afraid of what might happen in those six weeks."

"But you're not afraid of marrying me."

"I was wondering if you'd come back to that, or just wriggle out of it," she said. "No, I'm not afraid of marrying you, as we stand now. But I'm told that six weeks in Reno can be a hell of a long time. Don't you think you could work there?"

"I can work anywhere, but it's been going so well here I hate to interrupt it. On the other hand, it will be interrupted by your leaving. You have to go in two weeks?"

"Yes. My husband is a very impatient type—in more ways than one, I might add."

"Why can't *he* go to Reno?"

"Oh, that's just not done. The wife is always the one to go. And besides, he could argue very reasonably that he has a job, and I'm doing nothing," she said. "What if I go and you stay here? What happens to us? That thought makes me very jealous. It wouldn't have, at least not quite as much, before I saw your play. But everything is going to date from my seeing your play."

"You're speaking of sex, of course. Well, couldn't I go out there at the end of three weeks and we could be private for two or three days and I could come back?"

"I've gone without it much longer than that. Up here I stayed pure. I always have, up here. Of course I don't know about you. In a couple of weeks you might want to take on anybody. I don't quite see you getting so desperate that you'd creep in with Anna Phelps."

"Don't be so sure about that."

"I'm not sure about anything. As far as that goes, I wouldn't like to leave you and Mother alone for six weeks. There's a little something going there, more on her side than on yours, but she has a lovely figure even today. I'd almost give you my permission, just to keep you in the family, so to speak."

"She has, a very good figure."

"I didn't like the way you said that. No, you stay away from Mother. She has too much to lose. She and Seymour are being overpolite to each other, which means they're having some kind of a Mr.-and-Mrs., and she's susceptible. She's susceptible. Oh, I don't know what to do. I guess the best thing is for you to come out to Reno at the end of three weeks. Have you ever gone that long?"

"Not since I got married."

"When you came to East Hammond you were probably all fucked out. I studied Zena Gollum with a special interest. I doubt if she'd wait three weeks. I had a feeling that she hasn't been waiting."

"Well, why should she?"

"She and the leading man, Aubrey Scott—"

"Scott Aubrey."

"Whatever. The night before last, when I saw your play, I'd have sworn they were a thing, but I could be wrong."

"You could just as easily be right," said Yank.

"You don't really care, do you?"

"No. You have a hard time believing that, but you'll be in for a much harder time if you don't believe it."

"Why?"

"Because if you don't believe that I can stop caring what Zena does, you can't understand *me*. And if you don't understand *me*, you could give yourself a bad time by expecting too much. Please don't expect too much, Sheila. I seem to be a very peculiar man. I may turn out to be one of those men that grow three sets of teeth, or something like that. Lacking in some things, oversupplied in others. I don't know why I'm attracted to the women I'm attracted to, or repelled by the others. You say you're the girl that hates Mickey Mouse. Well, I don't like everything I'm supposed to like, either. I'm attracted to more women than I'm repelled by, and yet I often pass up the obvious pretty ones with good shapes. That girl in the post office, Helen MacDowell. A dish, and ready to go, but I'm not interested. I'd much sooner go to bed with your mother, who's at least twice as old."

"You're not saying anything that isn't true of me, too. I don't always respond to the obvious stimuli."

"Who knows that better than I? I have none of the obvious stimuli. As they say in the South, I don't pretty much."

"Maybe not. But you have a mean way of cutting into a woman's insides. You've certainly cut into mine."

"Just don't expect too much."

"There's no use warning me. I'm going to expect everything."

"Including marriage?"

"Yes, including marriage. You may be determined not to marry me, but I'm going to go on wanting you to and that might do it."

"To your regret."

"All right, to my regret. But I'd rather regret having married you than regret not having married you."

"You understand, of course, that if you and I were going to spend the rest of our lives in East Hammond, Vermont, marriage to you would be simple and delightful."

"Then why don't—"

"But much as I like living here now, this talk about my becoming a permanent resident fails to take into account the fact that some day I'm going to leave and never come back."

"Why?"

"Because I know that when I've finished this play, I'm

going to have to go someplace else. East Hammond, *and you,* are part of the creation of this play. New York was part of the creation of the other play. When I begin to be taken over by my next play, I'll have to settle down in new surroundings."

"With a new woman."

"Yes."

"So that all I really am is part of the play you're writing now?"

"Yes."

"It makes no difference that I love you—and I do."

"It makes a difference. But I'm not going to lie to you and say it makes the kind of difference you think it ought to make."

"If I were to take you home this minute and never see you again, would you be able to finish your play?"

"I'd finish it. It would take longer, but I'd finish it."

"Then I think that's what I'd better do," she said.

"We're not going to be private?"

"No," she said. "You're going to have to overcome your antipathy to Helen MacDowell. I'm terribly sorry that you won't get there before the post office closes."

"It won't be Helen MacDowell."

"Well, it won't be my mother, either."

"It might be. If you turn me loose, you know, you have no say in what I do."

"One word, the slightest hint from me to Seymour, and you don't stand a chance."

"Oh, that isn't much of a threat, Sheila. I can sleep with your mother any time I want to. And the last thing you want to do is alert Mr. Atterbury. If you were to do that, you'd be destroying their marriage. And why? Out of pique. I could have a brief affair with your mother and no one the wiser, provided you didn't go blabbing to Atterbury. I could finish my play and depart, never to return, and your mother would have her little secret, a final fling. But if you sick the big dog on us, there won't be any secrets."

"So far, you're right. But you've only thought of it from one angle. I have another ace in the hole."

"Ah? What's that?"

"Shall I tell you or not? Yes, I'll tell you. Suppose I go straight to Mother and tell her that you've decided to make her your temporary mistress? Do you think you'd ever get to first base? My friend, if you do you don't know my mother. She'd put the chill on you so fast, and so thoroughly, that you wouldn't thaw out till spring."

He smiled. "You are *so* right," he said. "I hadn't thought of that angle, but of course it's true. So Helen MacDowell, here I come."

"You won't like her. Zena Gollum and I have taken care of that."

"I'm afraid you're right there, too."

"Every time you went to the post office she'd put a strangle-hold on you. In a week's time there wouldn't be a soul in East Hammond that hadn't guessed that you were her boy friend. Not that she was your girl friend, but that you were her boy friend. I can just see her. And I can see you, too. They all know who you are, now, and they'd watch every move you made, every move she made. 'Looks like our Helen is humpin' that Lucas fella. Bet she gets him, with those tits of hers.' How are you going to like knowing that every Yankee in East Hammond will be thinking of you nibbling on Helen's jugs?"

"They have the same thought about you and me."

"Yes, but I'm not one of them, and Helen is. Helen's a bit of a tourist attraction. East Hammond folks are mighty proud of their Helen. She don't go nowheres without folks wond'rin' if she's humpin' or holding out. But when that rich writer fella comes into the post office, by gum Helen won't make no secret of it. He's Helen's new boy friend, and she ain't gonna let him get away, not him."

"You're doing a beautiful snow job."

"I'm doing my best. I can't tell a man that I love him, and then a few minutes later let him make a fool of himself."

"Then what do you suggest?"

"I suggest that I come back about nine-thirty and we go to the motel."

"Yes, that seems like the sensible thing to do," he said.

The new motel east of Georgetown was their place. The small deception they practiced was to leave the Atterbury station-wagon or Sheila's car in the vicinity of Anna Phelps's house, and use Peg McInerney's coupe. Yank had an arrangement with the manager, a York State man, whereby he paid a monthly rent and avoided the necessity of registering every time they occupied the cabin. P. McInerney, of New York City, license number 8C-855-433, was on the registry. She would not mind, and too damn bad if she did. For the next two weeks Sheila and Yank went there every day. The imminence of her departure for Reno removed the spontaneity of their earlier visits to the motel, but in its stead was desperation as the time grew short. She did not again bring up the subject of his breaking her stay in Reno, nor did he. Marriage was an even more verboten topic of their conversations. On the afternoon that was to be their final visit to the motel he said, "It's odd that we haven't brought this up before, but you've never actually said you were coming back to East Hammond."

"What's odd about it?" she said.

"It's odd because we usually say what's on our minds."

"Not lately. There are lots of things we don't talk about. Practically everything that has anything to do with the future. You don't even want to plan three weeks ahead. What do you think? Are you coming to Reno?"

"I don't know."

"There, you see?" she said. "So I'm not at all sure I'll be back here. They keep the house open all year round, but I'll have been here almost a year, and we're all beginning to get on each other's nerves. *They* asked me where I was going to be after Reno, so it's been on their minds. Just asking me showed that they weren't exactly counting on me to become a permanent fixture."

"Well, what did you tell them?"

"Well, if you must know, I told them—" She hesitated. "—No."

"You're not coming back?"

"They've been very patient with me. I've been difficult at times, and it's a strain on them. They really like to be by themselves. They've reached that age where they don't need other people. But with me in the house, Seymour trying not to behave as though I were in heat. Oh, hell. No, I'm not coming back."

"Where will you be?"

"Well, I don't relish the thought of that same old rat-race in New York. But that's where my friends will be, and New York in the fall can be pretty exciting. The new plays, and the really good parties. Autumn in New York is really spring, except for the weather. After Christmas everybody ducks out, and I might take a house in Nassau or some such place."

"You've obviously given the future a lot of thought."

"I've had to, haven't I? You haven't, and that's why I've had to."

"What if I do come to Reno?"

"If you have any plans to come to Reno, you must tell me now, or at least sometime before I leave."

"Why?"

"Because otherwise, once I leave East Hammond I won't be your girl any more. I've liked being your girl, but I must start learning to be someone else's girl. To *like* being someone else's girl. I'm too much of a person to go on letting you treat me this way. I don't blame you, entirely. We're all selfish. But it's time I got really selfish, before I turn into one of those awful self-pitiers that wait around for a man to throw them a bone."

"You therefore intend to have an affair with someone else."

"The first man I'm attracted to. It probably won't work out. I don't see how it possibly can. But I'll have put him between you and me, and the next one may turn out more successfully. I'm not trying to threaten you—not *you*. But I might as well tell you, I have a candidate picked out for my first experiment. He lives in San Francisco, and he's already written and told me he'd heard I was going to be in Reno."

"This is what you might call the society brush-off."

"Hardly a brush-off, but all right. A declaration of independence. An abdication. An emancipation proclamation. I don't care what name it goes by. You could just as easily call it a cry for help. Throw me a life preserver."

"Then this could be our last time together," he said.

"I think we've had our last time together," she said. She sprang out of bed, on the side opposite the edge on which he was sitting, and went to the shower bath. Presently he followed her in and stood with her. He ran his fingers everywhere on and into her body, but she shook her head. "It's no use. I couldn't," she said.

"I want you. You can see that," he said.

"Honestly, it's no use," she said. "I'm sorry, but you might just as well turn on the cold. Please don't do that any more."

He got out of the shower bath and handed her a towel. "I'll do things to you, if you like," she said. "But don't expect me to get excited."

"All right, do things to me," he said. She did, and it was too much like the impersonal ministrations of a paid whore.

"Are you all right now?" she said.

"Thanks," he said.

"It was probably better that way," she said. "There was no love at all to that, not this time. Other times—ah, yes. But not this time. Now will you please get dressed? I have a lot of last-minute packing to do."

"You're practically on your way, aren't you?"

"Yes, I guess I am."

"To your friend in San Francisco."

She halted in the midst of putting on her bra. "Actually, that's none of your business, is it?" she said.

The dead desolation of East Hammond on the next afternoon, when he knew that she had gone, was badly lighted by Nature. It was a warm, bright September day, and the people were walking around hatless and in shirtsleeves, squinting in the sunlight and making the faces of mirthless grins. He wrote a memorandum to remind him that the lighting for the second scene of his second act, the murder scene, must avoid the cliché of dimness.

◆ III ◆

Once more, for the third or fourth time, Yank Lucas was where he wanted to be—alone with his work. Rather to his surprise the adjustment did not at first seem difficult. He had two more or less ready explanations for the ease and rapidity with which he resumed the writing of his play. He had expected, and had been preparing himself for, some perturbation from the physical absence of Sheila Dunham. Yet, when a week or so had passed and the sunlit anguish of her departure was gone, he missed her not at all. He could not quite explain to himself *why* he was able to be undependent on her so soon, but the condition of his mind, the state of his mind, was a fact. Whatever the reason, he was able to get along without her. The *why* of it was deep inside among the atoms and cells and globules that comprised a being called Yank

Lucas, which would always remain something of a mystery to him as it does to everyone. His oculists could tell him why he was near-sighted, and a geneticist might be able to tell him why he was thin. But finally no one could tell him why he was Yank Lucas, why or how he had become Yank Lucas, and all the knowledge and information in the world was never going to suffice to explain anything more subtle than the wax in his ears. He prided himself in his instinctive understanding of the acts and motives of his fellow human beings, but he had the humility to know where to stop: he stopped where he could no longer implant himself in the souls of his fellow human beings and see and feel things their way. Beyond that point the artist was lost and could not breathe. (And even the philosophers and the theologians got confused and breathless.) The good explanations were usually the simple ones, the simple ones were usually good. In a billion light years it might turn out that God was a disembodied man with a long white beard; He might also turn out to be Yank Lucas! At the moment, lacking divine omniscience and divine omnipotence and divine omnipresence, Yank Lucas was satisfied with his mundane explanation of a mundane condition: he was able to do without Sheila Dunham because he had lost his appetite for her, and because he was engrossed in his play.

As nearly as it ever happens, the play was writing itself. The characters got fat—and thin—and they said the right things in the right language, at the right time. "Now it is my turn, Lucas," a character would say, and on he would come. There were moments of joy when Yank Lucas would tell himself that he was functioning as a medium, controlled by his creations. The play thus was writing itself through him, and it would be finished when his people said it was finished. He hoped and wished that that were true, but he knew that it never was: as the god of his own work he would have to intervene, with his instinct and craftsmanship and conscience.

"I thought you'd be grumpy when somebody left town," said Anna Phelps.

"Is that what you thought, Mrs. Phelps?" said Yank.

"Yes, that's what I thought, Mr. Lucas."

"Well, aren't you glad I'm not?" said Yank.

"Makes for a pleasanter atmosphere around here, to be sure. I don't object if a person's a little disagreeable before they had their breakfast. But having somebody grouchy to contend with, after two days of it my mother used to hand my father the bottle of castor oil."

"And did it always work?"

"Too well. It killed him," said Anna Phelps.

"Killed him?"

" 'Take this,' she said, when he'd been grouching a couple of days. He took it, flavored with a little maple syrup. That very same day he was dead."

"You're not going to tell me she flavored it with something else besides maple syrup," said Yank.

She interrupted her ironing. "No," she said. "He had the appendicitis. It broke open and pus spread all over his insides. Dr. Wells never told *her* it was the castor oil, but he told *me*. That was back when the appendicitis was still pretty new.

From then on I used to hide the castor oil like it was Paris Green. Some of these tourists, they come and ask me if I have anything for an upset stomach. Usually children. I tell them no. I'm the greatest enemy of castor oil in the State of Vermont."

"That's good," said Yank.

"Oh, if you ever feel the need of it, it's here. I guess you'd have sense enough to consider the appendicitis."

"I had mine out when I was ten years old."

"Dr. Wells took mine out when I was eighteen. There for a while the young girls used to postpone their operations and dental work till after they got married. That way the husband had to pay. But my mother didn't hold with that kind of trickery. When I married Mr. Phelps I didn't have a cavity in my mouth."

"Or an appendix in your belly."

"Huh." She smiled. "Change the subject. I hear you working away."

"Listen, if it bothers you—"

"I'd tell you if it did. No, I was thinking of the daytime, not the night. And now I guess you'll be at it day *and* night."

"It's going very well."

She put down her iron again. "I have a favor to ask you. You can say no and I won't blame you."

"How could I say no to you?"

"Now, now, don't get flirty. You put a double meaning into things where they don't belong."

"What's the favor, Mrs. Phelps?"

"Well, I have this nephew's going to college over in Burlington. He graduates next June. He heard you were staying at my house and he wants to interview you. He's something on the college paper."

"Would it be a favor to you?"

"Yes, it would. He has a hard time getting around, from the polio when he was younger. He's my sister's boy and they're very proud of him. He'd have to be driven here in a car, but that won't be any problem. He said if you gave him an hour of your time."

"All right. You arrange it, but make sure it'll only take an hour. I used to be a reporter, and an hour is plenty."

"His name is Charles Palmer," said Anna Phelps. "I'd appreciate it. I never did as much for him as I wished I could."

The next afternoon, shortly before the agreed-upon hour of four, a Ford four-door sedan stopped in front of Mrs. Phelps's. The driver was a young woman, who got out and opened one of the rear doors and unfolded an invalid's chair and steadied it for Palmer. He dexterously lifted himself out of the sedan and into the wheelchair, and the young woman pushed it to the downstairs front room.

Anna Phelps introduced Palmer and his companion, a Miss Thompson, and placed a trayful of cookies and grape juice on the table. "I'll be in again at five o'clock, on the dot," she said to her nephew, and left.

Before Palmer had said a word Yank disliked him. Palmer put a smile on his face that was the antithesis of the jolly cripple's, which Yank had anticipated. Instead it was the smile of supreme self-confidence, the big-man-on-campus. "Bessie is my transportation," said Palmer. "She takes me every-where."

"How nice for *you*," said Yank.

"Well, she's glad to do it. I took her up to Montpelier to meet the governor. We had a very interesting interview. I don't know if Aunt Anna showed it to you."

"No, she didn't."

"I sent her a tearsheet, to show you the way I go about it. I understand the governor wasn't too pleased, but politicians don't like anything that isn't a puff."

"I've known some politicians. I used to be a reporter."

"I know you were. You got fired, and I'll bet you get a charge out of that now."

"Actually I wasn't fired. I quit."

"The *Time* story said you were fired."

"The *Time* stringer in Spring Valley, Pennsylvania, knows what *Time* likes," said Yank.

"Uh-uh, Mr. Lucas. I happen to be the *Time* stringer in Burlington."

"Then you must know what they like, too. By the way, is this interview for *Time?* Your aunt didn't say anything about *Time*. I think we ought to have that understood at the very beginning. In fact, it might be a good idea to ask Mrs. Phelps to come back."

"Would you refuse the interview if it was for *Time?*"

"Indeed I would," said Yank. "Even without Mrs. Phelps here, Miss Thompson has heard me on that point. I don't want

Mrs. Phelps here during the entire interview, but I think it would be a good idea if she heard you say that this is not for *Time*."

"You kind of have me over a barrel," said Palmer.

"Well, it's only by the merest accident that I discovered what you're really here for."

"I don't know, you're pretty difficult," said Palmer.

"Not at all. Just not completely stupid."

"Suppose I write the interview and *Time* picks it up?"

"Who do you think you're kidding? They'll pick it up by air-mail special-delivery, sent by you, Mr. Palmer."

The dull film of hatred covered Palmer's eyes, and his mouth lay open. You could hear him breathing. He even hated Bessie Thompson for being present.

Yank stood up. "Obviously we're not going to get any-where, Palmer. Why don't you turn the trip into a visit to your aunt?"

"I'll go speak to her," said Palmer. "Bessie, you wait here." He spun the wheelchair around and made for the kitchen.

Yank looked at the girl, and she was smiling.

"Good for you," she said.

"Really?"

"Well, I couldn't say anything. But on the way over he had it all planned out. It didn't seem right to me, but it was none of my business either way."

"Why couldn't you say anything? Is he your boy friend?"

"He doesn't like girls. No, I'm getting paid for this. It's on the *Time* expense account. So was Montpelier."

"Are you a taxi driver?"

"No, I'm a student. But he uses me when he can. It's easy for him to get in and out of my car."

"And you're pretty."

She shrugged. "Well, I guess that helps," she said. "I don't get as many tickets."

"He's a monster," said Yank.

"Oh, I don't know if he's that bad. But he does trade on his affliction. I s'pose you can't blame him for that."

"Yes you can," said Yank.

"Yes, I guess you can."

"How about a date with me?"

"I go steady."

"How about an unsteady date with me?"

"I don't know," she said. She put a finger to her breast. "I was pinned."

"Sigma Nu. I noticed it when you first came in. It wasn't the very first thing I noticed, but almost. In that general direction."

"Oh, sure," she said.

"Well? Does an old Phi Gamma Delta get a date with you?"

"I don't know. I have a lot to lose, and nothing to gain. I couldn't even let on I ever knew you."

"As far as I'm concerned you could."

"As far as *you're* concerned. As far as you're concerned I'd just be somebody you were making out with. Where would we go?"

"That's always a problem, but it always gets solved."

"And when? My steady doesn't object when I take Charley Palmer someplace. But if I as much as look at anyone else he raises the roof." She stood up to pour some grape juice, poured less than half a glass, and turned and put her arms around Yank. He kissed her.

"All right," she said. "I just wanted to see," she said.

"And having seen?"

"I'll take him home and meet you later."

"Great. I'll be at Cabin Number 24, the big new motel on the other side of Georgetown."

She laughed. "Didn't take you long to solve that problem," she said. "A little after six. As soon after six as I can get there."

"And take off that damned Sigma Nu pin."

"Oh, I *couldn't* do *that,*" she said. "You'd think I was fickle."

"Well, you are, aren't you?"

"I guess I must be, but it's better to be now than later. I got all dressed up to meet you, the famous celebrity. Little did I realize that you'd want just the opposite."

"If you'd arrived here in overalls it'd have been the same."

"Oh, I look pretty good in overalls, so they tell me," she said.

"Nobody has to tell you very much, Bessie."

"No, but they all keep trying to. Especially *him.*" She touched the fraternity pin. "Maybe he started a little too soon."

"I hear the monster," said Yank.

"He's too stingy to buy some 3-in-1 for his velocipede," she said.

Palmer wheeled himself in. "All right, Bessie, let's get moving," he said. He did not look at Yank, did not speak to him. She stuck her tongue out at him and followed him out.

"Goodbye, Miss Thompson," said Yank.

"Pleased to have met you," said Bessie, and did a strip-teaser's bump.

Yank watched them get in the car and leave, and he was unconscious of Anna Phelps standing beside him at the window. "I guess I owe you an apology," she said.

"Why? It wasn't your fault."

"No, where I owe you an apology is giving you the wrong impression of him. I thought he was an altogether different kind. That's what I get for listening to my sister singing his praises. You shouldn't give a recommendation unless you know the person. I'm mortified."

"Well, don't be."

"I could have got you in all kinds of trouble," she said.

At that very fraction of a second he could have turned his fantasies of her into reality, and she wanted him to. But a funny, lewd little girl intervened. "Let's have a glass of grape juice," he said. "Waste not, want not, they say."

"It's the last time I'll ever ask you a favor," said Anna Phelps.

"Don't say that. I may want a favor from you sometime," said Yank.

The funny, lewd little girl arrived at the motel, and the

first thing he noticed was the absence of the fraternity pin. "What did you do with it?" he said.

"Oh, you took notice?" she said. "I swallowed it."

"How did it taste?"

"Tasted pretty good, going down," she said.

They laughed simultaneously, but soon there was the serious business of first-time lovemaking, fearful awkwardness and ignorance complicated by the separate desires to please and be pleased. Immediately after her orgasm he thought she had fainted. She lay with her eyes closed, breathing deeply and regularly. Presently she opened her eyes but she remained motionless except for the breathing. Little beads of sweat matted the hair at her temples. "That was almost too much," she said.

"You had me worried," he said.

"It took me by storm. Maybe because you're a famous celebrity."

"Maybe."

"I'm serious," she said.

"I know you are."

"I told you I got all dressed up to meet you."

"Yes."

"What I *didn't* tell you—when you were giving it to Charley Palmer, I got so excited I almost came. I've been excited ever since. It was as if we'd been making out for two hours, postponing it. Those women that watch bullfights. Something like that. When I kissed you I was hoping I'd come, but I didn't. I can't come from just kissing any more. Well, I'm all right now. Charley's such a bully, I guess I've been waiting to see somebody give it to him, but when it was you it took me by surprise. He's a complete sadist, but he's a masochist too."

"He's a monster."

"Oh, I guess he is. But he sort of fascinates me. He can't *do* anything, and he slapped a girl that made a pass at him. On a bet a friend of mine made a pass at him, and he clobbered her with one of those ugly hands of his."

"She deserved it."

"Not that hard. I'd never make a pass at him, and I really loathe him, but he fascinates me. So when I was watching you just take him apart, I can't tell you how excited I got. Oh, we're all crazy, in some way or other."

"How am I crazy?" said Yank.

"I don't know yet, but I'll bet you are. Is your watch right?"

"Within a minute or so," said Yank.

"I have to be home at seven. Charley *could* run into my steady. I don't think he will, but it's possible. I really feel great now, so stop worrying. It was nice of you to be worried."

"I wasn't being nice," said Yank.

"Are you as rich as they say you are?"

"Before taxes," said Yank. "Why?"

"Well, don't go thinking I'm a whore, because I'm not. But have you got fifty dollars you can spare?"

"Yes."

"Is that too much?" she said.

"No."

"What I was thinking—if you gave me money every once

in a while, I could stop driving Charley. I could meet you here, and you could give me twenty-five or fifty dollars. It doesn't have to be every time, but sometimes. That's not a whore. A whore will lay anybody, but I'd only go to bed with you. And my steady. Would it be worth it to you? Tell me honestly. I'd still *want* to go to bed with you, but if you didn't give me any money, I wouldn't want to take too many risks."

"It seems fair enough to me."

"Good. One thing, I could never give you any trouble, I guarantee you that."

"Why not?"

"Because he isn't my steady. He's my husband. We're secretly married. I've never told anybody but you. Not even the girls in my fraternity."

"I should hope especially not the girls in your fraternity."

"Oh, they'd keep it secret. We have two married girls and nobody knows about it except us. But I can't tell them about myself because he's Catholic and we're going to get married again next June. We only got married in case I got knocked up, which I thought I was last summer."

"What are you going to do with your money?"

"Buy a trousseau. I can't spend it now, but if I spend it on my trousseau, nobody'll ever notice how much I spend."

"I'll be delighted to help buy your trousseau. Of course I may not be here much longer. What happens then?"

"Oh—I'll find somebody. When I get married, publicly, I expect to settle down. With one exception."

"What exception?"

"You. That's because I like you. I don't care when it is. If it's a year from now or five years from now, any time you're hard up, or not that you'll ever be hard up with all those actresses. But if you get to thinking it would be fun to go to bed with Bessie again, you just send for me and I'll make some excuse. Word of honor. I know a girl that's happily married, with three children. But once or twice a year a certain person in Hartford sends for her and she goes. She doesn't love him, but she likes him a lot and he was always nice to her. It would kill her husband if he ever knew, but he's such a boring son of a bitch he ought to be grateful."

"Your steady is a bore."

"Oh, is he ever a bore! With one exception. Bed. In bed he's a stud, but to talk to him or be with him, if I had to do over again I never would have married him, pregnant or not."

"I don't get it. You don't have to remarry this bore, and yet you're planning to and to stay faithful to him. And he's not the only stud around."

"You want to know something? He is for me. In bed we're practically like some kind of a machine. Turn it off, turn it on. Faster. Slower. He keeps looking at me, I keep looking at him, and I give him the nod or he gives me the nod and away we go. Five minutes later I can't hardly bear to be in the same room with him, I'm so bored. But fifteen minutes later we're at it again. Always twice with him. The second time he really wears me out. The night we got married the second one lasted so long I had to stop awhile, but he did that on purpose. He wanted to set a record."

"For some other man to shoot at. Well, it's not going to be me."

"Oh, you're entirely different. You don't see me getting bored with you. But if there isn't going to be a second show I have to get dressed. I can be ten or fifteen minutes late, but not more."

"You'd better get dressed, then."

"Save it for the next time," she said. "I hope you didn't mind me talking about him so much. You didn't *seem* to mind, but did you?"

"Of course not."

"When we get on Topic A at the chapter house I never tell them what he's like. If I did, they'd be after him like a bird-dog. So I play it dumb. But I can tell you anything. I have that feeling with you. Last look before the bra goes on."

"Very pretty," he said. "Before I forget it, here's your fifty dollars."

"Save that for the next time, too," she said. "We can call this a demonstration. My father's in the garage business, if you're ever in the market for a second-hand car. He can't get a dealership for new cars. Doesn't have too good a reputation. But I'll see you don't get a screwing—at least from him."

"Bessie, do you know what you are? You're a card."

"Don't think I never heard that before. Well, how about the day after tomorrow, same time, same station? If I can't make it, I'll give you a buzz."

"Six o'clock, here, the day after tomorrow," said Yank.

"A nice kiss before I go," she said.

He kissed her.

"My own brother couldn't have been nicer," she said.

"That seems to be getting to be a habit with me," said Yank.

"Au 'voir, chéri," she said, and was gone.

He listened to the sound of her merry little heels on the blacktop, and the whine-and-catch of her car, and the too-fast takeoff. He smiled at the joke she would make of too-fast takeoff. She was funny and lewd, but she was not shallow and she was not evil. He would somehow find a way to be nice to her because she imparted such cheerfulness.

But four hours later, by way of the Burlington radio station, she was the cause of the deepest depression he had ever known. "In other local news, Elizabeth Thompson, nineteen, was fatally injured early this evening when her car, which police say was being driven at a high rate of speed, crashed into a tree. Miss Thompson, who was alone in the car, was a sophomore at the University of Vermont. Her father, Roy R. Thompson, proprietor of a used-car lot in Burlington, identified the body. Mr. and Mrs. Wendell Hitchcock will celebrate their fiftieth wedding anniversary tomorrow at their home on . . ."

"Why if I'm not mistaken that's the same girl that was here this afternoon," said Anna Phelps. "I'm sure it was. She was sitting in this very chair. Bessie Thompson. Age nineteen. Sophomore at the college. Pretty. You talked to her, right in this room. Oh, I certainly opened up a fine can of worms, I did."

"Don't talk that way, Mrs. Phelps. Your nephew wasn't with her. The radio said she was alone."

"Yes, but she would have been someplace else at that particular moment if she hadn'ta brought Charley here when she did."

"Oh, stop that kind of talk."

"You have just cause to be irritable, Mr. Lucas, but I thought you were over it. Why don't you go take a long walk and when you get back I'll have some fresh coffee and a little something for you to munch on. There's a good snap in the air this evening. We can be expecting the first frost any time now, Ed Cross thinks."

"A good suggestion," said Yank. He went out and stood in the dark protection of a chestnut tree. But he could not buy off the depression with easy tears, then or at any other time in his sleepless night.

He read the details of the accident in the next day's paper. There was a photograph of the car on the front page, followed by two others on an inside page. The sedan embraced the tree-trunk like a pair of calipers, the wrecked body was U-shaped from the impact. The list of the girl's injuries contained three that were usually fatal. From past experience Yank guessed that the doctor who performed the autopsy would note incidentally that she had recently had sexual intercourse, but he would be more interested in the contents of her stomach and the amount of alcohol in her circulatory system. A few drops of grape juice, unfermented, were all he would find. The multiple skull fractures presumably laid open the brain, for any of the early arrivals on the scene who had the power to read her last thoughts. There would be vestigial traces of a man's saliva for the chemists to ponder over. A very, very good heart man might be able to conjecture that shortly before the accident she had been under prolonged strain related to the reproductive organs, culminating in a blackout. The post mortem would probably be witnessed by medical students from the university who had been acquainted with Bessie— if only acquainted with her. Perhaps in the interests of medical science, Yank thought, he ought to volunteer to give all the information he possessed. The post-orgasm blackout might be a symptom of auricular fibrillation, do you think so, Dr. Lucas? No, Dr. Blank, in my considered opinion she was glowing from a wonderful piece of tail, in which I had the good fortune to participate, so please for God's sake give this mess to the mortician and let him set fire to it, she has third-degree burns already.

The ground—more poetically, the Vermont earth—had not yet become so cold that they had to postpone her burial. And Yank was not yet so lapidified that he could stay away from the funeral. He wondered why that word, lapidified, reappeared from some disremembered geology lecture, some crossword puzzle. He wondered if Bessie Thompson had ever seen a wonderfully funny comedian named Lou Holtz. Why Lou Holtz? Ah, yes. He told funny Jewish stories about a character called Sam Lapidus. He wondered if Bessie Thompson would have gone on being funny. Yes, anyone as cheerful as that would have stayed that way throughout her life, and probably did so until the very moment when her car hit the tree. He could imagine her saying, as the car went into its spin, "Hey, there, wait a minute! Don't get carried away," and dying in the middle of a laughing protest. He hoped that that was the way it had been. He wanted her at least to have had no fear. If that was the way it had been, God was forgiven.

He had to know more about her than the little he knew. He knew everything, of course, that lovemaking could tell him. If she had lived to go to bed with him a thousand times their lovemaking would tell him little more, and probably, as they got used to each other, somewhat less. With her, as with all the girls he had been to bed with, satiation would neutralize his passion. Two years was the limit of his desire for any girl, and that, the relationship with the girl he married, had been divided into two phases: the phase before and the phase after she had taken off all her clothes and prolonged the relationship by adding visual pleasure to the tactile. It was neither unreasonable nor harsh to suppose that Bessie's cheerfulness and sensuality would have become tedious. But the supposition was not factual, and the cheerfulness and sensuality were. He lived now and always would with memory of a perfect relationship—that had lasted less than three hours. Well, three hours could be enough. They had not had time for the bad things, the unpleasant things. In three hours she had not been unfaithful to him (nor he to her), they had not quarreled over money, or coffee not hot enough, or the air in the bedroom not fresh enough, or her mother's interference, or her stepfather's suppressed lechery, or his position in the world. Three hours had been only long enough to share passion and fun and perfection. The ugliness of life had intruded after those three hours, and Yank felt a chill at the thought of how he nearly had missed the good. But again, the nearness of the miss was not factual, and the passion and fun and perfection were.

The perfect thing would be in no danger from his curiosity, his need to know more about her. Nothing, really, that had happened before or after the perfect thing could affect it. He got in his car and drove to Burlington. He went to see her house. It was a two-story grey-shingled building with a gabled roof, and a porch that no one was meant to sit on. It had nothing to do with Bessie; it told nothing except that there had been a death in a house in a sternly middle-class neighborhood. A massive dark grey hearse was waiting at the curb, and behind the hearse stood an almost matching Cadillac flower-wagon and two limousines, a Cadillac and a Chrysler, both black, one older than the other, related by the sequence of their license plates. Not much was going on at the Thompson house, and apparently not much was expected; the big show was being saved for the church. Yank waited until the family came out of the house: the obvious father, shady dealer in used cars; the obvious mother hidden under a veil; an obvious and a less obvious sister, a possible brother, and an unmistakable Bore, the secret husband, the baffled stud, and the only one who could not control his grief. The obvious funeral director, in a dark grey suit that matched his hearse and black loafers that matched his Chrysler, held a piece of paper in his hand and assigned the mourners to their cars. A slight confusion when the Bore started to enter the second car and was redirected to the first. One last, gentle tug by the funeral director of his toupee and the cortege was under way. Yank followed at a disassociating distance.

The church was not far away, and if it had been larger the congregation would not nearly have filled it. Most of those present were young people; there were not two dozen persons more than twenty-five years old. The girls of Bessie's fraternity sat together in three pews. Just before the clergy-man came out, Charles Palmer was wheeled up the aisle by an undergraduate, who assisted him in the transfer from wheel-chair to pew. And that was all. Yank, covering his face with his hand until he spotted Palmer, stayed until the clergyman completed his duties, then ducked out before it was time to move the casket. The clergyman's flat Yankee delivery ob-scured half of what he had to say; two girls in the fraternity group had brief attacks of audible grief; the Bore moaned throughout. But the predominantly youthful congregation was more puzzled than deeply touched. Boys and girls cre-ated a jam-up at the conclusion of the ceremony, stopping to light cigarettes the moment their feet crossed the threshold. It was not good enough for Bessie Thompson, and Yank hurried back to East Hammond without remembering to look for her tree.

"You're to call New York Operator 989," said Anna Phelps. "Oxford 5-1417. They called twice. I said you ought to be back before lunch."

"My agent. I went to the Thompson girl's funeral."

"Oh, that ought to pleased the family," said Anna Phelps. He shook his head. "Nobody saw me."

"No Charley Palmer there?"

"He was, but he didn't see me."

"Well, it seems kind of a waste, going that distance and not calling on the family, but you always have different ideas."

"I went because I liked her."

"They give her a nice sendoff?"

"Not nice enough, but I'm a stranger up this way. Are you going to be wanting to use the phone?"

"You go right ahead."

"It doesn't go on your bill, so we won't have to keep track of this one."

"I don't lose any sleep over that. Only once I ever got stuck. Thirty-some dollars on a call to some Air Force base in California. But I got my money a couple months later. They forgot all about it till I reminded them. It's the forgetful people that give the most trouble. Leave the light on in the bathroom. Burn out the tubes in the radio. Sheer forgetfulness, that's all. Smoking in bed."

"Well, before I forget it, I'd better call that number," said Yank.

Peg McInerney was out to lunch, but in the world of agents and show people and the like, the world of creative advertising executives and creative coordinators and vice-presidents in charge of creative coordinating executives, co-ordination on the executive level consists in no small part of getting two people connected by telephone. By means of gadgetry Yank's voice went from Anna Phelps's cottage in East Hammond, Vermont, to Peg McInerney's office in New York, was monitored by Peg's secretary, was passed along to the restaurant at 21 West 52nd Street, through the restaurant switchboard, and finally to the table where Peg was having her lunch. "Hello, there," said Peg.

"Hello, Peggy. I hope you're not worried about your car."

"My car? Listen, I'm glad you took it off my hands. You saved me garage rent and all. In fact I'd just as soon give you the car. But that's not what I called you about. How are you?"

"I'm all right. You didn't call me about that either."

"No. How's the new play going?"

"Very well. I'll have the first draft finished in about three more weeks, I think."

"Great, just great. This is what I called about. Do you feel any great obligation to Ellis?"

"Ellis Walton? Yes, I guess I do. He's been behaving him-self, hasn't he? I mean no funny business about money?"

"I've been watching him like a hawk. You don't pay much attention to those reports I send you, do you? Those sheets with the number of tickets sold and so forth?"

"Not very much."

"I didn't think so. And you're not very good at answering letters, but I know you're working. But that's why I wanted to get in touch with you by phone. How would you like to pick up twenty-five thousand dollars for a week's work?"

"That kind of money only comes from Hollywood."

"It's Hollywood, but hear me out before you say no. Eli Harbenstein—does the name mean anything to you?"

"Not a thing."

"Well, it didn't to me two years ago, but he's one of the new breed out there. He was a major in the Air Force, a Dartmouth graduate, Phi Beta Kappa. During the war he made some Air Force films, or at least he had some hand in the making of them. He flew several missions with a camera crew. Oh, hell, I don't know what all he did. But after the war he went to Hollywood and worked his way up to where he's now one of the fair-haired boys at Metro. He has his own set-up, with complete autonomy."

"In other words, he's a producer."

"A creative producer. He works hand in glove with the writers and the directors. He starts with the basic idea. He's against paying big money for plays and novels, but he's paying big money for originals. I sold him a two-page outline last week for ten thousand dollars by a writer that nobody ever heard of."

"What does he want from me, Peg?"

"He wants you to go out there, all expenses paid, car with chauffeur, cottage at the Beverly Hills Hotel. The V. I. P. treatment, and twenty-five thousand dollars for one week's conferences. Frankly, brain-picking. He wants to sit down and talk to you about picture business. No writing is involved, not a line. He wants you to tell him what you think is wrong with pictures from the *creative* point of view."

"That's a hundred thousand a month, times twelve is a million-plus a year. If I came up with a good comment, it would be worth at least a million, but I'd only be getting paid twenty-five thousand dollars. So it really isn't so much money when you stop to think of it, is it?"

"Not if you look at it that way."

"Has he offered this deal to any other writers?"

"Frankly, yes. Three others. I'm not at liberty to give you their names over the telephone, but they're top people. The others have accepted. Well, two of them have and one is considering it."

"So for a lousy hundred thousand dollars, or maybe seventy-five, *and at Metro's expense,* not his, he gets the best advice, private tutoring, from the best brains in show business."

"That's one way of looking at it," said Peg.

"Tell me the truth, Peg. Air Force major and Phi Beta Kappa from Dartmouth to one side, this guy is a real phony, isn't he?"

"Oh—one of the worst phonies I've ever met," she said. "But he's fooling an awful lot of smart people."

"Then I tell you what let's do. I'm tempted to tell him to come to East Hammond, Vermont, and have our seminar here, but I'm not that important yet."

"Not yet," said Peg. "And the trip would be fun for you. Hollywood from the top, without getting involved."

"I'll go out there and commune with Major Harbenstein, Monday through Friday—that comes to five thousand dollars a day—from eleven A. M. to five P. M. But no dinner parties, no cocktail parties, no orgies, no social life. Between five P. M. and eleven A. M., my time is my own."

"He'll agree to that, but he's not going to like it," said Peg.

"I guessed as much. He sounds to me like the kind of jerk that would like to rediscover Thornton Wilder."

"He's that, all right," said Peg. "When would you go to the Coast?"

"At my convenience," said Yank.

"That's very good," said Peg. "Now, what about Ellis? Are you going to let him have first look at the new play?"

"Yes—at my convenience," said Yank.

"I think Vermont has done you a lot of good," said Peg. "It's made you much more sure of yourself."

"I just came from a funeral. That may have something to do with it."

"Oh, who died?" said Peg.

"A girl," he said.

Peg's hesitation was barely noticeable. "I was wondering about that. You found somebody."

"I lost somebody before I found her."

"I'm sorry, Yank. Truly I am. But I'm afraid you had it coming to you. You did some damage down here, you know."

"No, I didn't know."

"Well, you did," she said. "Quite a bit of damage. You know who I'm talking about."

"Naturally," he said.

"I'd have thought you'd be the last person to pull a stunt like that."

"Oh, no. The first," he said. "You follow your instincts in those things."

"No, you ignore, or control, your instincts."

"And let things drag on to the same inevitable conclusion, but meanwhile having damaged yourself as well as the other party. If you follow your instincts going into one of those things, it's perfectly permissible to follow them when you want to get out."

"I couldn't agree less," said Peg. "You don't seem to realize what you did, the extent of the damage. You drove her back to Barry, but on his terms."

"I don't agree with you for a minute. Nobody drove anybody anywhere. Your trouble, Peg, is that you're thinking like a man. That is, the way men are supposed to think. And I'm thinking like a woman. The way a woman does think."

"I guess I'll never understand you," she said.

"*Now* you're *talking*. But luckily for all concerned, you don't have to understand me. Nobody does. I often have trouble understanding myself, but nearly always, when I finally do understand some action, some decision of mine, the simple explanation was there all the time. In this case, I had to get away from the whole business. Zena was an important part of it, but only a part of it."

"You're a misogynist."

"Anything but. However, I won't argue the point. If a man

has a monogamous relationship with one woman, he's being misogynistic toward all the other women in the world. And yet you'd hardly say he was a misogynist. It's like the accusation of anti-Semitism. If a man says he loves all Jews, he's a damn fool or a liar. The Jews he doesn't like will accuse him of anti-Semitism, the ones he does like will deny it. The women a man doesn't like will accuse him of being a misogynist, or a fairy. The woman he does like will say he's the greatest lover, et cetera, et cetera. If Barry Payne chooses to tell a gossip columnist that I'm anti-Semitic, that's all right with me. Of course at the time he did that he kind of put Ellis and Zena on the spot. I was doing business with the one and going to bed with the other. If they didn't deny it, they weren't being very good Jews. In fact, they were being anti-Semitic, by having such a close relationship with such a gonif."

"I don't know that they ever did deny it," said Peg.

"You want to know something? I don't—really—care. If you want to think I'm a misogynist, or a fairy, for that matter, I may take the trouble to ask myself if the accusation is valid. I happen to know it isn't. But even if it is, I'm not going into deep analysis to have it cured."

"For somebody that wasn't going to argue the point—"

"Yes, I realize that now. But I've been having to give a lot of thought recently to my feelings toward women. If men had women's bodies, I'd be a monosexual. But as long as women have women's bodies, I'll be a hetero. Probably this indicates latent homosexuality on my part. But better latent than ever, I always say."

"Do you mind if I quote you?"

"In private. Oh, God."

"What?"

"I was just thinking of a girl who used to say, 'Let's be private.' I had myself convinced that I didn't miss her. But just that chance remark came up and hit me. The person you're having lunch with must be having a jolly time, sitting there ignored. Is it a man or a woman?"

"The former."

"I hope he's gone right on eating his lunch."

"He has."

"He sounds like a confirmed misogynist."

"Even more than that."

"A fairy?"

"Howling," said Peg.

"Tell him it's not good manners to howl with his mouth full."

"He'd tell me to keep out of his private affairs."

" 'Let go my ears, I know my business.' "

"I know that joke," said Peg. "Well, nice to talk to you and I'm glad the play is going so well. I'll go ahead with Harbenstein, on your terms."

"One thing more. How much do you want for your car?"

"I don't know. Fifty dollars."

"No, it ought to be worth at least a thousand."

"All right, a thousand. I'll send you the papers on it. Is there anything else you want?"

"Yes, a strong third act," said Yank.

"Who doesn't?" said Peg.

During their conversation Yank had transported himself back to the world he had abandoned, to the restaurant he had never been in, the men and women he had not seen since his arrival in East Hammond (and had not greatly missed). Ellis Walton, Barry Payne, Zena Gollum. One time when Yank was a small boy the Al G. Barnes Circus had come to Spring Valley, an unfortunate booking as the circus appeared in the midst of an epidemic of poliomyelitis and children were not allowed to attend. They had to be content with the big free street parade. Consequently Yank's recollections of the Al G. Barnes Circus were limited to the rolling stock, the cage wagons and the bandwagon, the wire-wheeled, rubber-tired runabouts, the cally-oap; and a sour woman in a plumed hat riding side-saddle, the driver of one of the six-horse hitches who had either a wen or plum-sized chew of tobacco in his left cheek, a war-painted Indian wearing a wristwatch, and a full-breasted living-statue girl whose tights had a rip in the behind. It was the last circus ever to visit Spring Valley. It was the one Yank remembered best, the only one he really remembered, all because he had got close enough to the equestrienne to observe her wrinkled neck and her disagreeable countenance, the wagoner's chew-tobacco wen, the Indian's Ingersoll Midget, the rip in the statue-girl's behind. The next time he saw a circus he was part of it, and he did not belong there.

Or did he not? Among the world's freaks and non-freaks, he belonged with the freaks, not merely because he had chosen to be a writer of things for the stage, but because even though he might never write a line, he saw things differently, could not long hate, could not long love, and did not think he should. Nor did he wish to convert the non-freaks to his ways. Now the non-freaks were willing to sit and listen to and to watch whatever he gave them to watch and listen to, and that would be so for the rest of his life. They would pay their money, they would part with their money, to be shown and told things they did not believe and did not wish to believe. He had no fear that they would not, and how Peg McInerney had so quickly sensed that he had grown into total self-confidence he did not know. But he did know that it had happened to him, that he had lived alone with his first success long enough to become a part of it and not only of his first successful play. What it had cost him he did not know; he seemed not to have paid for it in East Hammond, and he believed now that he had been paying for it all his life and would continue to pay for it, episode by episode, year after year, in small instalments of brief and scarifying passions. He had sold no piece of his soul to any devil but himself and his talent. But even then he had not bargained; it had only happened that way. He could not repudiate the bargain or improve upon it. He and his work were the product of his condition, which began no later than his birth. He could not be sure of anything, and least of all could he be sure that being a freak was not a warning hint of his divinity. He longed to know what had gone on in his mind during those minutes when he was partly dead, back in the kitchen in Chelsea. If he was part of God, the confirmation of that secret was discoverable during those minutes. But maybe he was not part of God and would never be God, but could properly trace the absence of fear of failure to those minutes during which he was at least part of death. But there might be a much simpler explanation for his total self-confidence, discoverable in those minutes: the gas could have anesthetized his capacity for fear. It could be something no more esoteric than brain damage. Well, the same condition could have been produced during his passage out of his mother's belly. You were probably never closer to death than at the beginning of your life. Some day he would write a fantasy in which Jiggs Muldowney first appeared as the obstetrician who attended his mother at his birth, and reappeared as the Jiggs Muldowney who found him in the kitchen. He would think about that. The world was full of people who could lead him to the inhabitants of his mind.

H e got over the anger and petulance caused by the brutal death of Bessie Thompson. The petulance, rather, gave way to the anger; nothing as good as anger, even a directionless anger, would go away so soon. It would always accompany his thoughts of Bessie. With deep feelings so scarce, he could not afford to throw away anything as positive as anger. The day after Bessie's funeral he made sure to buy a copy of the Burlington paper, and journalistically he was pleased to find that the coverage was thorough. (He had covered so many items just like it.) He was especially pleased that the reporter's routine chore could be enlivened by the following: "Seated with the family was Paul Sinowski, University of Vermont senior, whose secret marriage to Miss Thompson on Aug. 19 last was revealed by her parents." That wrapped it all up, no loose ends. He finished reading the story on the sidewalk outside Thayer's, the confectionery-tobacconist-newsstand, and headed toward the post office.

"Good morning, Yank."

Yank? Who was calling him Yank? He turned and saw Mrs. Atterbury. She smiled her own surprise. "It popped right out," she said. "Of course that doesn't mean you can call me by my nickname."

"What is it?"

"Pussy. Although I don't believe anyone knows it in East Hammond. There aren't more than two or three people that call me Catherine. Have you heard from Sheila?"

"No."

"We haven't had any mail from her, but I've spoken to her two or three times. She's getting in a lot of skiing. I don't know Reno, but there's a place fairly near." She was wearing an old polo coat and a little brown felt hat. There was no doubt about it; she possessed a swaggering style that neither old clothes nor casualness could give to the young. "What did I just read about you somewhere?"

"Oh—that I swam the English Channel? That?"

"Something less strenuous. Oh, yes. That you were probably going to get the Pulitzer Prize. Good for you."

"I don't think my play is eligible. Something about the time we opened, which puts us in last season."

"Do you know, I don't even know what got it last season."

"Neither do I, unless I think hard."

"Well, whether you get it or not, there doesn't seem to be any doubt about your having the big hit of the year. My sister saw it last week and people were standing. I want to see it again. I'd like to go see it alone, and not have to make polite conversation. The night we saw it, my husband and I were with two friends who know a great deal about the theater, and who had played in what and so on. That's all very well, of course, but not with a play like yours. So I'm going to see it and not talk to anyone. I may go out for a cigarette during the entr'acte, and I may not."

"Let me know when you want to see it and I'll get you first row in the balcony. That's probably the best place to see a play. How is Mr. Atterbury?"

"Much better. He had a series of colds, but that seems to have stopped, thank heaven. I hear in a roundabout way that you're working very hard, but do come see us. I *hate* that kind of invitation. Come for lunch Sunday."

"Thank you, I will. One o'clock?"

"One o'clock. Just the three of us," she said. "And if I call you Yank, you still mustn't call me Pussy." She looked away from him and then left. She of course knew the sexual meaning of the word, and he wondered why she repeated it unnecessarily.

He went to her house for lunch on the following Sunday. Atterbury was in good health, still free of his colds, but beyond his duties as host he did not extend himself. At two o'clock he said he had to see a man about a cow, and left them.

"Alone at last!" she said, and read the line as burlesque of an old Lonsdale comedy. Then, playing it straight, she said, "I could really be quite cross with you, you know. What makes you think I'd jump into bed with you? Oh, yes, Sheila got that in before she left."

"I didn't think she would."

"She needn't have, but she did. You know, you're an extremely talented and quite attractive young man, but you really mustn't overrate yourself. Not even in the case of my daughter, who apparently fell pretty hard for you. Hard enough, at least, to go plunging into a thing, as you'd call it, with someone in Reno."

"A man from San Francisco," said Yank.

"That's the one. Who, doesn't matter. But her going into it so cold-bloodedly does. And you apparently frightened her about me. I represent something to Sheila, something called stability, which she needs. All in all, Yank, for a man who's so sensitive in his work, you've got surprisingly little sensitivity about real people. Me, for instance. If you were really observant you'd know that I haven't the faintest desire to go to bed with you."

"Pussy, I don't believe that."

"I know what Pussy means, and I know why you said it just now. But you're wrong. I have my man, and I have him back. He'd hardly be normal if he didn't show some response to Sheila's attractiveness. And frankly, I'm glad she's gone. But she'd be disturbing even if she weren't attractive, and God knows she's attractive. In this big place we have here, there just isn't room for anyone else. If people stay too long, he has to go see a man about a cow. Eight master's bedrooms and we almost never have anyone overnight. My husband talks to me, and he talks to Adam Phelps, and that's really about all he needs."

"That may be, but it isn't all you need."

"It didn't use to be, but it is now," she said.

"I'm sorry, but I don't believe that. This place is reeking with sex, or has been. Your prize bull with that enormous thing of his. The cows. Then for several months, Sheila and I. And Sheila and your husband. And you. You haven't got some button that you can turn on and off. The things you've had to imagine affect you as much as the things you see. You can watch the bull from an upstairs window, but of course you never saw Sheila and me. That you had to imagine, and you've been imagining it all summer. Now don't try to tell me, Pussy, that somewhere along the line you didn't imagine what it would be like to be in bed with me."

"Not really."

"I don't believe you. You're not lying to me, you're lying to yourself. If you can have it with Atterbury, you can have it with Adam Phelps, or the butler, or me. Or all of us."

"This is really quite an obsession with you, isn't it?"

"Yes. Not to the exclusion of everything else, but I don't do what you do, which is to pretend that you have your sex life neatly compartmentalized with you and your husband. I'd like to give it a try."

"Oh, you would?"

"The next time your husband goes away—or in fact, any afternoon—come to bed with me, and if nothing happens, I lose."

"Ah, there you miss the main point. Once we were in bed together, I have no doubt at all that you could break down my feeble resistance. Oh, I like sex. But first you'd have to get me in bed, and that isn't at all likely to happen."

"You're stimulated right now."

"If I am, it's only so little that it doesn't matter. I'm sure everybody is stimulated a dozen times a day as much as I am now. I'm surprised you haven't said I'm afraid. Because I am afraid. I'm afraid to go to bed with you, because I know perfectly well what would happen. Not just then, the lovemaking. Oh, I said before, I like sex. But what happens to me? Even if no one ever found out that you and I had been to bed together, there'd be subtle differences in me that maybe my husband would never notice, but *I* would. I don't want you, the thought of you, in the same bed with me and my husband. I want just him and me, because I happen to love him. And he loves me. That, apparently, is your trouble, or so I gather from Sheila."

"She had no right to tell you that."

"Yes she had. Indeed, she owed me that much. She owed me some explanation of what happened to her, and what happened really was you. Sheila didn't go into any of the details of your lovemaking. And officially, I was not informed that you ever did make love. To this day she's never actually said that she went to bed with you. But she did tell me quite a bit about the non-physical side of your affair with her. And emotionally, you're impotent. Is that a fair statement?"

"Yes."

"Then you see why you're wrong about me, Yank. At my age, after about thirty-five years of an active sex life, most of it but not all of it with two husbands, I have to have more than the quick lay. The one-night stand, your generation calls it. I had one of those one time, a long while ago, and I don't remember now whether the man had blue eyes or brown. But it helped to break up my first marriage. The fact that I could lie on a beach and make love with a man who meant absolutely nothing to me except that he was there and I did nothing to stop him. How precarious, I thought. How un-something my marriage was when I could be so easily seduced. The intactness of my marriage was broken, if there is such a word, and very soon after that I had quite a serious affair with someone else. But he hadn't seduced me. The other man had. And then I fell in love with Sy Atterbury, dropped the other man, divorced my husband, and married Sy. You couldn't know these things, and neither does Sheila, but you must know things before you make the kind of judgment you made about me. That I was panting to have you seduce me. I don't as a rule pay much attention to things that are said about me, but you aren't just an ordinary person. Was it possible that you could be right? Then I realized that you may have gotten a lot of misinformation from my daughter."

"I won't use that as an out. My guesses were my own."

"Well, in that case, you have a lot to learn."

"*Please* go to bed with me," said Yank.

"Please? That's hardly the same thing as declaring yourself irresistible," she said.

"No, it isn't. But I want you to."

"I like that much better," she said. "You have no idea how much better I like that. And how much better I like you. It almost changes everything."

"Almost," he said.

"Yes, almost. But have you tried that girl at the post office?"

"No."

"I think you ought to. My husband once called her the town pump, which I don't suppose was original with him. But heavens, what if she is? You don't want complications, and I don't want complications either. She's young, and I'm old enough to be your mother. I'll tell you what you do. You try her, and if you have no success, come back to me."

"And after having pretended to make a try there, and told you that I got nowhere with her, what then?"

"Then I'll see if I can't find someone else for you."

"Someone else could be you."

"I'm aware of that. But you ought to exhaust all the other

possibilities first. If what you want is an older woman, I'm surprised you haven't tried Anna Phelps. Or have you?"

"What's suddenly made you think I want an older woman?"

"Well, I'm an older woman. I may be a year or two older than Anna Phelps. You had an affair with my daughter, and before that with the actress in your play. Then you somehow convinced yourself that I was dying to have an affair with you, which at least indicates that you wanted to have an affair with me. To someone your age, the most obvious thing about me is that I'm a lot older than you are. And—"

"Yes, and God damn it I think you may be a lot smarter than I am."

"But I should be, Yank. I'm so much older. I've lived so much longer."

"What was the technique of the man you laid on the beach?" he said. "What approach did he use?"

"Well, he arranged to have the Atlantic Ocean at the right temperature, and a full moon. And he also arranged to have me thirty years younger than I am now."

"Come on, tell me."

"No technique. If it hadn't been him it would have been someone else. Probably even you don't realize that a girl that's only been married a short time can't help herself where sex is concerned."

"Oh, can't I? Sometime I'll tell you about my ex-wife."

"Then you do realize. Everything had better be perfect with your husband, or you'll be ready for the first man that comes along. That's what happened to me, at least. I'm not smarter than you, and you don't think so, but I have learned a few things. The sad part is that I was never able to help Sheila. If anything, she helped me."

"By tattling."

"Yes."

"Then I'm to infer that we'll never share the same bed and the delights thereof?"

"That's correct," she said.

"Unless, of course, you change your mind again."

"*Change her mind? Change her mind about what? My wife never changes her mind about anything. Of course it sometimes takes quite a while for her to make up her mind,*" said Seymour Atterbury. "What are you two talking about, if it's any of my business."

"Something in my new play," said Yank.

"Oh," said Atterbury. "I didn't know she knew anything about your new play."

"I don't, very much. And now that you're back so soon, I guess I never will," she said.

"I turned my God damn ankle trying to leap a fence. Only four feet high. You'd think I could manage that. I got over it all right, but I landed kerplunk."

"Soak it in hot water and Epsom salts," she said.

"Exactly what I'm going to do, if you'll excuse me. I don't mind telling you, it hurts like a bastard."

"Come on, I'll take you upstairs. Yank, you'll excuse us."

"Of course. I've stayed too long anyway."

"You calling him Yank? Isn't that rather fresh?"

"I won't go on calling him Mr. Lucas when I'm old enough to be his mother."

"I'm old enough to be his father, and then some, but you don't hear me calling him by a nickname. There's too damn much familiarity. Oh, *Jesus!* I turned it again. I'm going to have Mother's old elevator put back in running order. We don't need a phone booth in this house. Chic. We don't need any chic around here."

"We converted the elevator into a phone booth, if you're baffled by all that."

"So I gathered. Thanks very much. Hope your ankle gets better soon. Couldn't I—" He was about to offer to help get Atterbury upstairs but his wife shook her head vigorously. He was being dismissed; he was not needed here. The butler appeared, putting on his black jacket.

"Never mind, William," said Atterbury. "Dear, you just give me a hand, get on this side of me, please. I haven't got a broken leg, you know."

They were oblivious of Yank's presence—or absence—and he took himself away. Through such a small crisis he had been shown the position he occupied vis-à-vis the Atterbury institution, with special reference to the Atterbury marriage, with extra-special reference to Catherine Atterbury. She could talk to him in terms so intimate that she was nearly describing the degree of her lubricity, and then in a few seconds she could effortlessly eject him from her presence, her house, her consciousness. She was more truly interesting than any woman he had ever known; she made all the others seem like girls, which of course they were. But she could also make him feel like an immature youth, which he had come to believe he was not. In more ways than one she represented a setback, and he hoped but was not sure that he could turn the experience to profit. It was not always easy to learn something about yourself, especially when it was something you should have discovered unassisted by a woman about whom the most obvious thing was her seniority in age. Perhaps, only perhaps, her original attraction for him was a subtler curiosity for what he could learn from her rather than an immature youth's curiosity for what she had under her skirt. Perhaps, but only perhaps. If he made the mistake of justifying himself on an intellectual level, he would be making the additional mistake of self-deception. In all honesty and humility he must admit that his original curiosity was directed at what was under her skirt, and that his retroactive intellectualizing was a fraud. There she was, fifty-five or whatever, and though she might *not* be smarter than he, she knew more. Be knowing, old girl, and let who will be clever.

He returned to her contemporary, Anna Phelps. "Well, did they feed you better than I do?" she said.

"Nobody ever fed me better than you do, Mrs. Phelps."

"Huh. I forced that out of you," she said.

"You're the first one that ever did," he said. "My mother was a terrible cook."

"Was?"

"Is, I'm sure."

"You never talk about your mother. I heard you talk about your father, a college professor, but nothing about your mother."

"It's a sad story, about my mother."

"Oh?"

"One of the saddest. She was about as dull a woman as I ever knew."

"Even if she was, you oughtn't to say that."

"But you forced it out of me," he said.

"There you go again, smart-alecking. Why do you say your mother was dull?"

"Why do I say it, or why do I think it? I say it because she was. I think she was—because she was. She never had an original thought. Everything she ever said to us was pre-digested by my father. And he was no intellectual giant either."

"A person that takes that attitude toward their parents, I don't know, I've seen children grow up without a family life and very few of them turn out well."

"Oh, but I've turned out very well. I sent my father eight thousand dollars not so long ago. That's what I figured it cost him to support me through high school and college, as much college as I had."

"You figure that fulfills your obligation?"

"Not quite. I'm going to send him fourteen thousand more. That'll be for the years before college."

"And then you'll be all square?"

"All square."

"Well—at least you didn't put some price on their love and affection."

"Yes I did. It amounted to zero. Actually, I could probably bill them for the love and affection I gave them up till the time I was eight or nine. That was when I began to get wise to myself, and to them."

"Why didn't they like you?"

"Because I was a damned nuisance. If they wanted to buy anything or go anywhere, they couldn't."

"They made you feel unwanted, is that it?"

"Yes, as commonplace as that, Mrs. Phelps. They never beat me, the way some children get beaten. No cruel and unusual punishment, as the lawyers say. I always had shoes, and enough to eat. My father wouldn't think of violating the laws against cruelty to children. But on the other hand, he thought nothing of squandering money on his base instincts."

"Meaning women?"

"No. Meaning his stupid bad taste in painting. He wanted to be admired, so he used to buy pictures by unknown artists —haven't I told you this before?"

"Not me."

"Good. Well, he was popular with phonies and incompetents because he bought their pictures. Instead of buying me the things I wanted."

"Such as what?"

"Oh—such as sending me abroad."

"When you were eight or nine?"

"A little older. Twelve or thirteen. I wanted to go to England, to visit George Bernard Shaw."

"When you were *twelve?*"

"Yes. I had already written seven or eight plays by the time I was twelve."

"You could have gone to England since then."

"Yes, I could have but I didn't want to, to see Shaw or Marjorie Daw."

"Who was she?"

"See Shaw, Marjorie Daw. That popped right out," he said.

"Oh. You make a habit of saying anything that comes into your head. I often noticed that. Some of your ideas would be better if you kept them to yourself."

"Impossible. The artist in me demands expression."

"Indeed? I didn't know you were an artist too."

"An artist, Mrs. Phelps. Not a painter. You've surely heard the phrase artistic temperament applied to others than practitioners of the graphic arts."

"I've surely heard about enough of this for one day, and a quiet Sunday at that. Do you want anything special for supper? I'm out for the evening, but I can fix you something beforehand."

"Some of your delicious tongue sandwiches."

"I never offered you a tongue sandwich since you've been here."

"That other stuff, then."

"I'll leave you some cold roast beef and potato salad."

"I'll save a few slices for Ed Cross."

"Won't be at all necessary. Breakfast is all he ever eats here."

"I was thinking of a snack when he brings you home. Oh, you might tell Ed that I'm buying my agent's car."

"Why would that interest Ed?"

"Because I'm going to trade it in, eventually, and when I do I want Ed to get the commission. When I buy a new car I'll buy it from whatever dealer Ed suggests. He refused to take any money for helping me get my driver's license, but I want him to know I haven't forgotten."

"How did you know Ed was a salesman?"

"I'm a small-town boy, Mrs. Phelps. I pick up bits of information."

She looked at him steadily. "Hmm. Bits of information," she said. "They're not always reliable, remember."

"About seventy-five percent of the time. And of course I rely to some extent on my imagination." He smiled back at her look. "That's more than seventy-five percent reliable."

"Don't let it throw you," she said.

"I'll try not to," he said. "Now I have a question to ask you."

"All right."

"If you were me, would you marry Helen MacDowell?"

"If I were *anybody* I wouldn't marry Helen MacDowell. But what's behind that question? You don't have any intention of marrying her."

"Well, then, if you were me would you invite her to have a Coke?"

"You're beating about the bush."

"Intentionally. I start with the question about marriage and then I go to the other extreme. What do you think about in between? If you were me."

"If I were you. Well, I'm going to fix you some cold beef and potato salad. When I get home this evening I'd be very much surprised if it was still there. That's if I were you. When you get hungry, maybe you'd rather have a steak. A filet mignon. But your filet mignon is out West, in the State of Nevada. So you take the cold beef and potato salad."

"I'm inclined to agree with you. I was wondering whether the cold beef and potato salad—not yours, but the one at the post office—might give me indigestion."

"Well, if you had a wife it might give her indigestion."

"Before this metaphor gets too complicated, I don't understand why Helen's never been married."

"There I can't help you. You'd have to ask one of her fellows, since you're so good at picking up bits of information. Certain things can happen to a young woman that's not too careful."

"It's unsanitary to drink at the town pump."

She nodded. "There was a rumor to that effect. A man friend of mine speaks of it as getting the hives. I don't know if Helen ever gave anybody the hives, but I couldn't swear she didn't either. But my goodness, I know a man over in Cooperstown got the hives from his own wife."

"In other words, a chance we all take."

"Everybody, young or old, rich or poor. On the other hand, there she is, with a pretty good job in the post office. Lives home with her mother that has a pension from the Rutland. Property all paid for. I can tell you from my own experience, staying single has its advantages. You're your own boss, and Helen likes to have a good time. She wouldn't be out two-three nights a week if she was married, that you can be sure of. Different fellows take her out. Salesmen. Strangers. During the war, you can imagine, the fellows from the Air Force. She was the one that had the cigarettes and never worried about gas rationing. A person gets into those habits, it might be pretty hard to settle down. I happen to know that some of the strangers she goes out with were originally Air Force fellows she met during the war. Any time they happen to be anywhere near East Hammond. Helen. That's not saying what it'll be like when she gets around forty, but I doubt if Helen ever thought that far ahead. Day to day is Helen. You could almost tell that by looking at her. Cheerful. Flighty. Her mother isn't from around here. Rhode Island. An altogether different breed of cat, your Rhode Islanders."

"Is that so?"

"Well, I understand there's over fifty percent foreigners there. A large Italian population. That's not saying Mrs. Mac-Dowell is Italian. She doesn't look Italian. But Rhode Island I know positively was where she came from. That's all I can tell you about Helen that isn't plain gossip."

"All right, give me some gossip."

"No, we'd be here the rest of the day, and you wouldn't recognize half the names. But there's one name everybody will recognize."

"What's that?"

"Yank Lucas," she said.

During his next few visits to the post office he relaxed his manner toward Helen MacDowell in order to establish in her mind the belief that at long last her friendliness was getting results. It was essential—he did not know why, but he knew that it was—to the nature of the relationship he wanted that she believe she had overcome his reserve. Her imagined triumph would be preferable to any aggressiveness on his part. Later, at the proper time, it would be simpler to break things off if she, not he, had been conceded her primary success. Otherwise that friendliness of hers could turn very sour and she would be a nuisance. He did not know what kind of nuisance, but he knew that in this game Helen MacDowell would be a hard loser unless she were able pridefully to blame herself.

It was, therefore, a pleasant diversion to go to the post office and day by day simulate the performance of a man who was unknowingly succumbing to her various charms. He began on the Monday, the start of a new week, and each day he bestowed upon her an increasingly warmer smile, a little extra time in casual conversation. By Friday it was apparent that she was ready, so to speak, for the kill. The weekend was coming up, and he gave her her opportunity. "Well, another Saturday and Sunday here already," he said. "East Hammond is a great place to work, but there isn't much to do when you want to relax."

"Oh, I don't know," she said.

"No, there isn't," he said.

"Did you ever try Cookie's?"

"What kind of cookies? Molasses cookies? You're kidding."

"No, I meant Cookie's, the place."

"Never heard of it. Where is it?"

"Oh, it's down there the other side of Cooperstown, about three or four miles."

"What is it, a juke box kind of place?"

"Well, they do have a kind of a juke box. That Muzak. You don't have to keep putting nickels in. It's quite a high-class place. French cooking. It's run by a family from Quebec City."

"Cookie's doesn't sound very French."

"Oh, they bought out Harry Cook several years ago, but we kept on calling it Cookie's. Now the name is Maison Blanche."

"Now I know where it is. I've seen the sign."

"About three and a half miles the other side of Cooperstown. *I* go there all the time."

"Well, take me sometime."

"No time like the present," she said.

"Do you mean that?"

"I never say anything I don't mean," she said.

"I'll just bet."

"Well, a little white lie now and then. Friday's always a

good night at Cookie's. Saturday they get pretty rushed, but Friday the service is better and they can take more time preparing the food. They have a pâté maison there that's out of this world. And if you like seafood, they give you a crab flakes au gratin. Don't mention it, it makes my mouth water to think about it."

"Well, what are we waiting for? What time shall I call for you?"

"Say around ha' past eight."

"As late as that?"

"Listen, nobody eats early at Cookie's. It's not a hamburger joint."

He called for her and she had obviously taken pains with her appearance. "I *guess* I'll wear my silver fox," she said, calling attention to her silver fox. On the way to Cookie's she was enjoying herself to the point of smugness, and when they entered the restaurant she was greeted by each member of the staff, from the hatcheck girl to the proprietor, who all carefully called her Miss MacDowell. "I called up and made a reservation," she said to Yank. "It's always better to, or otherwise you don't get a banquette."

"I'm going to let you order," he said.

"All right, glad to oblige," she said. To his astonishment she carried on the transaction with the proprietor in French.

"My mother was French extraction. Pawtucket, Rhode Island. My father couldn't speak a word of it and it used to drive him bats when my mother talked it to us. It comes in handy once in a while. Do you speak it?"

"No, but it doesn't drive me bats. I know a little Spanish. It's much easier than French."

And so on. Patrons came in, stopped at their table to speak to Helen and stare at Yank. Some she introduced, some she did not. "He's the senator over in Montpelier . . . That's the doctor that operated on my mother . . . He's a lieutenant-colonel but he's not wearing his uniform . . . Very prominent lawyer from Springfield, Mass. . . . They're nothing, those two. Watch me brush them off . . ." And so on. At one end of the room was a large open fireplace. There were hurricane lamps and tall peppermills on the tables. Jeroboam-size cognac bottles on a high ledge. Harness brasses on the door frames. The tunes from the Muzak were mostly Jerome Kern and Vincent Youmans. The food was rich and well served, and Helen ate every scrap and drank most of a bottle of Chambertin. When the bill came he had to cash a traveler's cheque. L'addition was $54.37.

"It isn't a hamburger joint, is it?" said Helen.

"I'm glad there is such a place to come to."

"Sunday they have a five-dollar buffet that's very popular, but I always spend Sunday with my mother. You know how they reach a certain age and everything seems to go all at once. First her eyesight, and then her hearing. She doesn't look old, but you know a funny thing is how they can listen to the radio. You'd have to raise your voice, but she can hear Jack Benny. Oh, that Rochester, he kills me. You know he has almost the same kind of a voice as Andy Devine, if you stop to think of it. At first I used to think he was Andy Devine, but then I found out there was such a person. Eddie Anderson, his name is. I guess you've met most of those people, or they're on radio and your writings are for the regular theater."

It was time to leave, a little past eleven. They got in his car, and only because he happened to look at her did he discover that she was waiting to be kissed. It was a full kiss, but with her it was also ritualistic: a fine, expensive meal, followed by love. He put his hand under her skirt and she parted her legs to accommodate him. Presently she said, "We better save that till we get home, Mama's asleep by now."

They drove to her house, went to her bedroom, undressed, got into bed, and she returned the favor of the fifty-four-dollar meal. There was hardly more to it than that. She was satisfied with a job well done, a logical sequence to their gustatorial pleasure. She had not said a word during the entire performance; it had proceeded, like a meal, in courses, and as with a meal it was not necessary to announce that this was the soup, to be followed by the entree. It was not to be a memorable event, and he lapsed into a state of disappointed silence. Now she spoke. "I'd let you stay awhile, but a man's coming to paint the kitchen early in the morning. He's doing it on his own time, supposed to be his day off."

"That's all right," he said.

"Did you enjoy your evening? I had a wonderful time." She reached out to the chair beside her bed and got her kimono, knowing exactly where it would be.

"What did you enjoy most?" he said.

"Are you kidding?"

"No. What did you?"

"The screw."

"You did?"

"Sure I did, didn't you? A man can't pretend. A woman can pretend, but not a man. You know what I'd like to do?"

"What?"

"Keep you here the whole weekend, till Monday."

"Really?"

"That's why I wish that fucking painter wasn't coming here so early. I'm just getting started. What's the most times you ever came in one night?"

"Twice."

"*Twice?* I don't call that much. Even with your wife? Didn't you ever just stay home and take the phone off the receiver and the hell with everything?"

"No, I never did. Tell me about it."

"Well, not mentioning any names, but during the war, my mother had to go to Pawtucket to see her brother, my uncle, before he passed on. And I was all alone here. So this boy from the Base, he got a pass and he arrived here at about eight o'clock in the morning and stayed till around four o'clock Sunday afternoon."

"And how many times did he get it up?"

"Five. And he was built like you. Slender. We never went out to eat or anything. I put all the shades down, and I want to tell you, he was really a character. A real character."

"He must have had some cooperation from you."

"*That's* what's bothering you. Well, listen, this was only

our first time. Goodness, you don't expect me to go all-out passionate the first time. I didn't know what you'd be like. *That's* what's bothering you. I knew there was something."

"How many men have you laid, Helen?"

"Twenty-two. You're the twenty-third. Laid, that is. Heavy-necked *about* that many, but actually laid twenty-two plus you. I started heavy-necking when I was eleven. I and another girl. We weren't the only ones. But she got into real trouble. She was thirteen years of age and one Saturday night she heavy-necked a whole bunch of fellows up at Atterburys' bunkhouse. They sent her *away*, and that taught me a lesson."

"Stay away from the bunkhouse?"

"That bunkhouse. I never went near that place. You know what they say about that bunkhouse."

"No, I don't."

"Well, I don't happen to believe it, but I heard it *said* that any time old lady Atterbury is hard up, that's where she goes."

"I don't believe it either."

"No, I don't believe it, although *he's* supposed to be sterile."

"Sterile, or impotent?"

"Impotent, I guess. Can't get it up, whichever that is. So he's supposed to not mind if she goes to the bunkhouse. They're all strangers, you know, and according to the story, when she gets tired of them she has them fired."

"But you don't believe it."

"No, she was always nice to me. Why should I believe a

story like that? But *your* friend, the daughter, I'd believe any-thing about *her*. She was up here to get over a dose, I heard. She must have got over it, though, because you don't have one."

"No. I had some strange notion that the East Hammond people were rather fond of the Atterburys, but apparently not."

"Wait'll you've been here awhile. I'll bet you there's not fifteen people in East Hammond ever set foot inside that house. Why, Adam Phelps's wife, living right there all these years, she's never even seen the upstairs."

"You don't tell me," said Yank.

"The Atterburys, you only have to go back to his grand-father and he was nothing but a farmer with two mules, according to my father. Then they made all that money in New York and bought up a lot of property, came back here to live. But I don't think there's fifteen people can say they ever set foot inside the house. And imagine Adam Phelps's wife, never even getting to see the upstairs."

"I thought relations between the Atterburys and the East Hammond people were very cordial."

"That'd be because you only get the one side. Anna Phelps isn't going around putting the knock on Seymour Atterbury, naturally."

"Why naturally?"

"Oh, that goes back before I was born, so I don't know how much there was to it, but they were always riding around in his pony cart. I have pictures of my father and Atterbury and Anna Phelps before she was Anna Phelps and Adam Phelps and his wife before they were married."

"In the same pony cart?"

"In the same pony wagon, this was a wagon with two ponies, a little miniature wagon. I'd show you the pictures but the album's in my mother's room. Not that she'd hear me but I'd have to turn the light on and that'd wake her."

She prattled on, lying on her side, her elbow on a pillow and her head propped up in her hand. She regaled him with two generations of gossip, hers and her father's, having her revenge for the unkind things that she knew were said about her, and she needed no encouragement. She did not spare her lovers. "You remember that senator I said hello to at Cookie's? I can get anything I want to out of him," she said. The senator was partial to little girls, she said. The recital was doubly fascinating, for its revelations of the private life of the community and for Helen's unawareness of the self-characterization it provided. Already Yank could hear himself described to some future lover as the famous celebrity, author of that dirty play down in New York City, but nothing much in bed. He was not quite sure of the tactful way to terminate her monolog, nor in truth was he altogether desirous of escaping. It was a monolog, but it was not monotonous, and it was having its effect on her. Unconsciously, or so deliberately that she deserved recognition as an artiste, her hand had strayed to his genitals, which she gently played with as she continued her talk. Abruptly she stopped talking; she had produced an undeniable degree of excitement in herself, and he now became a willing victim of a rape. Rather stupidly he had never expected such thorough sensuality in Vermont, but Helen had nothing to learn from any Oriental. When it was over he understood why this smiling voluptuary, standing behind her counter in the post office, had not married. Even the least confining marriage would have put some restrictions on her addiction. She got up and ran a tub for him, and when he came out of the bathroom she was reading a magazine and smoking a cigarette. "Did you ever meet this Humphrey Bogart?" she said.

"No," said Yank.

"When you go to Hollywood you tell him he has a great admirer in East Hammond, Vermont," she said. She took a last look at Bogart's picture before laying the magazine down.

"What makes you think I'm going to Hollywood?"

"That's what you write plays for, isn't it? New York? New York is nothing compared to Hollywood. Who would have ever heard of Humphrey Bogart if he stayed in New York?"

"That's true."

"Well, we do it again sometime, eh?" she said.

"With your permission."

"With my permission? That's a laugh. You know, you'd look better with a bow tie."

"I've never worn one. I can't tie them."

"You can get them ready-tied. You have a pretty long neck, and if you wore a bow it would kind of shorten the effect, if you know what I mean. I'll buy you one for a present. Goldberg over in Cooperstown has them, or as far as that goes, you can get all kinds of men's clothes in Burlington."

"Well, I'm not much of a dude."

She stood up, rather shorter and vaguely appealing without her high heels. "I'm glad you like Cookie's. Of course you'd have been crazy if you didn't. Next Friday there won't be the God damn painter coming the first thing in the morning. Do you want to make a date now for Friday?"

"Well, of course."

"If Anna Phelps starts asking you a lot of questions—but she's too smart for that."

"Yes, she's very smart."

"And who is she to talk? Her and Ed Cross, for Christ's sake." She opened the door with her right hand and held her kimono with her left. "You know what I'd like to do sometime?" She opened her kimono wide, stepped out on the porch, and quickly stepped back. "Just give them a *good* look. But I'm a government employee. Goodnight, sleep tight, don't let the bedbugs bite." She squeezed his behind, pushed him out and closed the door. He had a conviction that she wanted to get back to her magazine and Humphrey Bogart. He also had a conviction that he would not wear a bow tie, and some doubt that he would meet her the next Friday. But that was a week away.

At the post office the next and succeeding days she smiled at him as always, but now she added an extra salute by the extension of the tip of her tongue, innocent enough if she had only been wetting her lips but she had never wet them before.

All of a sudden East Hammond, with all she had told him and with Helen herself, was becoming oppressive. Was there no place to go that would not become oppressive? No, there was not, and he wondered how many times he would have to relearn what he had always known. Spring Valley. New York. East Hammond. Eventually the planet Earth. Eventually? Already. He had known that all along too. He had begun by knowing that, but learning it and relearning it took time. There *was* a place where he was omniscient and omnipotent: it was in any room in any chair that faced his typewriter, where he could play God. Anywhere else he was a skinny man with defective vision, subject to mortal confusion at the sight of a strumpet's tongue. Beethoven and Edison were deaf, and Milton went blind; Gibbon and Chesterton were fat, and Poe was mad; Plato a fairy and Gauguin a syphilitic. The kinship he felt with all of them was tentative and hesitant until he touched the keys that gave life to Nancy the Snatch and Harry the Queen, but then he was in the company of Ludwig and Thomas and John and Edward and Gilbert and Edgar and Paul, and of George Herman Ruth, the Sultan of Swat, of those who were set apart from those who were not set apart.

Thus fortified from his own resources, he went back to work, and on Friday morning in the post office he said to Helen MacDowell, "Our date's off for tonight. I have to work."

"Oh, that's all right," she said. It was not all right, and her smile could not hide her chagrin, but he had made a positive statement and in the life that Helen MacDowell led the men who made positive statements went unchallenged. She hated him, but she would have hated him in any case. This time she did not extend the tip of her tongue.

In another week he finished the first draft of his play, and he telephoned the news to Peg McInerney. "That's the best news since they discovered penicillin," she said.

"Why penicillin?" he said.

"Oh, no reason. I could have said since the invention of the wheel. When are you coming down?"

"Well, I'm not sure. I'm going to sleep for a couple of days and then read it over again. There's no hurry, is there?"

"None whatever. You get your sleep. When you do come down I'd like to talk to you again about Eli Harbenstein. He's still very anxious to have you go to the Coast. And it'd be a complete change for you."

"I thought he'd have cooled off by this time."

"Anything but," she said.

"Well, his idea fits in with my plans," said Yank. "When I leave here it'll be for good."

"You've had it?"

"Just about had it," said Yank. "The place has served its purpose, and I see no use in hanging around any longer."

"Then by all means get out. Those small towns can be death, once the novelty's worn off."

"Or once you've discovered that there *is* no novelty," said Yank.

"Then I can look forward to seeing you in about a week?"

"About a week, give or take a day or two," he said.

He did not immediately notify Anna Phelps of his decision

to leave East Hammond. He did, however, tell her that he had finished his first draft and that he wanted to sleep around the clock.

"Then I guess you'll be off for New York," she said.

"Yes, I don't dare entrust my manuscript to the U.S. mails," he said.

She smiled. "You mean the U.S. mails, or the local post office?"

"Actually I wasn't thinking of the local post office," he said.

"That's not saying the local post office isn't thinking about you," said Anna Phelps. "Anyhow, talking about you."

"You wouldn't by any chance be referring to Helen Mac-Dowell?"

"I guess I would," she said. "As far as I know, you only had the one date with her—even *that* you didn't say anything about to me. But you know these little bits and pieces of information, in a small town. You're the expert on bits and pieces."

"Give me some bits and pieces," he said.

"Couldn't," she said. "I wouldn't know how to begin."

"Oh, that kind of bits and pieces. Well."

She smiled. "Maybe I should have told you, Helen has a habit of saying things a lady keeps to herself. But being the expert on bits and pieces, you were supposed to know that."

"You seem to be enjoying yourself, Mrs. Phelps. And at my expense."

"Do you blame me? It does strike me funny somehow."

"Then have yourself a good loud laugh. Don't just snicker."

"It isn't worth a good loud laugh. It isn't *that* funny."

"Probably not. And of course *you* can take a joke, even if it's on yourself."

"That'd depend," said Anna Phelps.

"Well, it isn't a joke, exactly, but I was quite surprised to pick up among the other bits and pieces that you and Seymour Atterbury had once been such great friends."

The transformation that occurred was amazing in a face that normally presented a minimum of expression. From good-natured taunting of him on the undisclosed topic that ladies kept to themselves she changed to sad and passionate defense of something, of something and not of herself. "Watch what you're saying, Mr. Lucas. You—watch—what—you're—saying, that's all," she said, and left the room.

Throughout the rest of the day and the following day she rebuffed his efforts to apologize. She had, of course, inferred that whatever he had heard about her and Atterbury had come from Helen MacDowell, a source which for Anna Phelps would besmirch a relationship. He decided to put off no longer his announced intention to sleep around the clock. "I'm going to bed for twenty-fours, Mrs. Phelps," he said. "If I want a glass of milk or anything, I'll get it myself. Any phone calls for me, tell them to call me the day after tomorrow."

"Very well," she said.

He took a Thermos jug of milk and a plate of cookies and retired to his room, undressed, had a warm bath, and went to bed. He knew that if he stayed off his feet he would relax sufficiently to sleep in three-hour, four-hour stretches, with periods of wakefulness in between. He did not attempt to hasten sleep—and it came, the first long stretch of nearly seven hours. He got out of bed to urinate, returned to bed and slept again. In that manner he stayed in bed two hours beyond the twenty-four, and he awoke pleased with the discovery. He washed his face and went downstairs to the kitchen. Anna Phelps was not there, but there were notes to him on the kitchen table. He made some coffee and drank it before putting on his glasses to read the messages. Someone, giving no name, had called at three o'clock in the morning. Two messages to call Miss McInerney, urgent. Two messages to call a Mr. Leeds at the *Journal-American*. More messages in twenty-six hours than he had had in any week since the departure of Sheila Dunham. He had a second cup of coffee and Anna Phelps came in with the dog.

"I see you got the messages," she said.

"Yes, thank you."

"The one that wouldn't give her name, I finally had to hang up on her. Then Miss McInerney was almost as bad. She phoned at about eleven this morning and again around two. She's your agent, I know, but I must ask you to tell her I'm not accustomed to being spoken to that way. Swearing and cursing. I said you left orders and I wasn't taking orders from her."

"That isn't like Miss McInerney."

"The other fellow, Leeds. He wanted to know if any other papers phoned. I said you left word you didn't want to be disturbed and that's all I was authorized to say. Then he wanted to know if I was sure you were asleep. I said to him, I've told him all I was going to tell him. No manners, none of them. City people. Well, I guess you ought to be ready for something to eat."

"Some fried eggs and bacon, please. Excuse me while I use the phone."

He reached Peg McInerney at her office. "Did you just wake up?" she said.

"Drinking my coffee, the first in twenty-six hours."

"Then you don't know about Zena?"

"About Zena? No. But I'll bet it's not good."

"No, it isn't good, Yank. Brace yourself. She committed suicide last night. An overdose of sleeping pills, but definitely suicide."

"Definitely suicide," he said.

"I got the whole thing from Ellis. It's not good, Yank. It's not good at all. She met Barry after the theater and they went to Sardi's for something to eat. They had a terrible fight and she walked out and left him there. He's been absolutely horrible to her, that's all over town. Absolutely horrible. She went home to the apartment and she called up any number of people, but if you want to know the truth, she's been doing that lately and some of them turn off their phones. Marc DuBois told Ellis she called him and was incoherent. Rambling on, saying anything that came into her head. Finally Marc said to her he had to get some sleep. She called Scott Aubrey and got his wife on the phone and told her all sorts of things about Scott. She called me. She said if I didn't give her your phone number she'd hold me responsible. Responsible for what, I asked her. Never mind for what, she said. She sounded so desperate that I gave her the number. She didn't get you."

"No, I've been in bed. Left word that I wasn't to be disturbed, no matter who called."

"Oh, it probably wouldn't have made any difference. The police said she tried to call Stalin."

"Stalin? In the Kremlin?"

"Well, she was mixed up with the Commies a few years ago."

"Yes, she told me. To get jobs."

"After that, nobody knows. But sometime between three and four she emptied a bottle of sleeping pills. The maid found her when she came in this morning. She was lying on the bathroom floor."

"Still that doesn't necessarily mean she committed suicide," he said.

He heard nothing and said, "Peg, are you still there?"

"Yes."

"I said it didn't necessarily mean she committed suicide."

"She left a note. For you. Just a piece of paper that said, 'Dear Yank, thanks for nothing.' "

"Oh," he said. "That's all?"

"That's all. But it's in the headlines. I'll read you one. 'Zena to Yank: Thanks for nothing.' There's one story that practically comes right out in print with what everybody's saying. That you drove her back to Barry and that he'd been giving her a bad time on account of you. Stuff about quarrels in public. No secret that the reconciliation had failed. That kind of stuff. I don't know what ever happened to the libel laws in this country, but believe me it's all there."

"Is that true, that he'd been giving her a bad time?"

"Everybody knew it. He'd say to people, 'You know my wife, Yank Lucas's *re*-ject.' "

"The son of a bitch," said Yank.

"Well, yes, but I tried to tell you, you did some damage."

"And now you're trying to tell me I killed her. Is that it?"

"If I really believed that I wouldn't be talking to you."

"You might," he said.

"No, I was kind of hoping that when you came down to New York you and she would either get together again or if not, at least she'd have the chance to tell you off. One or the other."

"I was coming down the day after tomorrow," he said.

"The funeral is tomorrow. Just don't come tomorrow," she said. "Some kind of a memorial service at a place on Madison Avenue. It could be very unpleasant for you."

"I wasn't going to be there but now I almost have to," he said.

"What for? To prove how brave you are? If somebody makes a scene, decides to punch you in the nose, what good will that do Zena? Show her that much respect. All the big people in the theater will be there. Let her take her bow, for God's sake, with some dignity."

"Dignity? All right. Then you don't want to see me till the day after tomorrow?"

"Right, and I'll get you a reservation at someplace like the Pierre or the St. Regis. You don't want to stay at the Algonquin."

"You don't want me to stay at the Algonquin. All right."

"And I can have you on a plane to the Coast the following day."

"You advise that, too?"

"Yes, I do. Out there—well, out there isn't here."

"I'll only be there a week."

"If that's all you want to be. You may want to stay longer. As a friend of mine once said, the girls grow much thicker out there. The same man said there was a rapid turnover, but of course I never knew what he meant by that."

"If I find out I'll explain it to you," he said.

"I want you to know, Yank, I've been through a lot of these things. Suicides. One murder. And God knows how many divorces and so on. No matter where my sympathies may lie, I always do my best for my client. Otherwise I wouldn't take his money."

"I figured that," he said. "And I know where your sympathies lie."

"Do you? In this case I'm not so sure. In the long run, I mean."

"Well, I hope we end up on the same side," he said. "On the same side at the same time."

The conversation ended there. So too, in effect, ended his sojourn in Vermont. "I'm leaving here the day after tomorrow, Mrs. Phelps," he said.

"For good?" she said.

"Yes."

She nodded. "Well, of course there's nothing to keep you *here*," she said.

"I'm sorry I offended you with that remark about Mr. Atterbury," he said.

"From what I've been able to deduce, Mr. Lucas, you'd have trouble knowing why it offended me."

"Tell me why," he said.

"I'll be glad to tell you, but I doubt if it'll clarify it in your mind," she said. "You see, Mr. Lucas, a person's memories are her private property. Somewhat like a child's toys. And the child doesn't relish coming home and finding a couple of strangers playing with her toys."

"Meaning me and Helen MacDowell?" said Yank. "I can see why that would be."

"Sticky with syrup off someone else's fingers. It'll come off with cold water, but you were always very careful never to play with your toys when you had sticky fingers. At least I always was. Now then, there's one or two phone calls to be accounted for, but outside of that you're all paid up to the end of the week. You could insist on a rebate for what's left of the week, but you're not giving me much notice, are you?"

"I'm not going to insist on anything, you ought to know that."

[294]

"I know you were never mean about money. I guess you gave up that idea of trading in your car?"

"Afraid I have. I'll be going to California this week, and I'm going to put this car in storage."

"Ed would have liked that commission," she said.

"I'll leave him a cheque for fifty dollars."

"No, I wouldn't do that if I were you. He wouldn't accept it. If you gave him something to do to earn it, that'd be an altogether different proposition, but don't offer a man like Ed Cross a tip."

"All right, Mrs. Phelps, I'll find some way to make it up to him. I'll have him look up my ancestors in the county records."

"As long as it's earned. Cash would be better, if you wouldn't mind."

"Right. I'll give you an address in New York. My agent's. She'll forward any bills or anything like that. I'll be leaving very early in the morning, day after tomorrow."

"I'll have your breakfast all ready."

"Between now and then I still have some work to do, but it won't be typing. So you'll start getting used to the quiet."

"The typing never bothered me," she said.

"What did, Mrs. Phelps?"

"No, we've as good as said goodbye."

"Now I am going to insist. What bothered you?"

"Well, sometimes those nightmares you get. I used to want to go in and wake you up, but I guess you always woke yourself up."

"I'm sorry about that."

"Oh, it was worse for you than for me. Although occasionally frightening."

"I yell, don't I?"

"More like groans. Lower down than a yell. No words, just groans. Maybe you drink too much coffee. Mr. Phelps used to get them if he ate anything with cheese in it, so I never left any cheese out for you. So I guess it was the coffee."

"Well, only two more nights you have to put up with it."

"Didn't happen every night."

"I doubt if it was the coffee, and I'm almost sure to have one tonight. The leading lady in my play committed suicide. That's what all those telephone calls were about. It'll be in the papers."

"It was on the radio."

"Oh, you knew?"

"That much, yes," she said.

"But you didn't say anything."

"Not till you did," she said.

"That was—courteous."

"We believe in manners," she said.

He commenced the reading of his play, the read-through that was comparable to the run-through in an actual theater. At first he was grateful to have it to read. It was absorbing, and it demanded his concentration, reading the lines, hearing the lines as they would be spoken, visualizing the performance. Then, in the second scene of the first act, Zena came on. It was the character he had created for her to play, denying all the while that he *had* created it for her but knowing that he was lying to himself. You did not like to think that a living person could so thoroughly permeate and saturate and dominate your artistic invention, but Zena had done so. Zena, and no one else, real or imaginary, was in every word and every pause. He read with eagerness, as though to discover what Zena Gollum had been in life. This play was now a recording and a record of Zena Gollum alive by an author who had observed her truly and well. Parenthetically, in an aside to himself, Yank commented that he knew now why, early in the writing of the play, he had believed that the play was writing itself. He had not known, however, that he had become the instrument of a creature that he had already destroyed. The splendid irony was in the manner of her revenge. It was sickening to confess to yourself that you would never again do anything as good as this. All those happy confusions of himself with God, those identifications with divinity and genius, and that supreme self-confidence—all of them were as lost as the smoke of Gettysburg, the tears of Gethsemane. He read on rapidly through this obituary of Zena Gollum that was correspondingly the obituary of the talent of Yank Lucas.

Unless, of course, he could find someone else.